Praise for
CHARLIE HERNÁNDEZ
AND THE LEAGUE OF SHADOWS

★"Filled with action with fast-paced chapters ... a perfect pick for kids who love Rick Riordan's many series, particularly for those eager for mythologies beyond Greek and Roman stories." —*Booklist*, starred review

★"A winner for all kids, but it will be especially beloved by Latinx and Hispanic families who may recognize some of the characters." —*Kirkus Reviews*, starred review

"This magical adventure brings the Hispanic mythologies ... to life ... the detailed attention to various Hispanic folkloric and mythological traditions is accessible to readers new to the legends as well as old hands, and this multicultural story proves to be a satisfying read for anyone interested in fantasy action." —*BCCB*

"The story is fast paced and jam-packed with many encounters with mythological creatures loosely based on folklore from around the Spanish-speaking world. The glossary at the end is helpful with a description and country of origin for each mythological being. VERDICT A great start to a new series that will be devoured by fantasy fans who enjoy action with ample doses of mythological inspirations." —*School Library Journal*

The adventure continues

Charlie Hernández and the Castle of Bones

CHARLIE HERNÁNDEZ&
THE LEAGUE OF SHADOWS

RYAN CALEJO

Aladdin

New York ✦ London ✦ Toronto ✦ Sydney ✦ New Delhi

ALADDIN
An imprint of Simon & Schuster Children's Publishing Division
1230 Avenue of the Americas, New York, New York 10020
First Aladdin paperback edition October 2019
Text copyright © 2018 by Ryan Calejo
Cover illustration copyright © 2018 by Manuel Sumberac
Also available in an Aladdin hardcover edition.
All rights reserved, including the right of reproduction in whole or in part in any form.
ALADDIN and related logo are registered trademarks of Simon & Schuster, Inc.
For information about special discounts for bulk purchases, please contact
Simon & Schuster Special Sales at 1-866-506-1949 or business@simonandschuster.com.
The Simon & Schuster Speakers Bureau can bring authors to your live event. For more information or to book an event contact the Simon & Schuster Speakers Bureau at 1-866-248-3049 or visit our website at www.simonspeakers.com.
Cover designed by Karin Paprocki
Interior designed by Hilary Zarycky
The text of this book was set in Adobe Jenson Pro.
Manufactured in the United States of America 0919 OFF
2 4 6 8 10 9 7 5 3 1
The Library of Congress has cataloged the hardcover edition as follows.
Names: Calejo, Ryan, author. | Title: Charlie Hernández and the league of shadows / by Ryan Calejo. | Description: First Aladdin hardcover edition. | New York : Aladdin, 2018. | Summary: Steeped in Hispanic folklore since childhood, middle schooler Charlie Hernández learns the stories are true when, shortly after his parents' disappearance, he grows horns and feathers and finds himself at the heart of a battle to save the world.
Identifiers: LCCN 2018014304 (print) | LCCN 2018020929 (eBook) | ISBN 9781534426603 (eBook) | ISBN 9781534426580 (hardcover)
Subjects: | CYAC: Shapeshifting—Fiction. | Folklore—Latin America—Fiction. | Secret societies—Fiction. | Good and evil—Fiction. | Missing persons—Fiction. | Hispanic Americans—Fiction. | BISAC: JUVENILE FICTION / People & Places / United States / Hispanic & Latino. | JUVENILE FICTION / Fantasy & Magic.
Classification: LCC PZ7.1.C312 (eBook) | LCC PZ7.1.C312 Ch 2018 (print) | DCC [Fic]—dc23 | LC record available at https://lccn.loc.gov/2018014304
ISBN 9781534426597 (paperback)

To my parents.
Who always believed.

To my abuelita.
Who helped me believe.

CHAPTER ONE

Myths, my abuela used to say, are truths long forgotten by the world.

Which is probably why she collected them the way some people collect stamps. Or mugs with pictures of kittens on them. She gathered tales of enormous, horned, snakelike sea creatures, of two-headed vampire dogs with glowing red eyes, of terrifying man-eating ghouls that stalk the night, searching for naughty children to kidnap.

The myths came from all over the Spanish-speaking world. From Madrid to Quito. Mexico City to Buenos Aires. Most of them were hundreds of years old, almost as old as the cultures that had inspired them. Some had spread quickly around the globe, spread like wildfire. Others never even left the tiny rural towns where they'd first been told.

All her life my grandma had been obsessed with Hispanic mythology, with all the legends and stories and folklore, and had spent years teaching them to me.

When I was little we used to hang out in the kitchen on lazy Saturday afternoons, me in my Power Rangers pj's and chancletas, my abuela telling her favorite tales from memory, making the epic battles and ghoulish monsters come to life with every gesture of her brown and wrinkled hands.

Afterward, she would quiz me on what I'd heard; we played this little game, sort of like Pictionary, where she'd draw a quick sketch of one of the characters, and I would have to guess who—or, in most cases, *what*—it was. If I got four in a row, she'd let me eat leche condensada right out of the can, which might've been the only thing I enjoyed more than listening to her stories.

At the time I thought it was all just for fun, a cool little game between the two of us. But I should've known better; my abuela hated party games.

CHAPTER TWO

I still remember the first night in the police station like it was yesterday. The tall sheriff's deputy telling me that everything was going to be okay, that there was nothing for me to worry about, that they'd find my parents—promising me that.

Then he handed me a chewed-up number two pencil, dropped a yellow notepad on the desk in front of me, and told me to write down everything I remembered. Told me not to leave anything out. Not even what I was feeling.

I'm not sure which was more embarrassing—the fact that I could barely hold the pencil in my sweaty, trembling hands, or that I didn't have anything to write. See, I wasn't there the morning my parents went missing—I was at the local guitar shop. And I wasn't there later that afternoon when our house burned down—I'd biked over to Zoo Miami for the day.

So forty-five minutes later I'd gotten down only two words, but they were the truest words I'd ever written:

I'm scared.

So scared I could barely breathe. So scared I could actually feel the blood pulsing through my hands and feet. But I didn't write any of that down.

Instead, I sat frozen in the small interrogation room with tears running down my cheeks, waiting for the deputy to come back. Waiting to wake up from this horrible nightmare.

And that was when the pain came. It felt like two little bee stings up near my temples. Hot and sharp, but lasting for only a moment.

I remember running my hands through my hair and feeling something strange. I remember getting up and walking to the tiny half bathroom at the end of the hall for a closer look. I even remember the small, squeaky sounds my sneakers made on the scuffed and dirty tiles.

But what I remember most was the pair of stubby horns I discovered growing out of the sides of my head.

They were a dark golden color. Like honey mixed with dirt.

CHAPTER THREE

That day was the single worst day of my life. But the days that followed were almost as bad. Since I didn't have any living relatives (my abuela died when I was nine) and child services was having a hard time finding a place for me, I spent the next two weeks sleeping on a scratchy cot in one of the empty cells at the front of the police station. Every night I planted myself on the folding chair outside the station's 9-1-1 call center, listening in on the dispatchers, hoping to hear something—*anything*—about my parents. And every night I was disappointed.

Obviously, with a pair of *horns* growing out of my head, I couldn't help but think back to my abuela's myths—especially the one about the Morphling. In those stories, the young hero would always defeat his nemesis—an evil, narcissistic, twice-cursed witch—by manifesting some kind of animal trait. It was usually something odd, like fins or hooves or an armadillo shell, and even though it seemed sort of similar to what was happening to me (minus the whole fighting-an-evil-witch part, of course), I honestly didn't see how a fairy tale could have anything to do with my current situation. They were just made-up stories. You know, kid stuff.

Then, about a week or so later, the horns suddenly vanished. I couldn't explain it. I just woke up one morning, felt around underneath my hoodie, and they were gone.

At that point I just assumed (like most people probably would) that I'd had some sort of nervous breakdown, my terrified mind frantically mixing reality with fiction, trying to bring me back to a time when I felt safe, back to a time when I was surrounded by people who loved me and cared for me and would never let anything bad happen to me.

At least that's what I kept telling myself.

That is, until the unthinkable happened.

Again.

CHAPTER FOUR

This time it happened in the worst place imaginable—*middle school*. Ponce de Leon Middle, to be exact. And just like the first time, I was caught completely off guard.

See, by then my life had almost started to feel normal again. More than four weeks had passed since the horns, school was starting back up, and my two best friends had come home from summer camp. Not only that, but I wasn't sleeping at the police station anymore; the state had found me a temporary guardian who lived in the same South Florida neighborhood, and I'd moved into her dusty upstairs attic. Not perfect, sure, but it definitely beat the heck out of a crummy six-by-eight cinder-block cell.

So anyway, there I was, just sort of dozing off in third-period history, when my life took another crazy detour into Freaksville.

Unlike the horns, this particular manifestation started with an itch. A hot, sort of painful itch way down on my back.

Then the itch began to spread. Up my sides, along my shoulders, down the backs of my arms. It felt as if an army of creepy bugs were crawling all over me!

I started to scratch and scratch, but it didn't help. The itching only got worse, my skin growing hotter and redder and ridiculously flaky.

And that's when it happened. That's when a fat gray feather burst through the skin on my forearm like a zombie hand busting out of a grave.

For half a second I wondered if Mr. Henry's snooze-inducing lesson about the French Revolution was somehow making me hallucinate. (Which, by the way, wouldn't have been the first time.) But then another feather sprang up, this one through a tiny pore in the crook of my left arm, and I felt my blood turn to ice.

¡Dios mío! I screamed on the inside. *Not again!*

Jumping to my feet, I raced for the door, snatching the big red hall pass from the pegboard on my way out. Behind me, I heard Mr. Henry shout, "Hey, Charlie, where're you going?" But I didn't stop. Didn't even look back.

Thankfully, the hallway was empty—no eighth graders

making out by the stairs, no hall monitors lurking with their bright yellow T-shirts and walkie-talkies.

I pounded past the wall of lockers and around the corner, through the heavy metal door next to shop class, my breaths coming fast and shallow, then up a short flight of stairs and into the boys' bathroom, which—thankfully—was also empty.

I ducked into the first stall, peeled off my shirt—and gasped.

My chest, smooth and hairless as a baby's bottom a minute ago, was now covered in a forest of ugly little feathers.

I didn't think, just started plucking. And the first thing I learned: ripping feathers out of your body isn't any fun. It's actually *insanely* painful. Sort of like tweezing your eyebrows, except these "eyebrows" were as long as my pinky finger and had hard keratin roots that sank down deep into my pores, deeper than any hair follicle.

My skin stung. Tears ran down my cheeks, and I had to bite down on my tongue just to keep from screaming. But I didn't stop. In fact, I started plucking even faster, squeezing my eyes shut against the tiny stings of pain and tossing the feathers into the toilet by the handful. Rip, wince, toss. Rip, wince, toss.

I'd almost sort of started to get into a rhythm, too,

when I opened my eyes again and saw something that made my heart stop. The toilet bowl was full of feathers—almost up to the rim of the seat—but my body was still covered with them.

Which could mean only one thing: They were regrowing faster than I could pluck them!

"*No!*" I screamed. "*No, no, no, no, no!*"

My mind was reeling. I didn't know what to do. I tried flushing the toilet, but nothing happened. I tried again, jiggling the handle this time, but instead of the feathers disappearing down the hole like they were supposed to, water filled the bowl and an unhealthy gurgling sound rose from the bottom.

I froze for an instant. Froze with horror. Watching as the water rose up, up, up and began to spill over the sides of the bowl and onto the floor. The gurgling sounds turned into choking ones. The sharp stench of number one—and its even stinkier numerical compadre—stung my nostrils.

Do something!

In a panic, I peeked into the toilet, trying to see if there was anything I could do to help get the freakin' thing to flush.

Huge mistake.

Because just at that moment, a fountain of whiz-scented nasty sprayed straight up from the center of the bowl, blasting me in the face and knocking me off balance.

I crashed through the stall door and landed on the floor with a wet splash. My breath exploded from my lungs in a painful *whoosh*. The world teetered. My head spun.

Just when I thought things couldn't get any worse, the choking, gurgling sound spread to the other toilets, and suddenly all five fudge funnels were overflowing—the urinals, too!

For a crazy second I thought about trying to clean this mess up, maybe spreading some paper towels over the floor to soak up the water. But then I realized there weren't enough paper towels in the dispenser—there probably weren't even enough in the *entire school*!

Scrambling to my feet, I ran to the bathroom door, cracked it open enough for one eye, and peered out. The hall was still empty, which was awesome. But how much longer would it stay that way? There couldn't have been more than fifteen minutes left of class when I'd Speedy Gonzales'd it out of there, and I had no idea how much time had passed.

Doesn't matter, I told myself. Either way, I had to get out of here. Either way, I had to find something to cover up the feathers.

Unfortunately, I could think of only one place to look.

CHAPTER FIVE

The school's main office was on the first floor of the building near the entrance. My target, the lost-and-found box, was usually kept in the teachers' lounge, which happened to be on the far side of the room, making it just about the hardest place in the entire office to get to without being seen. But I didn't exactly have a lot of options.

I made my way there as quickly—and *sneakily*—as humanly possible, arms hidden inside my shirt, my soaked-through sneakers squeaking on the chipped gray linoleum. The office had a large window, chest-high, through which I could see the receptionist, Mrs. Ambers, sitting at her desk. She seemed super busy, flipping randomly through a tall stack of yellow papers while yelling at someone over the phone.

This was my chance.

I took a deep breath, let it out slowly through my nose, then eased open the door (its rusty metal hinges practically screaming INTRUDER ALERT!) and slipped inside.

I walked quickly past Mrs. Ambers, who was still yapping away, and into the small room with its faculty-only vending machine and cappuccino maker.

The moment I stepped inside and saw the lost-and-found box sitting on the big laminated desk in the middle of the room, I was so excited I almost burst into a full-on theatrical rendition of "La Cucaracha." But there wasn't any time for that, so instead I just gave a little fist pump and started for the box.

I was just reaching for it when a deep, gruff voice spoke up from behind me:

"What are you doing in here?"

I whirled around in surprise. Mrs. Kirilenko was standing in the doorway, arms crossed. Mrs. Kirilenko was one of the new teachers at our school, and even though she taught only a small group of students—only eighth grade and only those in the gifted program—her reputation for being a ruthless disciplinarian had spread through the student body like a bad case of pinkeye. She was *literally* the last teacher on earth I wanted to run into.

"Uh, I—I'm just looking for something I lost in homeroom," I said. "My, uh, my jacket-sweater-hoodie thingy."

Translation: Anything in that box with sleeves, it's mine.

Her dark eyes narrowed in an *I know something's up* kind of way. "Is that—*feather* sticking out of your sleeve . . . ?" she asked in that thick Russian accent of hers.

"A feather? Ha! What?" I took a tiny, terrified step back, bumping up against the freezing-cold wall. "No feathers here! Just skin and bones! Like your average *completely normal* middle school s—"

She cornered me with her bulky frame. "Take your arms out of your shirt."

"Excuse me?" I squeaked.

"Now!" Her voice was so loud, so intimidating that I had no choice but to obey. Slowly, grudgingly, I pulled my trembling arms out of the sticky sleeves of my T-shirt—and watched as Mrs. Kirilenko's eyes nearly popped out of their sockets.

"I can explain," I started to say (although I actually *couldn't*—not even a little), but she never gave me a chance.

"No need," she said, shooting up a hand to shush me. "I already know what is going on here. . . ."

My eyebrows shot up. "You do?"

"*Da, da,* of course, I do! You are part of Mrs. Tannenbaum's upcoming play."

"I—am?" Then, realizing I should probably go with this: "I mean, *yes. I am!*"

"Granted, it is not her best work. Maybe she is losing bit of her *magic touch*, as you Americans would say, but it is not bad. . . ." She plucked a feather from the already tender underside of my forearm, making me flinch. "Something wrong . . . ?"

I shook my head. "Nope. Didn't hurt one bit."

"'Course not. They are glued to your arm with some sort of specialized adhesive." She plucked another—this one from higher up on my arm, near my armpit——and I *screamed* on the inside. She could've stabbed me with the world's sharpest thumbtack and it probably would've hurt less. "Bell-Horn roll-on, perhaps?"

"That's the one." I could barely get the words out.

"What most around here fail to realize is that I was member of Russian intelligence community before becoming teacher," she said. "So one must wakey-wakey *pretty early* in the morning to pull the old bear carcass over this Muscovite's eyes."

Then, with a hint of a smile (which I suspected was the most you ever got from Mrs. Kirilenko), the not-so-friendly giant strode briskly over to the big round desk and peered into the box. "I tell you, with how little money the state government is giving to schools nowadays, it is no wonder Mrs. Tannenbaum is raiding lost-and-found box for wardrobe. Fortunately, we have very resourceful teachers in this school."

She tipped the box toward me, and I almost burst into tears right then and there. The only thing inside was a hideous purple jacket decorated with splotches of red paint and a dusting of sparkly yellow glitter. Some poor kid had probably gotten it as a Christmas gift from a kooky aunt and had conveniently "lost" it here at school.

On the bright side, it *did* have long sleeves. . . .

Cranking out another smile, I said, "Yep, that one's perfect!"

"Really?" she asked, frowning as she held it up. In her huge gorilla hands, the purple abomination looked like doll's clothes. Still, it couldn't have been much bigger than a youth small—*if* that.

"Uh-huh, fits my part like a glove. We—we're doing, uh . . . *Shakespeare*! And I'm playing a sort of colorful jacket-wearing human-bird hybrid of . . . of Hamlet!"

Mrs. Kirilenko raised her eyebrows in surprise. "You are?"

"Yeah, it's kind of hard to explain. But it's gonna be a lot of fun. You can trust me on that."

She didn't look convinced but handed the jacket over anyway.

I quickly shrugged into it, forcing myself not to think about how ridiculous I was going to look. Up to this point the most outlandish thing I'd ever worn to school was a guayabera, which is a style of Latino dress shirts that I'd become obsessed with after seeing a black-and-white photograph of my abuelo wearing one out in the campo as he chopped sugarcane. I'd worn one almost every other day during the first few months of second grade, and even as much as I'd stuck out dressing that way in an American public school, it was *nothing* compared to how bad I was about to stick out walking around in this sorry excuse for clothing.

Mrs. Kirilenko studied me closely. "So Shakespeare and feathers, *da?*"

"Yep. But I don't want to go giving away any more spoilers, so that's all I'm gonna say. I've been sworn to secrecy, you know!"

"Ah, yes, *secrecy.* I am very familiar with the concept. KGB is *all about* secrecy. . . ." She gave me a wink. "Just one more question—why do you smell like toilet?"

CHAPTER SIX

As I was making my way back to class, wondering what excuse I was going to give Mr. Henry for why I'd run off like that and why I'd come back wearing this ridiculous purple ski jacket, a huge banner hanging over the glass trophy case caught my eye. The glittering tinsel lettering read:

MRS. TANNENBAUM'S UPCOMING PLAY:

A FLIGHT OF FEATHERS

Auditions in the auditorium!

More details to follow!

For a moment I just stood there, stunned. I couldn't believe Mrs. T's upcoming play *actually* had something to do with feathers. The only explanation I could come up with was that the big guy upstairs must've really enjoyed messing with me because, like, what were the chances? I half expected to see another sign somewhere that read, CHARLIE HERNÁNDEZ IN THE ROLE HE WAS BORN TO PLAY!

Shaking my head, I was about to start walking again when something else drew my attention—one of the faculty photos on the wall next to the trophy case. It showed a woman in a dark business suit, with long reddish hair swept over one shoulder, smiling at the camera.

Lynda Eloise Hernández.

My mother.

Just the sight of her brought a huge lump to my throat. Today made it exactly two months since my parents had gone missing. Exactly two months since I'd last been able to hug them or watch TV with them or tell them how much I loved them. The only good news in all this was that they hadn't been in the fire. (The firefighters had been very clear about that.) But the bad news was that the police still hadn't been able to turn up any leads.

Without thinking, I slipped my hand into my pocket and pulled out the big silver locket that had come in the mail last week. It was my mom's, the only thing I had left of hers. According to the little evidence card it had come with, the locket was the one item in the entire house that had survived the fire. A fire that the chief over at the station house was pretty sure had been caused by a freak toaster-oven malfunction. And the weirdness didn't end there. I still hadn't been able to figure out how to open the darn thing. It was locked by a row of tiny combination wheels, like the ones on briefcases and bicycle chains, that had me totally stumped. But I figured eventually (or whenever I got my hands on the world's tiniest crowbar), I should be able to—

"Hey, check it out!" shouted a voice behind me. "It's Barney the dorky dinosaur!"

I turned, surprised, and saw Alice Coulter standing behind me, her army of lady-jocks gathered around her. Alice was a six-foot-tall fastball-crushing all-state softball player who looked like she belonged in the majors. She had thick tree-trunk legs, forearms like pythons, and biceps that were the envy of the boys' varsity football team. Her softball jersey and cleats were always spotless. Her dark, brownish hair was cropped close to her head in a faux-hawk, the tips frosted blue for a little extra school spirit. Her pirate-inspired crossbones nose ring glinted dully in the overhead lights.

In third grade, she'd earned the nickname "Alice the Terrible" after pegging one of our PE teachers with a fifty-mile-per-hour curveball and then proceeding to strike him out in front of the entire class. Mr. Plummer, who was also our school's basketball coach, was never again seen on school property.

"Hello, boys and girls. I'm a big purple *loser!*" Alice said, doing her best Barney impersonation, and big surprise, her gang of morons burst out laughing.

One of them shouted, "*Burn!*" right in my face. Another one—the starting catcher, I was pretty sure—shoved me into the water fountain with her shiny black mitt while popping a bubble of gum between her teeth.

I looked around for a hall monitor. Nada. Which was the problem with hall monitors: They were never around when you needed them.

Alice gave me a big, wicked grin. "Honestly, is dressing like that considered cool wherever it is you're *really* from?"

"I'm from *here*," I reminded her for what felt like the *zillionth* time. This whole thing started back in first grade when we'd been partners for a cultural heritage project and she learned that I was born in Puebla, Mexico. (My dad's family is Mexican and Portuguese, and my mom's is Cuban.) I'd tried to explain to her that my parents had moved here when I was only one, so America was the only country I'd ever called home, but she didn't seem to get that. It sucked that some people would never accept me just based on my parents' nationalities and the color of my skin.

"Sure you are, ese . . ." Alice's gaze narrowed. Then she stepped forward and snatched my mom's locket out of my hands before I could react.

"Hey, gimme that back!" I shouted, lunging at her. But two of her henchwomen grabbed me. They slammed me roughly against the wall of lockers and held me there. I could only watch, shivering with anger, as the bat-swinging Neanderthal raised the locket to her face and grinned.

"Pretty fancy," she said with an evil wink. "Let me guess, a going-away gift from Mommy and Daddy when they got deported?"

My temper flared. "Don't talk about my parents!"

"Yes, sir, Capitán! I beg your pardon, Capitán!"

Most of her crew was almost falling on the floor, they were laughing so hard. Then Alice gave me a mocking salute, and they all started laughing even harder.

Gosh, what was wrong with these people? Did they just wake up in the morning thinking about whose life they could make miserable?

"Tummy tuck!" Alice suddenly shouted, and punched me right in the stomach.

Pain exploded inside me, and I doubled over, letting out a weird, high-pitched gasp as more cackling laughter echoed through the hall.

"You're lucky I'm in such a good mood," Alice said, bending down to whisper in my ear, "or that would've just been the opening pitch."

I managed to choke out, "So this is your good mood,

huh?" But I had a feeling she wasn't kidding about that.

Ignoring me, she held my mother's locket up to the light like some wannabe jeweler examining a precious stone. "You know what?" she said. "I think I'm gonna hang on to this for a while. Yeah, that's a good idea. . . . Matches my nose ring pretty good. Plus, it might help with your lip." She looked around at her friends. "What do you think, girls? Add it to my collection?"

"Yeah, I'm thinking maybe not," said a new voice.

I looked around and felt my face flush with a mixture of relief and embarrassment. It was Violet Rey, also known as Ultra Violet. The prettiest, smartest girl in our entire school. And probably the world. Violet was captain of both the debate team and the cheerleading squad and was editor in chief of the school newspaper. The crush I had on her went all the way back to first grade, when she tricked me into eating a carrot-shaped stick of orange Play-Doh. I puked. Saw stars. Had a thing for her ever since.

"In fact," she said, strolling right up to Alice, "I'm thinking these two bozos should let him go, and you, queen of *all* bozos, should apologize and give him his stuff back."

"Or what?" the queen bozo sneered. "You gonna go *tattle* on me?"

A couple of her sidekicks laughed at that, smacking hands like it was the comeback of the century. *Morons.*

"Sort of," Violet said, "but not exactly how you're thinking. See, a very reliable source told me not too long ago that you spent the summer bulking up on performance-enhancing drugs your daddy bought for you off the Internet. So, I was thinking maybe I'd run with it. Make it the front-page story of the *Leon Gazette* and see what all the high school and college scouts think about that." Violet grinned mischievously. "Would you like me to forward a copy to your place of residence? Maybe sign you up for a year's subscription? As always, all proceeds go to support our local PTA." She let that hang for a moment before adding, "Next move is yours, Allie. But my advice, you and your baboons make like polynomials and factor out."

I saw Alice's expression darken. Saw her teeth grit as she aimed a long, meaty finger at Violet. "You wouldn't *dare* print something like that. . . ."

"Then call my bluff, poker star." Violet stepped up to her, getting all up in her face. Her blue eyes were like chips of ice and just as sharp. "'Cause I'm all in."

Alice thought for almost twenty seconds—yeah, I counted—and I swore I could hear the gears grinding in her head. Finally, her toxic brown eyes narrowed on me, and she slammed the locket into my chest. "You lucked out this time, amigo," she said. "But hey, there's always mañana. . . ."

The moment they were gone, I turned to Violet and

said, "Thanks." But what I really wanted to say was, *Hey, would you mind being my personal bodyguard for the next thirty-six weeks?*

The pay wouldn't be great, but at least I could guarantee she'd get to see plenty of action.

"No sweat. I can't stand racists or bullies—and especially not *racist bullies.*" Then she looked at me and laughed. "What in the world are you *wearing* . . . ?"

Kill me now, God. "Just, um, a little something I picked up at the mall."

Violet made a face. "Listen, for the record, no one hates bullies more than I do. But I gotta be honest, dressing like that—you're making yourself an easy target."

"I was cold," I lied.

"Then wear a jacket that fits. And preferably one that's less *sparkly.*"

"I'll try to remember that." I rubbed my chest, feeling a red-hot blush creeping up my neck.

"Hey, your dad is Edward Hernández, right? The animal scientist?"

Whoa, she knew that? "Uh, yeah . . . he's an animal geneticist. He studies their DNA and stuff like that."

"You remind me of him," Violet said, and it was easy to understand why. My dad and I were basically twins. We had the same honey-colored skin, the same dark hair, and the same chocolate-brown eyes that proudly showed our Latino heritage. My mom says I'm his mini-me, which I guess is a good thing since most of her friends like to call my dad (when he isn't around, of course) Señor Tall, Dark, and Muy, Muy, Handsome. But, *unlike* me, my dad has this cool Spanish accent that everybody loves but that he thinks makes people underestimate him. I never understood that.

"I still remember that presentation he gave about dogs," she said. "It was really eye-opening."

"You remember that?" I couldn't believe it. That must've been, like, two years ago, on Bring-Your-Parents-to-School Day.

"How could I forget? When he explained how pure-breeding dogs actually hurts the animals and messes up the gene pool, I ran home and worked all night to get a story ready to publish the very next morning in the school paper. I mean, it really is a modern form of animal cruelty, wouldn't you agree?"

"Totally . . ." I was too stunned to come up with anything more intelligent-sounding.

"So, what is that thing, anyway?" Violet asked, nodding at my mom's locket.

"You mean this?" When I held it up, her eyes got all huge and excited.

"Oh my God, it's beautiful! Where did you get that?"

I caught a whiff of her—she smelled like strawberries and cotton candy—and "Uh," was all I could manage.

"You don't remember?"

"No, no—I do. It's just . . . something I found." I hoped I didn't sound as stupid as I felt. Though I was pretty sure I did.

"Well, looks to me like a hybrid of a bola necklace and a locket. Definitely silver. Throw in the chain and the oddity value, and my guess is that it's probably worth somewhere in the neighborhood of six hundred bucks. You could probably pawn it for around three hundred if you needed to score some quick cash." I must've looked pretty stunned because she quickly added, "My dad owns an antique shop downtown. Sometimes I work the register."

"I had no idea," I said. But the truth was I knew all about her dad's shop. I'd probably made my mom sell off about half her old clocks and china just so I'd have an excuse to go in and maybe catch a glimpse of Violet hanging around the back somewhere. Pathetic, I know.

"Yep." She was nodding now, eyes fastened on the locket. "Anyway, it's definitely vintage. Maybe early nineteenth century. Definitely rare."

"I was thinking the same thing, actually . . . about it being rare and stuff."

"Have you checked to see if there's anything inside?"

"Yeah, yeah, I tried. But I couldn't get it open."

"Here, let me." She took the locket and went to work on it. "I'm good with locks."

"Yeah, I don't think you're going to be able to open it so easily. . . . I've been trying nonstop for, like, five whole—"

The locket clicked open in her hands. "There."

"—*seconds*." I gaped, shaking my head. "How'd you do that?"

"I'm good with locks, remember?" Her lips curved into a dazzling smile. Then she turned her attention back to the locket. "Where did you say you found it again?"

"In my house. My *old* house."

"Check it out. . . ." With the tips of her fingers, she pulled what appeared to be a small square of dyed animal skin from the locket. She held it up, and I could see that the edges were all crinkled and frayed like some ancient scroll. "Looks like some kind of map," she whispered. "An *old* one . . ."

When she passed it to me, I realized she was right—it *was* a map! There was a legend in the bottom-left-hand corner, a scale (1 cm = .5 acres), and a little red *X* in the middle. But why was there a map hidden inside my mom's locket?

"What do you think that symbol means?" Violet asked. "On the other side?"

I flipped it around. On the back was some sort of decorative marking: two long horns curving up toward a fan of plumy feathers.

My fingertips went numb. Horns and feathers.

No flippin' way . . .

"Hey, you okay?" Violet asked, jabbing me on the shoulder.

I gave a shaky nod as she handed me back the locket.

"Where did you say you found it again?" she asked.

"It was in my room. In my other—"

"*Excuse me!*" rasped a voice from up the hall.

We both turned to see Mrs. Porter, the school's home ec teacher, poking her head out of her classroom. She had a crusty wooden spatula in one hand and was pointing it at us threateningly. A glob of spaghetti sauce dripped off the spoon-shaped end, splattering to the ground between her feet. "This isn't a coffee shop," she said. "You two need to get back to class. *Now.*" Her beady little eyes narrowed on me. "And what in *God's name* are you wearing . . . ?"

"He's cold," Violet said.

Mrs. Porter looked like she'd just been told the earth was actually square. "But it's over ninety degrees out!"

"Might actually be closer to eighty-eight with the windchill factor," I threw out. What else could I say?

Mrs. Porter stared at me for another long moment, as if her brain absolutely refused to let her accept what she was seeing. Then she said, "Your generation lacks any sense of propriety. And style. Now get back to class!"

CHAPTER SEVEN

When the final bell rang, I headed out to the bleachers by the PE field to meet up with Alvin Campbell and Sam Rodriguez—my two best (and only) friends. I jokingly called them "Los Jimaguas," which means "the twins" in Spanish, because I don't think there were two people on the planet who looked less alike. Where Alvin was tall and portly, with a milky complexion and curly orange hair that fell over his face like a mop, Sam is rail-thin, dark-skinned, and had thick black hair that stuck straight up in a perfect three-inch-tall flattop. If I had to compare them to creatures in the animal king-dom, I'd say that Alvin most closely resembled a manatee in shape and overall athleticism (which I guess is kind of ironic since manatees recently became his favorite animals when one started hanging out in the canal behind his house last year), while Sam probably reminded me most of a flamingo, with those bright, tropical-colored T-shirts he liked to wear and his long stick-thin legs than could really move when they had to. But as different as they looked on the outside, the bonds that united them on the *inside*—that united all three of us, really—were strong and unshakable: video games, Hot Pockets, and our three-man Latin rock band called Los Chicharrones. So, naturally, the guys were rocking out on air guitars when I got there, probably leveling up through the latest mobile version of Guitar Hero.

"Dude, where's the blizzard?" Alvin said mid-solo.

"Not today, Al." I blew out a breath. "Definitely not today."

As we started across the field toward the line of parked cars, Sam put his shiny new NY Red Bulls–skinned iPhone away and said, "So, are you going to explain the jacket, or you want us to pretend we don't see it?"

"Guys, it's not a big deal," I said. "I just felt like adding another layer of protection."

They both stared at me.

"What? It's not *that* weird."

Alvin was shaking his head. "Dude, I just need you to understand that when you wear stuff like that, you bring down our entire group average. People are going to start thinking we're weird."

"They already think that," I pointed out.

"Yeah, but I mean, like, *everyone*'s going to start thinking that. Not just the cool kids."

Sam looked me up and down. "You look like you're about to pass out, hermano. Sure you don't want to take that thing off real quick? Give your cells a second to breathe?"

"It's actually more comfortable than it looks," I lied. "The material's soft. Breathable. I can really see it becoming a staple in my wardrobe." *At least until I* molt, I thought.

"Well, thanks for the heads-up," Alvin said. "Guess I'll be avoiding you for a while."

"Laugh it up, chico." I wiped a stream of sweat from my forehead and glanced down at my watch. It was a couple of minutes past four, which meant Sam's mom was almost twenty minutes late. Again. When she happened to be on time (which wasn't very often), she usually parked on the far side of the field, waiting along with the rest of the other parents, but I didn't see her blue Oldsmobile anywhere. *Magnífico.*

"You know, this whole ski-jacket-in-the-summer thing kind of reminds me of this loco story my mom told me," Sam said. "Last year, a friend of hers started wearing winter coats in July after giving birth to triplets. Then she started carpooling and . . ." He suddenly trailed off, his gaze drifting over my shoulder.

"Is this supposed to be a cliff-hanger or something?" Alvin asked, giving Sam a funny look. But Sam didn't answer; he just kept on staring, and it took me a couple seconds to realize he was actually looking *at* something. Or some*one*.

I spun around and saw Violet Rey coming up behind me, her glittery JanSport over one shoulder, her big purple cheer bag over the other. I thought there was a hint of a smile on her pretty pink lips, but I could have just as easily been imagining it.

"Hey, Charlie. What's up?" she said.

"Nothing much, Violet. . . . Wh-what's up with you?"

Out of the corner of my eye, I could see Alvin and Sam with stupid, OMG expressions plastered across their faces; Alvin looked like he'd swallowed a dinosaur egg and realized it had just hatched in his stomach. I couldn't exactly blame them.

Violet held up a finger and crooked it at me. "Think we can chat for a sec? Alone?"

"Uh, sure . . ."

We walked a little way together, and once we were out of earshot of the guys, she whispered, "So, when are you going to find out where the map leads?"

"Oh, I wasn't really gonna," I lied.

"*What?*" She sounded like I'd just told her to paint her

face green and start cheering for the G. W. Carver Hornets, one of our rival schools. "What do you mean you weren't really gonna?"

"Don't get me wrong; it's cool and all. But I don't think it's going to lead to some . . . *undiscovered treasure* or whatever."

"And you're not even *a little* curious to find out where it *does* lead?"

"Not really," I said. But that was an even bigger lie. Of course I was curious. I mean, how could I *not* be? Just a few hours ago I'd found a map inside the only thing on the planet that I had left of my parents. A map that *also,* by the way, happened to have a big decorative stamp of horns and feathers on it. But I simply couldn't let her get involved. With my current feather situation, now was not the time to be making new friends—*especially* ones as popular as Violet Rey.

"You're *so* lying right now," she said, eyeing me suspiciously.

"Wh-what would give you that impression?"

"Yeah, I *wonder.* . . ." She rolled her eyes. "And why are you still wearing that ridiculous jacket? You look like you're about to pass out."

"I . . . heard there was a cold front coming."

"So why don't you wait for it to actually *get* here?"

"Because I like to . . . be . . . prepared." I winced, wondering just how stupid I could make myself look in a sixty-second conversation. My guess was very.

"Fine." Violet crossed her arms over her cheer jersey. "But I should warn you that I'm a curious girl, Charlie Hernández. A *very* curious girl. And the fact that you're being all dodgy is only making me *even more* curious."

"I—I'm sorry?"

She eyed me for another moment, then dragged a hand through her thick blond bangs. "Charlie, your feathers are showing," she said with a sigh.

"My *what?*" I nearly shrieked. I looked down and saw it was true—a couple of feathers were poking out of the cuff of my sleeve. "My jacket's got a little rip," I said, quickly stuffing them back in. "I've been trying to get it fixed for a while now, but my, uh, tailor's on vacation. . . . You know tailors." I could hear the fear in my voice, could feel the sentences spewing out like vomit, but couldn't seem to shut myself up. "I'm not stressing, though. I've heard things like that can happen to even the best winter coats. They say it's quite common, actually."

Violet gave me a doubtful look. "Who would tell you something like that?"

"Just . . . people." My cheeks felt like they were on fire; my face was probably redder than a habanero chili pepper.

Her eyes never left mine. "*Right.*"

And just then, a miracle happened.

Honk! Honnnnnk!

Sam's mom pulled up to the edge of the PE field, saving me from the Violet Inquisition. (Which was beginning to feel even more intense than the Spanish one where they burned people at the stake.)

She honked again, then rolled down her window and shouted, "C'mon, guys! I'm gonna be late for hot Pilates!"

"That's my ride," I said to Violet. "Gotta run . . ."

She fixed me with those brilliant baby blues. "Don't think this is over, Charlie. I'm going to be keeping my eye on you . . . *both* eyes." Then she made a gun gesture with her fingers and fired it at me.

Ay, que bueno. My very first psycho stalker. "'Kay." Swallowing hard, I gave her an awkward wave and then hurried after the guys.

CHAPTER EIGHT

The entire car ride home the guys pestered me with questions about Violet: What did she want? What did she say? What does her breath smell like? Glitter? Cupcakes? Chocolate-frosted fairy dust? Unfortunately for them, I wasn't in a question-answering mood. And fortunately for *me*, the whole trip took less than five minutes, as Sam's mom broke almost every traffic law known to man, blowing through stop signs and traffic lights, weaving madly from lane to lane, honking and hollering at anyone who dared to get in her way.

Honestly, after all I'd been through today, I was just glad to be alone, glad to be off school property, and glad to be home—even if that home wasn't my *real* home.

Mrs. Wilson—my temporary guardian—lived in a small two-story bungalow half-hidden behind a tangle of mango trees and crooked palms with their trunks painted white. The house was an oldie from the fifties, and even though she'd spent the last five months remodeling it, the place still showed its age, with sagging gutters, creaky wood floors, and old-school jalousie windows that protested with an annoyingly loud groan when cranked open.

Mrs. Wilson was in the living room, dusting her dolls, when I walked in. Like the house, Mrs. Wilson was getting up there in years—and by getting up there I mean she'd probably shared a carriage with Benjamin Franklin at some point in her life. She had a dandelion fluff of frizzy white hair and skin so crinkly it reminded me of an old photograph someone had folded and unfolded too many times. Her back was a little hunched and her legs were a little wobbly, but her eyes were still a sharp, piercing green and didn't miss much. Didn't miss any dust particles on her dolls, that was for sure.

"Oh, hello there, dear," she said when she heard the door close. "How was school?"

"Hot." I armed sweat off my face. "Very hot."

She set her duster down and smoothed the front of her floral-print nightgown. (Mrs. Wilson was an early sleeper and therefore always in a nightgown.) "Maybe that's because you're wearing a snow jacket," she said, catching my gaze in the mirror behind the old-fashioned antenna TV. "Don't think it's the right season for one of those."

When I didn't say anything, she gestured around the room at her dolls. "So, this is all of them. What do you think?"

"It's . . ." I searched for the right word. "*Wow.*"

Over the last few weeks, Mrs. Wilson had been bringing her "prized collection" out of storage. Every couple days, she'd go and fetch another box or two, usually about seven or eight dolls. But today she'd brought home close to forty, and now the living room basically looked like one giant showroom for her vast—and *freaky*—collection.

There were literally dolls everywhere—sitting on sofas and armchairs, perched on shelves, staring blankly across the room from pint-size rocking horses and cribs. Some of them were big—well, *big* for dolls—and sported even bigger smiles, while others were tiny and had terrified expressions on their pale, plastic faces. They wore everything you could imagine, from miniature vaquero jackets to extravagant baiana dresses that must've taken months to sew.

According to Mrs. Wilson, she'd started her collection when she was only five years old and had since traveled the world, buying a doll or two in every country she visited.

"There are certainly a lot of them," she said with a proud sort of grin. "But they fit the space quite nicely, no?"

I nodded, trying to be supportive. "Yeah, very nicely."

"Oh, I almost forgot. Are you interested in a little dinner, dear?" She nodded toward the kitchen, where I could smell somthing rich and creamy bubbling away in one of her huge, old-school cast-iron pots. "I whipped up some *escargots à la Bourguignonne*. That's snails finished in a delicious herb butter sauce, just like they make in France."

"That sounds amazing," I said, but it was all I could do to keep my tears in check. Ever since I was little, my mom would cook up all kinds of tasty traditional dishes for me. She'd make seafood paellas in the old Spanish way; chiles rellenos using real Mexican chilies; arroz con pollo with the exact spice combination her family had used in Cuba for generations. My mom taught Spanish and Hispanic culture at my school and always said you can learn everything about a people from what they ate. I missed her. *A lot.* And now, anytime someone mentioned any kind of cultural dish, I missed her even more.

"I'll prepare a plate for you," Mrs. Wilson said, moving past me.

"Oh, no. Actually, I think I'm gonna have to pass. I have a ton of homework. I'll just have a Snickers or something if I get hungry." Usually, just thinking about my parents made me lose my appetite. Today I had even less of an appetite than usual because I was so anxious to take a closer look at that map. And the whole snails-in-butter thing didn't exactly get my digestive juices doing the salsa either.

"Candy bars aren't a real meal, dear," I heard her call out

as I pounded up the creaky stairs to the attic. "You should always try to incorporate multiple food groups."

"Don't worry," I called back. "I'll throw in a bag of tortilla chips to get some veggies in. ¡Hasta mañana!"

In my room, I stripped down to my underwear (which were soaked through—TMI, I know) and dropped into the rolling chair in front of the laptop Alvin had let me borrow.

Then I pulled the map from my pocket, typed the words "horns," "feathers," and "map" into my favorite search engine, and hit go.

Nothing came up—nothing useful, anyway—so I tried my second-favorite search engine, but I didn't get anything there, either. Not even a page of results this time.

Sighing, I leaned back in my chair, wondering what to do next. Unable to come up with much, I took a picture of the little horns-and-feathers symbol with my webcam, uploaded it into Google, and ran a reverse image search. Honestly, I really wasn't expecting to get a hit, but next thing I knew, *bingo*, I got one! A link to the La Rosa Cemetery website had come up in the results.

More than a little confused, I clicked it and was greeted by a colorful banner that read, LA ROSA, THE MOST TRUSTED NAME IN ESTATE PLANNING. Below it was the slogan, PICK A PLOT, SECURE YOUR SPOT! It sounded like they were offering cruise reservations, not a six-foot-deep hole in the ground. In the center of the page was some sort of family crest (a shield flanked by two huge birds—eagles, maybe), and inscribed along the edge of the shield was that symbol again—the horns and feathers!

Interesting . . .

I browsed the site. There was some history about the place, a little background on its founder—Mr. Juan Garcia, an old Spanish industrialist—and a couple of pages about pricing and payment plans. Nothing jumped out at me (except the half-off sale on coffins—because who doesn't need to get in on that deal, right?).

Just when I was about to close the page, I randomly clicked on the directions tab, and an aerial view of the cemetery came up on the screen, freezing me in place.

It was a mirror image of the map—right down to the little hill in the middle and the long stretches of trees that bordered it.

At first I couldn't believe my eyes. But looking at it from this angle, there was no doubt about it. This was a map of the old cemetery up on Bonita Avenue!

Then something else hit me: Whatever the *X* marked was *inside* that cemetery.

The idea hadn't even fully formed in my brain, and already I could hear my parents telling me that it was a bad one, my mother saying something like, *¡Mijo, ni lo pienses! Who in their right mind follows a map they found in a locket to a cemetery? It's stupid. And dangerous. What do you even expect to find?*

And she'd probably be right. It *was* stupid. And dangerous. Heck, the trip alone was a six-mile bike ride in each direction. Not to mention the fact that the only way there was through a super-shady part of town.

But as sure as I was that my parents wouldn't approve, I knew I had to go. If there was any chance of figuring out what was happening to me, any chance of finding my mom and dad, I had to give it a shot. Regardless of the consequences.

CHAPTER NINE

That evening I waited for Mrs. Wilson to go to bed—which wasn't a very long wait, because she tucks in promptly at seven p.m. every night—then waited a little longer for the sun to start going down before I snuck out my bedroom window and headed over to La Rosa. The ride took almost an hour, and by the time I got there, night had fallen and the wind had really picked up, gusting through the narrow two-lane street that curved into the cemetery's parking lot. Fortunately, I'd put something on to hide the feathers—my own normal, full-size, *non*-sparkly hoodie this time—so the drop in temperature was more of a relief than anything.

I laid my bike by the entrance and looked around. The cemetery on Bonita was supposedly one of the oldest establishments in all of Miami. According to their website, it had been founded in the late 1800s, right around the time

Miami was declared a city. The graveyard itself, a rolling carpet of ankle-high crabgrass, was surrounded on three sides by tall, spindly trees. A twisted wrought-iron gate guarded the entrance, hanging from a pair of giant rusty hinges. The gate shivered slightly in the breeze, making this sad, high-pitched whine that sounded like a wounded animal. Beyond it, sunken tombstones and towering mausoleums created a haphazard maze of stone and marble that seemed to run on forever. I could hear a chorus of spooky sounds coming from somewhere deep inside—low moans and echoes, creaking branches, and a constant *tap-tap-tap* on stone—but I told myself it was just the wind. Had to be.

Still, standing there, staring at this huge, creepy place, I instantly regretted not asking Alvin or Sam to tag along.

But it was too late now.

Stuffing my hands into my pockets, I walked in through the main gate (which someone had forgotten to close—if it even closed anymore, that is) and began picking my way around the grave markers, trying not to think about the bodies rotting just six feet under. Wispy tendrils of fog wound through the grounds, creating a freaky 3-D effect. The headstones poked up through the fog like hundreds of crooked teeth. I tried not to think about those, either.

About twenty yards in, I stopped to check the map. It was dark in here, much darker than by the entrance, but the yellow glow of the streetlamps across the road provided just enough light for me to see. And judging by the little pictures, I wasn't too far now—another fifteen yards or so and whatever the *X* marked should come up on my right.

Almost there, I told myself, pocketing the map. Somewhere in the distance, I heard the low roll of thunder and started walking again, faster, knowing I had to pick up my pace. A storm was coming—if it wasn't already here. And sometimes when it really poured, Mrs. Wilson would come upstairs to check on me, to make sure the attic wasn't leaking or something. She was always keeping an eye on me—I guess she felt responsible for my well-being now or whatever—and I appreciated that. The last thing I wanted was for her to walk into an empty room and—

A flicker of movement to my left drew my eye.

I whirled in that direction, scanning the shadows.

Nada.

No movement or sound except for the *wham-blam-blam* of my heart.

I squinted into the gloom, listening. Still nothing.

This place is getting to me, I thought. *A few more minutes in here and I'll be seeing a zombified Justin Bieber doing the claws-up move from "Thriller."*

Up ahead, the branches of the ancient oaks creaked and snapped. I tried not to stare at the creepy mosaic they made against the starless sky, tried to ignore the nagging feeling that I was being watched, followed even.

"Get it together, chico," I said out loud. "There's nothing to be afraid of . . . *cero*." But my voice sounded weak and scared even to my own ears. There was a vibe to this place . . . a sort of lurking, uneasy feeling that put a chill in my bones. And even though I knew it was probably all in my head, I also knew I didn't want to spend one more second in here than I absolutely had to.

In fact, part of me was already beginning to think I should turn around, when I passed a row of shallow graves and saw something that made me stop in my tracks.

It was an enormous statue of an angel—a big ol' tough-looking dude made of solid white marble. He was kneeling down, both wings folded over the top of his head with a serious expression that was all like, *Hey, whatchu lookin' at?* One of his huge stony hands was pointing down at the ground, and I could just make out a pair of tiny symbols chiseled into the concrete slab between his legs: two horns and five long feathers. The exact image from the map!

My skin prickled. *This has to be it. . . .*

Just below the symbol, pressed lightly into the concrete, was the vague imprint of a hand. A big one. And smack-dab in the middle of the palm was a tiny gem that seemed to be radiating a dull greenish glow. Without thinking, I stretched out my hand to touch it, and just as I did, that creepy *someone's watching* feeling came over me again.

Holding my breath, too scared to move, I flicked my eyes from left to right, scanning my surroundings, but at first it was too dark to see much of anything. Only shifting shadows and the blocky, bulky outlines of the gravestones. Then a sliver of moonlight sliced through the cloud cover, and I felt my mouth go dry.

Someone *was* watching me. Maybe a hundred yards away. Some dude in a dark jumpsuit and a beanie. At this distance, I couldn't make out his features—they were just a shadowy blur—but it looked like he was holding something. Something big. Like a huge steel s—

Leaves rustled nearby. Then I heard the dry sound of a twig snapping.

I whirled but didn't see anyone. Not even a stray cat.

Geez . . .

Sucking in a breath, I rubbed a hand over my racing heart and turned back to the creepy guy in the jumpsuit—but he was gone!

A chill of fear skittered down the middle of my back. Had I *imagined* him . . . ? Was I now hallucinating freaky-looking dudes in jumpsuits? The angel's stony eyes stared down at me. *You're losing it, muchacho*, he seemed to say.

And he was probably right.

Somewhere far away, an owl hooted. Closer, leaves stirred in a cold gust of wind. I shivered. Wrapped my arms around myself.

And then nearly jumped out of my skin when I felt a hand clamp down on my shoulder!

Shrieking, I whipped around.

Violet Rey screamed and leapt back.

Wait. Violet Rey is here?

"You almost gave me a heart attack," she said, panting. Her wavy blond bangs hung in her eyes, and she had one hand pressed over the breast pocket of the long brown trench coat she wore.

"*I* almost gave *you* a heart attack?" My voice was high and shrill. "¡Estás loca!"

"Why'd you freak out so bad, huh? I only touched your arm."

"Because I thought you were a grave-robbing serial killer!" I rubbed the spot of pain on my shoulder. "Man, you got one heck of a grip. . . ."

"That's what seven years of nonstop cheerleading and gymnastics will do for you." Violet smiled, making my stomach flutter even through the fear and shock. "I could probably snap your back like a twig," she confessed. When I didn't say anything, she shrugged, looking embarrassed. "Just kidding—*kinda* . . ." Then she stepped up to the statue of the angel. "So, this is where the map led you, huh?" She ran a hand along one of the marble wings. Her shiny pink nails glinted in the moonlight. "*Creepy.*"

I looked around wildly. "Where the heck did you come from, anyway?"

"I followed you," she said, like it was the most natural thing in the world. "I know what you're doing here, Charlie."

"You do?"

"Of course I do. You're trying to find out what happened to your parents. That's why you didn't want to tell me what you were going to do with the map."

My mouth opened and then closed. Dang, this girl was sharp.

"Don't be embarrassed," she said. "It's perfectly natural. In fact, I probably wouldn't have told me either. And full disclosure? I knew that locket I opened for you was your mother's. I'd seen it before. She wore it to a PTA meeting once, and my mom tried to convince her to sell it at our shop." She took a step toward me, her eyes soft. "I wanna help, Charlie. . . . I wanna help you find them."

"Aw, I don't know—" I started to say, but she cut me off.

"Charlie, this is what I *do*. Investigative journalism. I hate to sound like Liam Neeson or whatever, but I have a very particular set of skills." She paused. "You've seen *Taken*, right?"

"Yeah, I've seen it. But I—I just think don't think it's a good idea. . . ." I was staring down at my feet now, shaking my head, but I could feel her eyes on me. "I'm usually pretty good at following clues and stuff, anyway. I mean, it's *pretty rare* when something catches me by surprise."

"Know a lot about sleuthing, huh? Keeping your wits about you? Noticing every *little* detail . . . ?"

"I know enough."

"Know a lot about spiders, too?"

"In fact, I *do* know a lot about spiders. I know a lot about *all kinds* of animals and insects."

"Know anything about tarantulas?"

Is that a challenge? "Kingdom, Animalia. Phylum, Arthropoda. Class, Arachnida. Order, Araneae. Burrowers by nature. Roughly eight hundred different species worldwide. They spin silk, but unlike most spiders, they don't use webs to catch their prey. They have eight eyes but can't see very well." *Take that!* I always knew all my dad's animal talk would come in handy one day.

Violet smirked. "Bad eyesight, huh? Well, that's ironic, because I bet the one on your arm is getting a pretty good look at *you.*"

"Ha. Nice try. But I see what you're doing. . . . You're trying to get me to freak out and look down so you can prove that I'm *not* aware of my surroundings and therefore need your help. Unfortunately for you, I'm not that gullible."

"Charlie, I'm serious. . . ." Her expression became earnest, urgent. "It's *literally* crawling up your arm right now."

"You're funny. I like that. But, for your information, I also happen to have a pretty keen sense of danger, so I think I'd know if a *tarantula* was crawling up my—"

Just then something tugged on my sleeve.

I glanced down. My body went numb.

A huge black tarantula was crawling up the side of my arm!

"*¡AY MI MADRE!*" someone shrieked—must've been me, I guess—and then I was tearing off my jacket, swatting it against my arms, my legs, my back, spinning in wild circles and stomping on anything that moved or even came *close* to resembling an eight-legged arachnid.

"*DID I GET IT?*" I shouted frantically. "*DID I GET IT? HUH? HUH? HUH?*" When Violet didn't answer, I danced right up in front of her and yelled, "*DID I GET IT OR WHAT, CHICA?*"

But she just stood there, staring at me with wide, bulging eyes.

And then I realized why: my jacket! I was EXPOSED! *¡Corre!* my mind screamed. *Run, run, run!*

But I couldn't run. I couldn't even *move*. I could only

stand there, frozen with fear and shock, waiting to hear the next words out of her mouth.

I expected something like, *Freak!* Or, *Animal!* Or, *Freaky animal!* (At least that's what I probably would've said to me had I been in her position.)

But what she finally said was: "*Awesome . . .*"

CHAPTER TEN

"You're like—like a beautiful blood-speckled angel!"

I could feel an embarrassed blush creeping up my neck. "The blood is on account of my pores being too small for the feathers, so they bleed a little. But you think I'm beautiful? I mean, my plumage?"

"Duh!" Violet was circling me now, looking me up and down like I was Michelangelo's *David* or something. "But no wings, huh? That's too bad. I've always wanted to fly. You know, like Lois Lane in the original *Superman* movie?"

"Gimme a day or two," I said. "Wouldn't be surprised if I *sprouted* a pair."

She held my gaze, her eyes electric. "So—what are you . . . ?" she asked finally.

"What do you mean *what am I?*" I snapped. "I'm a boy. A real boy!"

She put her hands up. "Easy there, Pinocchio. I was only asking."

"Kind of a *rude* question, don't you think?"

"Listen, I know as the head of the student newspaper I'm probably the last person on earth you wanted finding out about this, but it's not like I'm going to write a story on you or anything." She paused like she was considering something. "Though I have to say, the headline would be one heck of a grabber: 'Charlie Hernández, the half-avian man-child that stalks our halls.' I mean, *c'mon*, tell me that's not must-read stuff!"

"I don't *stalk* the halls," I grumbled. "And I am *not* half-avian."

"Nephilim?"

"Ne—*what?*"

"Shape-shifting mutant?"

I raised a brow. "Like Mystique from *X-Men?*"

"Is that a yes?"

"No! It's a definite *no!* I'm just a normal guy, okay?" I started pacing back and forth in front of the angel, thinking, *I can't believe I'm having this conversation right now. I can't believe I have to defend my humanity of all things!* "Listen. *This,*" I said, gesturing at the feathers, "todo esto— feels like a nightmare. And it's definitely *not* something I've been dealing with all my life. *Believe me.*"

"So, when did it start?"

"The day my parents disappeared," I said before I could catch myself.

Her gaze sharpened. "I should probably start there, then."

"What? *No*. You're not investigating this! This isn't some local fast-food place putting horse meat in their burger patties. This is *my life*!"

Violet looked surprised. "You read that story?"

"Yeah. And I loved how you worked in the factory farms and animal abuse angle. . . . But no! This is not some—some *investigative journalism piece*!"

She gripped my shoulders, the sudden intensity in her eyes more than a little freaky. "Charlie, I don't know if you realize this or not, but your feathers and your parents' disappearance are linked. Just consider the circumstantial evidence. All your life you've been normal, right? Your words. Then your parents vanish, and all of a sudden you start experiencing this kooky transformation. It's *one* case. And you're going to need someone with *extensive* investigative experience to help you crack it. Again, not that I'm thinking of doing a story on you or anything, but a chance to investigate something like this—the hours of painstaking research, the thrill of the hunt, the exhilaration when all the pieces finally click together . . ." She trailed off. Her eyes were huge, her dark blond hair whipping around her face in the breeze. "Charlie, this is what I live for. . . . And how many times in my life do you think I'm going to get a chance to be a part of something like this? Do you seriously want to deprive me of that kind of life experience?"

"Yes!" I said. Then I turned and started walking away.

"You're so not being fair right now, Charlie Hernández!" she shouted after me. "You're acting like a selfish little boy! A selfish, *selfish* little boy!"

I whirled on her. "*Me?* I'm the one who's *selfish?* Look at my arms. Look at where I am. In a cemetery. At almost eight o'clock at night. Trying to figure out what's happening to me. What happened to my parents—who, by the way, have been missing for more than *two months!*" I was trying to catch my breath, trying to keep the tears from smarting in my eyes. "You really want to go there . . . ?"

Violet's expression softened; her voice was low as she said, "What if I can help?"

"What if you can't?"

"Fine, let's say I can't. What do you have to lose?"

I ran the back of my hand across my eyes. "Besides my dignity?"

Violet sighed. "Look, I just wanna help. And I don't want to have to resort to cheap threats or blackmail, but if you don't agree to let me, I'm going to have no choice but to rat you out in the school newspaper."

"I believe that's the *exact* definition of blackmail," I said, putting my jacket back on. "And a cheap threat."

"You're burning moonlight. We should see what's under that statue before it gets any later."

"*Under that statue . . . ?* Please tell me that was a joke."

"You have a better idea?"

I felt my eyes bug. Was she kidding? "Better than *grave robbing*? Uh, *yeah!*"

"Oh, don't be so dramatic, Charlie. Plus, we wouldn't *technically* be robbing anything, since I fully intend to return whatever it is we find once we're done with it."

"Oh, well, when you put it like that . . . Just be sure to explain that to the police when they *arrest* us!"

Just then lightning flashed overhead, momentarily turning the night into day and revealing row after row of whitewashed stones. It flickered again, and out of nowhere a figure appeared in front of us. A man, tall and skinny, with a hard, bony face and eyes sunk so deep in his skull they might as well have been empty sockets.

"Getting arrested should be *the least* of your worries," he said.

CHAPTER ELEVEN

Aaaaaaahhhhhhh!" I screamed.

"Aaaaaaaahhhhhhh!" Violet agreed.

She whipped out a can of Mace while I struck my fiercest-looking karate pose. When I was little my mom had signed me up for Brazilian jujitsu classes, and even though I'd only made it to a gray belt (which is a rank-two belt for juniors), I'd learned that looking like you knew what you were doing was enough to deter most attackers.

And I guess it worked, too, because the guy didn't take another step. Instead, he stabbed his shovel into a hump of dirt and leaned heavily on it like it was a cane.

"The cemetery is closed, muchachos," he said with a thick Spanish accent. "Cerrado. You're both trespassing." His voice was *seriously* creepy; it sounded all raspy and distorted, as if coming through a pair of ancient, blown-out speakers.

"Uh, sir, if you could just gimme a minute to look around—" I began.

"Kid, you deaf? I said we're *closed*." His fingers tightened threateningly around the shovel's rusty handle. "Now move along or I'll bury the both of you. *Side by side*."

I frowned. *The heck did he just say?*

"We're very sorry, sir," Violet suddenly piped up. She tugged on my arm, then began pulling me back the way I'd come. "We'll be going now. . . . Sorry for bothering you."

As we threaded our way through the maze of tombstones, I whispered, "Wow. You sure talk big for someone so ready to tuck tail and *run*."

She threw a fast look over her shoulder. "Who said anything about running?"

I turned, trying to follow her gaze. "¿Qué haces? What are you looking at?"

"I'm timing it."

"Timing what?"

"*This!*" And she shoved me to the ground behind a row of tall headstones.

"*What'd you do that for?*" I rasped as she ducked in next to me.

"Because this guy knows something," she said. "Did you see his pinky ring?"

"No. I was too busy praying he wouldn't *murder us!*"

"It has the same symbol from the map. The horns and the feathers."

I blinked in surprise. "Really?"

"Yep. Which means we're going to have to follow him."

"But you told him we were leaving!"

Violet gripped my shoulders and squeezed. "Get ahold of yourself, Charlie. And remember, I'm the professional here. Just follow my lead."

"Yeah, you're the professional, all right . . . professional *crazy person!*"

She peeked over the top of the tombstone. "Look!" she whispered, tugging excitedly on the sleeve of my jacket.

The gravekeeper had turned to face the statue of the angel. Now he crouched down and put his hand to the handprint in its concrete base. Before either of us knew what was happening, the ground started to tremble and the entire statue—giant stony angel and all—slid silently to one side, revealing a gaping hole in the ground. I rubbed my eyes, unable to believe what they were seeing, but nothing changed: the groundskeeper dude had opened up some kind of hidden passageway!

"That's why you always keep pulling on the thread," Violet whispered, as if talking to herself.

I shook my head. "*What?*"

"Never mind."

After a quick look around, the groundskeeper started down the hole, his enormous shovel dragging behind him like a limp leg.

The moment he was out of sight, Violet grabbed my arm and yanked me forward. We skidded to a stop at the edge of the hole, and when I peered into it, I was surprised to see a set of dusty stairs leading down into a narrow corridor.

"Ready?" Violet asked, her eyes all big and blue and sparkly. The girl obviously lived for stuff like this. When I hesitated, she tilted her head, grinning at me. "You're not *chicken*, are you?"

I glared at her. "Seriously? You're going to make chicken jokes with my whole feather situation?"

Her grin widened.

"By the way, just 'cause something's got feathers doesn't mean it's chicken." I grabbed her hand. "¡Vamos!"

The tunnel was cold and damp and smelled like clothes that had been left wet after washing. A few torches burned on either side, casting long, spooky shadows on the rocky-dirt walls, but otherwise it was pitch-dark.

As we walked, Violet inspected the torches, the beams of rotten wood supporting the ceiling, even the little fluffs of moss that had gathered *between* the beams. She reminded me of a bloodhound. A bloodhound on a scent.

"This is *incredible!*" she whispered excitedly. "This thing shouldn't even exist. We're in Florida! Which is, like, what? Eight feet above sea level?"

"Six, actually," I said, but she had a point. How *did* this thing exist?

A couple of yards later, the tunnel curved left and opened up into some kind of underground boarding station: about a dozen rusty old mine carts sitting on even rustier steel tracks that ran off into the black mouths of the tunnels in either direction. As we looked on, the lead cart shot off into the tunnel to our left while another cart—this one just as rusty and rickety-looking as the others—emerged from the opposite end, joining the back of the line.

"They're automated," I heard myself say. "Like a theme park ride."

"And look!" Violet pointed at the side of one of the carts. Etched into the corroded metal were those symbols again: the horns and feathers.

I felt the hairs on my neck prickle. Okay, this was getting weird. . . .

"C'mon," Violet said.

We climbed into the lead cart, and it lurched forward almost immediately, sending us to our butts. As we entered the dark tunnel, a rush of cool air washed over us, blowing my hair back from my face and making me shiver. The cart's single headlamp snapped to life then, but it didn't show much—only the arched brown ceiling above and the rocky red earth beneath.

"Feels like we're moving at a slight incline," Violet said, struggling to sit up.

I squinted into the dark. "I can't see a thing. . . ."

"Me neither." She gripped the sides of the cart and gave them a firm shake. "At least this thing feels pretty sturdy. Safe."

The wheels on the cart rattled and groaned as we began to pick up speed.

"I think we have very different definitions of the word 'safe,'" I said.

"How about we try to stay positive here, Charlie?"

"I *am* positive. Positive this was a really, *really* bad idea."

And as if to make my point, the cart took a sharp corner, picking up even more speed—and we suddenly dropped into nothingness.

CHAPTER TWELVE

'd like to say that I bravely stared down certain death without so much as a blink or a squeak of fear. But the truth was that when the mine cart made that first awful plunge, leaving my stomach floating somewhere above us, the first thing I did was squeeze my eyes shut so hard I felt it all the way down to my toes. Then Violet and I threw our arms around each other and began to kick and scream like a couple of terrified newborns as the cart twisted and turned and abruptly shot back up again. Hot air rolled over us in a vapory wave. My insides shriveled like pork rinds. Still gaining speed, we rocketed through a narrow section of tunnel, and the world became a blur of shapes and shadows. I was pretty sure Violet was trying to tell me something, but I could barely make out her voice over the rattling thunder of the cart on the tracks.

"We have to do something!" I yelled as I hunkered down as best I could.

Violet glared at me. "Yes, *the lever!*" she shouted, pointing back over my head. "Pull it already!"

I turned. Saw a skinny metal bar poking out over the rear of the cart.

"On it." I struggled to my knees, fighting the g-forces while the cart rattled and jumped.

"Hurry, Charlie!"

Leaning hard against the back of the mine cart—well, more like being *sucked* into it—I wrapped my fingers around the rusted hunk of metal—and pulled. My arms shook, the skin on my palms burned, but the bar didn't give. Not even an inch.

"It's not budging!" I shouted, glancing back at Violet. "Help me!"

Struggling over to me on her hands and knees like a baby learning to crawl, she gripped the bar with both hands. "On three," she said. "One . . . two . . . THREE!"

We pulled. The shaft bent. Gears shuddered and strained. And then—

SNAP!

We were holding the rusty old bar in our hands.

For a moment we looked at each other in disbelief. Then, in perfect unison: "AAAAAAAAHHHHHHH!"

The cart hurtled forward, wheels screaming, sparks shooting up in a wide spray as we thundered furiously along the tracks. A hard left, and I slammed into Violet. A sharp right, and a mass of stalactites zoomed by close enough to stir my hair. Close enough for me to actually *smell* the minerals.

"What's your plan B?" I shrieked as we veered through another tight passageway.

"The lever *was* my plan B. And my plan A and C and D, too!"

There was a rusty screech of springs, and we flew into another hard left. The tracks rumbled. The cart vibrated and bucked like a massage chair gone bonkers. I felt my lunch rise into my throat and clapped both hands over my mouth to avoid giving Violet a face full of our school's gluten-free mac and cheese as we plunged into another drop, this one so steep I literally felt myself float for a full second.

When we hit the bottom, the cart lunged right, and I smacked my head on the sidewall with a thump. A galaxy of bright lights burst across my eyes. The world spun. I opened my mouth to shout something like, *We have to do something!* But Violet was already on it: She had a coil of thick rope in one hand and our half of the broken brake lever in the other.

"Where'd you find the rope?" I shouted.

"I was sitting on it!"

I watched her fasten one end to the brake lever. Then she tied the other end to the rear of the cart and looked up at me.

"The plan is, I toss this bar behind us, it catches in the tracks, and if the rope is strong enough, it should slow us down. You know, like an anchor."

"That's brilliant!"

Violet shouted, "We'll see," then tossed her makeshift anchor onto the tracks. It hit the ground with a flash of sparks, dragging behind us for several yards. Bouncing once, twice, three times—

And then miraculously catching on the rails!

"It worked!" I shouted triumphantly. "It actually worked!"

But half a second later, the rope pulled taut and then snapped like a shoelace.

My heart instantly plummeted to my toes. "I don't suppose you have a plan E?"

Violet's gaze drifted past me. "No time," she said.

And now I saw what she meant: Twenty yards up ahead, just over a hump of rocky earth, the tracks fell away into empty space.

I barely had time to whisper, "Dios mío," before the cart came to a sudden screeching stop and tipped forward, launching us out over the pitch-dark chasm.

CHAPTER THIRTEEN

'd never plummeted to my death before—*obviously*—but I was pretty sure about three things. One, we'd fall for a while, screaming and flailing and hoping for something soft and squishy to break our fall. Two, there wouldn't be anything soft or squishy to break our fall. And three, when we finally *did* stop, that would be the end of the road for us. Like, *forever*. (That's the one I was *most* sure about, in fact.) So you can imagine my surprise when we hit the ground less than a second later, landing face-first on the dusty cavern floor, and neither one of us went *splat!* I suddenly realized two more things—facts, this time. One, we weren't going to die (not right this second, anyway). And two—which was important, because it was the whole reason for number one—we hadn't been launched out over a gaping pit . . . just a really, really dark area of the cave.

Somewhere to my left, I heard a low, grumbling moan

and turned my aching neck to see Violet pushing unsteadily to her knees.

"You okay?" she asked. In the darkness, I could just barely make out her face: Her cheeks and nose were coated in a thick layer of brownish dirt, making it look like she'd taken a big ol' cinnamon pancake to the face. I almost burst out laughing, but then realized I probably didn't look any different.

I sat up, dusting myself off. My neck ached. My knees were throbbing. But, hey, at least I could still move them. "Could've been worse . . ."

"You can say that again."

Looking around, I saw we were sitting in the middle of a huge, semicircular cave surrounded by masses of dripping stalactite columns. Ahead of us was the opening to a narrow tunnel, carved right into the rock. It glowed with pale, flickering light. For a second I thought it was moonlight, but that would've been impossible—we were too far down.

"Looks like there's only one way out," I said, pointing.

Violet blew a strand of hair out of her face and nodded. "C'mon."

Just like in the entrance, the tunnel walls were hung with torches. These, however, burned with a strange green flame that was almost black. Violet guessed the combustible ends must've been dipped in boric acid. That, she said, or there had to be high levels of copper sulfate in the air. Violet was in Pre-AP Chemistry, so I didn't argue. Either way, the greenish fire was awesome (if not a little freaky). But even more awesome—at least to me—were the walls themselves. Carved with beautiful geometric patterns of triangles, zigzags, circles, and squares, they looked like something straight out of the National Museum of Anthropology in Mexico. In fact, the stepped-fret design that ran along the base in thick vertical bands looked *exactly* like one of the display pieces that had been on the cover of the brochure my mom had brought back from her trip to the Mitla ruins site in southern Mexico (aka the Place of the Dead) last year.

Mesmerized, I ran my hand along the intricate carvings. "Magnífico, huh . . . ?" I reached up to trace my thumb along one of the triangles, then quickly yanked my hand away as a gnarly black tarantula came scuttling out of a hole in the middle of it.

"Looks like you found another friend," Violet said with a grin. "I've already seen a bunch. The entire place is crawling with them. . . ."

"In that case, let's keep moving."

Every few yards, the tunnel curved and split off in

different directions. Violet always chose middle, and I just followed, because she looked like she knew where she was going. (And because I'd never been any good at multiple-choice tests.)

About thirty yards in, we began to hear a weird *tink, tink, tink* sound.

"Sounds like dripping," Violet said. She walked out ahead of me and peered into a soccer-ball-size hole in the wall. A moment later, she whirled around, her eyes huge as a startled deer's. "Charlie, get over here!" she whisper-shouted.

I hurried over. "What is it?"

"Look into the hole!" she said, stepping back.

"Huh?"

"Just do it!" she hissed.

So I did—and felt my eyes bug. *Whoa . . .*

Below us, about five or six hundred feet straight down, was a hollowed-out cavern the size of the Grand Canyon. A vast network of platforms and bridges spanned it, criss-crossing like the web of a crazy spider. On the platforms, hundreds of tiny little men in miners' uniforms swung hammers, worked crosscut saws, and fit hinges to rectangular wooden boxes twice their size.

Some of the men were brawny with long white beards and no necks. Others had hairy, reddish faces and feet so big they waddled when they walked. The brawny ones hacked away at minerals embedded in the cave walls, while the hairy-faced ones collected the fragments into buckets and then passed the buckets along a complicated system of pulleys to other hairy-faced dudes, who stood over giant bubbling cauldrons, forging the minerals into what looked like carpenter nails. As I watched, one of the dwarfs—a brawny, bearded one—placed his hairy-knuckled hand on the wall of the cave, and thick yellow veins suddenly appeared in the stone, spreading out from around his tiny palm like the crooked branches of some enormous tree. At first I didn't understand what I'd just witnessed. But then it clicked: The little guy had somehow managed to turn plain old rock into gold ore just by touching it! I counted nine separate bands, each one as thick as a giraffe's neck and at least twice as long.

"Santo cielo," I breathed. "Those things must be mukis!"

Violet, squeezing in next to me, whispered, "What are they called?"

"Mukis. They're like . . . like, *cave dwarfs*. I heard stories about them when I was little. They help miners sometimes—make pacts with them. They supposedly live in mines all over Central America."

"So, they're, like, *good guys?*"

"Not always. They also sometimes *kill* miners and

cause cave-ins." I blinked. Then I rubbed my eyes, hardly believing what I was seeing. "But . . ."

Violet was shaking her head. "But what?"

"I thought those were just myths my grandmother used to tell me . . . stories to scare little kids from wandering into mines alone. How can they *actually* exist?"

"Oh, you'd be surprised what *actually* exists," said a familiar voice at our backs.

I whirled around.

And what I saw made me doubt my own sanity.

CHAPTER FOURTEEN

t was the groundskeeper . . . only he wasn't *really* a groundskeeper. In fact, he wasn't even *human*! In the dim green glow of the torchlight, he looked like nothing more than a shovel-wielding skeleton. His nose was gone; his eyes were two black holes. Through the sheer fabric of his jumpsuit (which he now wore unbuttoned), I could see his pointy shoulder blades, the hollow birdcage of his ribs, every bump and curve of his bony spine. And even though my brain refused to believe what it was seeing, I still knew exactly what he was, what *it* was—a calaca. Yet another creature my abuela had told me stories about!

I vividly remembered the stories, too—tales of walking, talking skeletons. Sometimes they were friendly, jovial spirits who would, on special occasions, sneak out of the underworld to celebrate with the living—like on the Day of the Dead in Mexico. Other times they were grim reapers sent to fetch those whose time on earth was up.

But those were just stories! a panicky voice in my head shouted. And yet there was one right in front of me, standing literally less than two feet away, its bony fleshless face gleaming bright white in the flickering torchlight.

"Hola, muchachos," the calaca said as it stepped forward.

"AAAAAAAAAAAHHHHH!" Violet and I threw our arms around each other. We started to backpedal and bumped painfully against the rocky wall of the cave.

We're trapped! I realized, and my legs instantly turned to jelly.

"Charlie, please tell me you are seeing this . . . ," Violet said, her grip tightening on my arm until it hurt.

"If you mean the walking skeleton—er, calaca—then it's a definite *yes!*"

"Ah, muy bien," the skeleton dude said, sounding impressed. "I see you know your Hispanic mythology. That's very good. It shows you have a curious mind, and that's important for a boy your age. Unfortunately, I still have to kill you now that you've trespassed into my home. . . ." And he raised the shovel, preparing to whack us.

In a panic, I reached into my pocket and pulled out the map and all my loose change. It seemed ridiculous, I know;

I mean, how are you supposed to fight a shovel-wielding maniac skeleton with an old map and a couple of quarters? But I had a plan. See, I remembered my abuela telling me a tale of a shrewd teenage drifter, an orphan named Juancho Ramirez, who'd cheated death, which in his fable had been personified by a calaca. According to the tale, Juancho had learned at a young age that calacas were traders by nature, so he spent his life collecting little trinkets he thought he could use to bargain for his life when one eventually came for him. In my abuela's story, Juancho successfully traded his way to become the oldest living man in Mexico's history. I just hoped that part of the story was as real as the rest of it seemed to be.

"¡Un intercambio!" I shouted, holding out a pair of quarters in my shaking hands. "Two shiny new quarters in exchange for our lives!"

Violet looked at me like I'd lost it (not that I could blame her; I probably would've looked at me that way too), but my ridiculous plan actually worked! Or at least it seemed to, because the calaca's shovel froze in midair. His dark, empty gaze narrowed on my hand, and he whispered, "Niño, where did you come by such a thing . . . ?" I realized he wasn't looking at the quarters; he was looking at my map.

When his bony fingers stretched toward it, I pulled it back an inch, just out of his reach. "It was in a locket that belonged to my mother," I said.

The calaca went dead silent (no pun intended) for several moments. Then a long, pale finger snapped out in my direction. "Listen here, muchacho, I *will* make a trade with you. But not for those worthless coins. For that map. You hand it over, and I'll spare your lives. ¿Cómo suena eso?" He looked between us. "¿Sí? Sounds good?"

"Only if you agree to answer a few questions as well," Violet said, surprising me. It was incredible; the girl was obviously terrified—I mean, I could *literally* hear her heart trying to beat its way out of her chest—but she'd somehow managed to keep her wits about her.

"Deal," the calaca agreed, holding one misshapen hand out toward me.

And did I think this undead skeleton could be trusted? Heck no! But I didn't really see another way out of our current situation. Fortunately, as soon as I handed over the map, Mr. Tall, White, and Bony dropped the shovel.

I let out a breath I hadn't realized I'd been holding.

"Madre mía," the calaca murmured. His voice shook with both awe and fear. "I cannot believe any of these still exist. . . ." He raised the map reverently before him, as if holding a sacred object. "I thought the last had been destroyed in the great fire of Oaxaca."

"Is that map, like, *special* or something?" I asked without thinking.

"No!" the skeleton suddenly snapped. "It's *FORBID-DEN!*" For a terrifying second, I thought he was going to pick up the shovel again and go all Whac-A-Mole on our heads—but he didn't. Instead, he turned his attention back to the map and began to speak slowly, quietly, as if talking to himself. "Once ninety-nine existed, each the hand-sketched work of the most ancient among us, La Calavera Catrina herself. As the head of our order, she took it upon herself to map out the way to the world between worlds so as to create a reliable record for our kin. But soon these maps found their way outside our circle, and those who should not have been able to navigate the deep places of the earth now could. Estos mapas have caused us a great deal of trouble—a *great* deal—which is why in the six hundredth year La Sociedad ordered their immediate collection and destruction. I—I had no idea any had survived...."

The calaca trailed off for a moment, lost in memories. Then he seemed to blink out of it as he lifted his hollow eyes to mine. "Pues, a bargain's a bargain," he said, his nimble fingers quickly slipping the map into his shirt pocket. "What are your *questions* . . . ?"

"First thing," Violet said. "*What. The heck. Are you?*"

The skeleton's glossy white jaw curved up to grin at her as he stooped to pick up his shovel. "Ask your little boyfriend. He seems to know."

"But I—I don't get it. . . . You didn't look *anything* like this when we ran into you up in the cemetery. . . ."

He looked at Violet like she was missing a couple of screws. "Claro que no. It's the torchlight; it reveals my true form. As do the headlights on cars, for some reason. Though this second one I cannot explain. . . ."

"But you're not *real!*" I blurted out. "You're just a Central American *myth!*" I wasn't sure why I was yelling it; I guess I just figured if I said it loud enough maybe the universe would wake up, realize I was right, and fix itself—in other words, send this crazy skeleton dude back to where he belonged: the pages of a Hispanic fairy tale!

The calaca laughed. A sound like bones rattling. "You humans are so silly. . . . You stand in judgment of ancient beings that have existed long before any of you were even born and will be around long, *long* after you and everyone you know is dead and gone." He pointed behind us. "You see those mukis working down there? Most are over three hundred years old. And me? Well, let's just say I once played ulama with an Aztec chieftain. Don't believe me? Ask him yourself. Oh, wait—you *can't*. Because he's *dead!*"

His voice echoed loudly through the cave. Loose dirt and pebbles rained down. Beside me, Violet made a face that said: *Please don't antagonize the psychopathic skeleton with the giant shovel in his hand.*

Still, I couldn't let this go.

"Hold up," I said, shaking my head. "So you're saying that *all* Central American myths are real . . . ?"

"Not just Central American myths, tonto—all *Hispanic* myths!"

Yep, I'd just been called a dummy by a mythological sack of bones. Guess there really was a first time for everything.

"But what you're saying can't be true!" I shot back. "There's *no way* all those myths can be real!"

"*No way? Really?* Then how do you explain how quickly those stories made it around the globe? How do you explain them finding their way into more than *twenty-two* different countries or the fact that they have, over the course of *thousands of years*, influenced *every* aspect of Hispanic culture, from the way people dress, to traditional dances, to what they name their favorite foods—even to the holidays they celebrate?! Do you honestly believe some *make-believe* stories could've accomplished all that? Face it, if people didn't keep encountering things like me generation after generation, the tales would've died off centuries ago. And trust me, you humans might be *a lot* of things, but not one of you, dead or alive, is creative enough to come up with stories like those all on your own."

The calaca was making some strong points. Really strong

ones. Plus, I was finding it sort of difficult to argue with a talking skeleton about what was real and what wasn't.

There was a moment of silence as the calaca composed himself. Then he leaned lightly on his shovel and sucked in a wheezy breath (which, by the way, was pretty freaky considering the dude clearly didn't have any lungs).

"Discúlpame," he said in a sort of embarrassed voice. He looked away, staring down at his bony toes as he wiggled them like worms on a hook. "My tirade was uncalled for. I just get a little irritado when *humans* try to deny my very existence—and the existence of beings like me—to my face. That, and I am going through a bit of a difficult breakup."

"Like with your backbone or something?" I guessed.

The dark sockets of the calaca's eyes bored into me. "No, not *with my backbone*, tonto . . . with a lover. Not that it's *any* of your business."

Definitely not my business, I thought. And *definitely* not something I wanted to picture. I mean, could you imagine going in for a smooch with that bony face? Yikes!

"Uh, excuse me, Mr. Calaca," Violet said, raising a hand like she was back in school, "if it's okay to call you that . . . But I was wondering why you specifically singled out *Hispanic* myths? As I'm sure you are aware, plenty of other cultures have myths too."

"I *am* aware, señorita," the calaca replied. "But Hispanic myths are the only ones that are *consistently* true."

Violet was shaking her head. "Why? That doesn't make any sense."

"Simple. Because the landmasses currently known as Central America, South America, and the Iberian Peninsula are closer in metaphysical proximity to the spirit realm than anywhere else on the planet. Hence the land, the animals, and yes, even *the humans* living in those areas are liable to give birth to all sorts of strange and fantastical beings. Not to mention the fact that there are more *pasillos* across those very same lands than the rest of the world combined; and because the spirits and creatures that cross back over tend to become *viciously* territorial, they usually choose to stay close to the area of their crossing."

"What are *pasillos?*" Violet asked.

The calaca crossed his arms over his chest. "Things niños like you two shouldn't concern yourselves with, señorita . . ."

"Hey, we made a *deal,*" she reminded him firmly.

The skeleton sighed. "They are passageways between the Land of the Living and the Land of the Dead. Links, you could say." His joints creaked and popped as he gestured around the cave. "Like this place . . . *okay?*"

One of my abuela's old sayings came back to me—a phrase frequently used in Mexico when someone dies: *Se lo llevó la calaca.* Or, in English, "The calaca took him." "You're a grim reaper, aren't you?" I said, feeling a cold chill run down my spine.

The calaca gave me a wicked grin. "Think of me more as un guardia . . . a station guard. I make sure none of you skin-people wander over to the other side without good reason. For example, your *deaths* . . ."

I felt my eyebrows press together. "That happens a lot? The people-wandering-over thing?"

"It *does*." He tapped his breast pocket. "Thanks to maps like these."

"But why would someone who's *alive* want to go to the Land of the Dead?" Violet asked.

"To hide from living authorities. To visit long-lost relatives." The calaca shrugged. "The list is long, believe me."

Suddenly, a crazy thought hit me, and I looked at Violet. "Are you thinking what I'm thinking?"

"Think so," she said.

I turned back to the skeleton. "My parents went missing two months ago. Do you think they might've come down here? Maybe to hide from someone?"

The calaca shook his head, and I instantly felt my heart sink. "I've been guarding this particular *pasillo* for more than nine hundred years, and *you two* are the only humans to ever get this far."

"But the map I traded you was in my mother's locket. That means she probably knew about this place."

"Your mother might not have even been the one who put it in there. Did you consider that?"

"Well, did you consider that his parents might've snuck past you?" Violet said.

The calaca's expression darkened. "*No one* sneaks past me, comprende? And they'd need my help to reach the other side, anyway, so you can toss that little theory out the window. Olvídalo." He popped up on his tippies, cracking the knuckles of his toes one by one. The whole thing was pretty gross—and freakishly loud, the sound bouncing off the walls like party poppers.

"Just one more thing," Violet said. She yanked back the sleeve of my jacket, revealing my feather-covered arms. "Explain this."

CHAPTER FIFTEEN

If the groundskeeper had eyes, they would've shot right out of his skull. "¡¿QUÉ ES LO QUE ESTÁ PASANDO AQUÍ?!" he burst out. "EXPLAIN YOURSELVES!"

"They're just *feathers*," I said. "Take a chill pill."

"WHAT KIND OF ABOMINATION ARE YOU?"

"*Abomination?* Hey, at least I have *skin and blood*, hermano. Which is a heck of a lot more than I can say for you!"

"WHAT ARE YOU? ¡CONTÉSTAME!"

"He's just a normal guy!" Violet shouted.

The groundskeeper snatched my arm and raised it—rather rudely, I might add—over my head. "Does this look *NORMAL* to you?" he roared at her.

I yanked my arm away. My cheeks were flaming with embarrassment. As if I didn't feel enough like a freak already, some bareheaded skeleton had to rub it in my face. "Hey, I've been normal all my life, all right? Stuff like this only started happening to me a couple months back."

"Get out!" The bones in his knobby knees made an odd grinding sound as he whirled to point up the tunnel. "¡Váyanse! Follow this tunnel the rest of the way, and the torches will lead you back to the surface!"

"First tell us what you know," Violet demanded.

"No! I won't speak a word about any of this! ¡Ni una palabra!"

"Why not?"

"Because I will not defy La Mano Peluda!"

I shook my head, confused. "The Hairy Hand?"

"Yes, *the Hairy Hand*. I will not allow you to bring their wrath down upon our heads! We are simple stewards, ferrying spirits from one place to another. You'll condemn us to an eternity of nothingness!" His voice once again echoed through the corridor, causing more dirt and bits of stuff to rain down on us.

"Just tell us what you know," I said. "Or at least tell us what the symbol on the back of the map means—the horns and the feathers. I've had both of those manifestations. ¡Los dos!" At Violet's shocked look, I shrugged. Then, to the calaca: "What's *happening* to me . . . ?"

"Read my jawbones," he said. "I. Don't. Deal. In. The.

Dark. Arts. And even if I were still on friendly terms with the *only* lady I know who *does*—which, by the way, I am not—I *still* wouldn't even give you the fifty-two dollars and twenty-five cents that it would cost you to get to her! And would you like to know why? BECAUSE I WILL NOT DEFY LA MANO PELUDA!" He paused, as if trying to catch his breath. "They have spies everywhere. I will say no more. Now get out!"

When we made it back topside a few minutes later, Violet said, "Did all that really just happen?"

I shrugged, feeling dazed. "I think so. That, or one of us is about to wake up from a *seriously* freaky dream."

Violet rubbed her dirt-streaked temples. "Honestly, I'm kinda hoping for number two," she said.

Suddenly, the ground began to shake under our feet, and I peered over my shoulder at the statue of the angel, which was now sliding noiselessly back into place. The thing must've weighed close to two thousand pounds, but it moved as easily as some hollow stage prop set on invisible tracks, hardly disturbing the ground around it at all. It was actually pretty amazing.

"Maybe we should get out of here," I said. "You know, before the earth decides to swallow us or something." Hey, it wouldn't have been the weirdest thing to have happened to us tonight. Maybe not even top three.

A few minutes later, we reached the rusty iron gate of the cemetery. Beside it, lying next to my bike, was a top-of-the-line Mongoose racing bike. "Is that your ride?" I asked Violet.

"Yeah, it's my work bike."

I helped her pick it up.

"Thanks," she said, dusting off the seat. Her eyes, sparkling in the moonlight, stared deeply into mine. "So, crazy night, huh?"

"More like, *psycho* . . . And the cherry on top is that that stupid skeleton didn't give us a freakin' thing."

"No one ever gives *nothing*, Charlie. He said a lot more than he realized. *Trust me.*"

"What do you mean?"

"We'll talk tomorrow. But now I have a few more puzzle pieces to push around in my head."

I had no clue what she was talking about. "Okay . . ."

"By the way, you said the mukis and Skeletor back there are Spanish myths, right?"

"Yeah. Hispanic and Latino myths."

"'Kay, then I better get up to speed on those. Always good to have at least some working knowledge of all things related to your investigation."

I was about to say, *We're not* on *an investigation.* But

the truth was—we were. And she was a pretty darn good detective.

Violet stared at me for a long second, the hint of a smile on her face. "We should probably get home," she said finally. "Before people start to worry." She jerked a thumb over her shoulder. "You'll get home faster if you go down Hibiscus. I should probably take Calle Ocho."

"Sure you don't want me to ride home with you?" I asked. "You know, so you're not alone?"

"Thanks for the offer, but I don't think much is gonna scare me after what we just went through." She hopped on her bike and started pedaling. "Meet me in the library tomorrow after lunch. Oh, and try to get some sleep. . . . Something tells me you're going to need it."

Halfway to the corner, she turned and shouted, "¡Buenas noches, Charlie Hernández!"

Her voice echoed through the night like a sweetly sung lullaby. I could've happily closed my eyes and sailed off to Neverland right then and there. But I didn't want her thinking I was any weirder than she probably already thought I was, so instead I just gave a little wave and watched her until she was nothing more than a tiny brown dot in the night.

"Buenas noches, Violet Rey."

CHAPTER SIXTEEN

I went through the next day in a total haze. My brain felt mushy, like undercooked flan, and I literally couldn't concentrate on anything for more than five seconds at a time—if that. Thoughts buzzed in and out of my head randomly. Nothing seemed to stick. Nada. Which, I guess, was really no surprise considering that just four-teen hours ago my entire concept of reality had been oblit-erated in a short two-minute conversation with the local cemetery's groundskeeper. And the worst part? I couldn't get the freak's bony, fleshless face out of my head. Or his laugh—that haunting rattle that sounded like someone rocking out on a bass drum with a couple of dusty old shinbones.

I was so out of it, in fact, that in second period when Mrs. James, my science teacher, asked me what was the first step of the water cycle, I answered, "Pi equals three point one four." Which *technically* wasn't wrong, but also had nothing to do with the water cycle.

Naturally, the entire class erupted into laughter, and pretty much everyone made fun of me for the rest of the period. Even Mrs. James got in a jab, calling me William Jones (after the guy who came up with pi) when she handed back some old homework. Then, a couple of periods later, it was apparently Alvin's turn.

"Earth to Mr. Three Point One Four. Hellooooo, Mr. Three Point One Four. Are you still with us?" He snapped his fingers between my eyes, making me flinch. "Anyone home?"

The two of us were making our way upstairs after lunch, Alvin on his way to fourth period, me to my previously scheduled meeting with Violet. All around us, kids were laughing and shouting and just generally goofing around, and it wasn't doing my poor fried brain any favors. "Dude, you gonna answer me or what?" Alvin asked, sounding annoyed.

"Answer what?"

"I asked if you were amped."

I shrugged. "Amped about *what?*"

"What do you mean, *about what?*" he practically shouted in my face. "Auditions are, like, *literally* less than seventy-two hours away!" He dodged a couple of huge eighth graders fighting over a pack of gum, then smacked me on the side of my arm. "Oh, I was going to ask—do you think Mrs. Wilson would mind driving us? I don't trust Sam's mom to be on time, and there's not going to be any space in my mom's van once we load up all our instruments."

"Uh, yeah . . . I think she'll do it." Mrs. Wilson was cool like that. If it was something where she could keep an eye on me, she'd pretty much agree to anything. In fact, she'd been nice enough to rent me a brand-new Gibson from the local music shop so I could keep playing with my friends as long as we held practices at her house. She also thought it was pretty rad that the three of us wanted to try out for *Así Que Piensas Que Puedes Cantar* (or *APPC*, for short), which is a very popular Spanish television version of *So You Think You Can Dance*, except it was for bands rather than dancers.

"*Tight.*" Alvin held out his fist, and I bumped it. "Hey, that reminds me. I've been working on my vocals—gimme a sound check." Then he sucked in a big breath and belted out the opening line from the Carlos Santana song we'd chosen for the audition: "*¡Oye cómo va, mi ritmo bueno pa' gozar!*"

A few people turned to stare. Someone booed and shot a spitball at us. One of the hall monitors told Alvin to shut up.

Alvin gave him a little bow as we walked past. "He definitely dug it. . . . So what do you think, bro? How's my accent?"

"Está bien," I said. "It's fine."

"Just *fine* . . . ? I've been working on it for, like, *two whole weeks!*"

"Alvin, it takes more than fourteen days to master a foreign accent."

"What's your point?"

"Nothing. You did great. It was awesome. You're the next Vicentico."

"Nah, see, now you're just saying that," he grumbled. "And not for nothing, Charlie, but I'd like to see you looking a little more excited about all this. I mean, you still care about the band, don't you?"

"Of course I still care about the band," I said, and it was true. I *did* care about the band. Making music with my two best friends was probably the one thing that had kept me sane over these last few months; I loved it. But with everything else going on in my life right now, an audition for a talent show—even one as big as *APPC*—was the least of my worries.

"Just wanted to hear you say it." Alvin gave me a toothy, sideways grin. "Anyway, where were you last night? You didn't answer any of my texts."

"I was with Violet," I confessed, and he snorted out a laugh.

"Yeah, and I was with Selena Gomez. We should've made it a double date."

"I didn't say I was on *a date* with her," I corrected. "We just ran into each other, that's all."

"Wow, what a coincidence. Same thing with Selena and me!"

"Laugh it up, Al."

When we reached the second floor, I spotted Violet standing by the double doors of the library. She was leaning back against the wall, head down, earbuds in, shoulders rolling to One Direction or whatever pretty-boy boy band was hot these days. But she surprised me by looking up and waving to me.

Giving Alvin a little shove, I waved back. "Now, why don't you go tell Selena about *that*, hermano?"

Alvin's face had gone full-blown Casper. "Dude, I think *Violet Rey* is waving at me. . . . How's my hair?"

"Greasy as a Mickey D's twenty-piece," I said. "See you in PE!"

"Dude, wait—" He tried to grab me, but I juked him and fast-walked (our school has a super strict no-running-in-the-halls policy—automatic three-day detention) over to Violet.

"Hey, how are you holding up?" she asked, yanking out the earbuds as I approached. "Let me guess—taking it one feather at a time?"

"Hilarious," I said dryly. But I couldn't keep the stupid grin off my face. "How about you? Blackmailed anyone today?"

"Not yet. But it's only fourth period." Flashing me one of her million-watt smiles, she opened the door to the library. "Shall we?"

There was a bank of computers along the rear wall. We went over and took seats, Violet jabbing the enter key as she set her cheer bag down on the table.

"All right, so I did a little research last night," she said, lowering her voice, "and I have some bad news, some good news, and some better news. Which one you want first?"

"Let's get the bad out of the way."

"Okay, so the bad news is I ran a quick preliminary search of your symptoms and wasn't able to find much. I spent, like, two hours on WebMD, researching cases of weird bodily manifestations—skin abnormalities, autoimmune disorders caused by stress, that kind of stuff—but really didn't come across anything even remotely similar to your case."

No surprise there, I thought. "That's seriously disappointing."

"Yeah. And after that I spent another couple hours ransacking the online databases of local newspapers for missing persons reports, trying to see if anyone else had gone missing around the same time as your parents. You know, looking for a pattern."

"And?"

"Unfortunately, I didn't find much there, either."

I sighed. Apparently, not even Ultra Violet could crack my case. "You said something about good news?"

"Yep. So, remember last night when the calaca mentioned some lady he claimed might be able to help us?"

"Uh, kind of . . ."

"Remember the dollar amount he threw out? The fifty-two dollars and twenty-five cents he said it would cost us to get to her?"

I tried to think back. "Sorta . . ."

"Well, he unwittingly spilled the beans," she said, her voice giddy with excitement.

I shook my head, not following. "What do you mean?"

"He was talking about cab fare, Charlie. See, my working theory is that the calaca has visited this lady before—probably a bunch of times. And the dollar amount he threw out was how much each trip cost him to get from the cemetery—which I'm assuming is his home—to wherever she is. So, this morning I called, like, five local cabbies and got rough estimates of how far from La Rosa Cemetery I could get with exactly fifty-two dollars and twenty-five cents. They all gave me pretty much the same answer, roughly eighteen miles at a rate of two dollars and seventy-five cents per mile, including the drop-off charge. Now check this out. . . ."

She slipped a purple thumb drive out of her pocket, plugged it into the computer, and double-clicked one of the little icons. A second later, an aerial map of South Miami with La Rosa Cemetery dead center blipped to life on the screen. A thick yellow ring (something Violet had probably done in Photoshop) highlighted a bunch of nearby streets, homes, and businesses. "See the areas in yellow?" she asked.

"Uh-huh."

"That's what I've termed our Ring of Probability. It includes every place a person might live or work that a cabbie would charge fifty-two dollars and twenty-five cents to drive someone to from La Rosa." Her eyes locked onto mine. "Charlie, you see where I'm going with this . . . ? The lady we're looking for is somewhere *inside* that yellow ring. Now we just gotta find her."

Oh man, this girl was good. . . . She was really, *really*

good. "All right, so, um—what now? We just go door to door or something?"

Violet was shaking her head. "I thought about that, but it would take too long to canvass all those neighborhoods; so I did a little more research and found *this*." She double-clicked another file in the thumb drive, and an old newspaper article from the nineties popped up. The headline read: DRUNK DRIVER CRASHES INTO STREETLIGHT—BLAMES A WALKING SKELETON.

I couldn't believe my eyes. "What the heck . . . ?"

"Yep. According to the police report, the guy said he was driving and saw a skeleton crossing the street. He claimed that was why he crashed. Of course, no one believed him, but guess what? It's not the only time that's happened around there." She double-clicked another file, and a second article popped up, this one a scan. "Three years ago someone else claimed to have seen a skeleton walking along the shoulder of the road. They also crashed. Hit a telephone pole."

"And that area falls in our *Ring of Probability?*"

"More like falls *squarely* in it. In fact, it's this little strip mall right here on Krome Avenue. . . ." She circled it on the screen with her finger. "It's right by the Everglades." Then she leaned back in her chair, grinning proudly. "What d'ya think?"

"I think you have a gift," I said. "*Scary* . . . but definitely a gift." This girl was basically Sherlock Holmes with pom-poms!

"And you wanna hear the even better news?" she asked, still grinning.

"What?"

"I'm free tonight."

CHAPTER SEVENTEEN

Before heading off to fifth period, Violet and I agreed to meet up at her house later that night so we could ride out together to find this lady— whoever she was—and see if we could convince her to help us. So, at around six, I took a nice, long shower, downed a bowl of lobster bisque (which, by the way, Mrs. Wilson wasn't about to let me leave the house without doing; not that I minded, since it was so delicioso that I had to go in for seconds), then jumped on my bike and headed over to Violet's.

Violet lived in a nice single-story house at the end of a cul-de-sac. The outside was a bright sunshine yellow, and the flower boxes under the front-facing windows were overflowing with reddish-purple flowers. Violet was waiting for me out front, and fifteen minutes later we were pedaling up the bike lane on Calle Ocho, Violet riding on the extreme right, me checking over my shoulder every few seconds, hoping not to get clipped by an elderly driver. The night was crisp and clear, the sky heavy with stars.

"Pretty nice out," she said, brushing hair out of her eyes. She was dressed very detective-esque with a fancy brown trench coat, dark jeans, and light blue ankle boots. The tail of her coat flapped out behind her like a cape as she picked up speed.

"Yeah, very nice." I pedaled faster, trying to keep up with her. "Oh, I was thinking maybe we could swing by my old house first. It's on the way. Plus, I never really got a chance to look around after the fire. And you never know—we might find some clues or something."

Her lips split into a dazzling grin. "Now you're thinking like an investigative journalist, Charlie Hernández."

"Hey, it's all one case, right?"

"You can say that again," she said.

"Hey, it's all one case, right?"

Violet laughed. "You're funny."

"Gracias. It's kinda my thing."

She let off the pedals a little, but the wind was still whistling in the spokes of her tires, and it didn't seem like she'd lost much, if any, speed.

"You training for the Olympics or something?" I asked.

I mean, I rode my bike *all the time*, but my legs were already burning from trying to keep up with her.

"Nah. I'm just used to going fast," she said. "Been riding that way since I was, like, four. Never used training wheels, either."

"No training wheels? That's pretty rad."

"I guess." She took her hands off the handlebars, resting them lightly on her knees as she rode. "When I was little my dad told me training wheels were crutches and that winners didn't use crutches." She pulled back the sleeve of her coat to show me a thick white scar near the tip of her elbow. Thing must've bled like crazy. "Guess crutches aren't always such a bad thing, huh?"

"Dios mío."

"Yeah, and that's not the only messed-up story I have about my parents. One day a lady brought this really old poster of Doublemint gum into our shop. It was the one with the two girls riding a tandem bike. You know, the Doublemint Twins?"

"Sure."

"Well, I was, like, five, and I thought it was the coolest thing I'd ever seen. But when I asked my mom if we could get one so we could ride together, she said no because it would be a poor life lesson."

I frowned. "What does that mean?"

"That's the same question I asked. And you know what she said?"

"What?"

"She said life's a one-person bike. You don't get a pedal partner."

"Dang," I said. "That's harsh."

She smiled weakly. "That's my mom."

Exactly sixty-two days ago, my house would have been described as a nice, single-family ranch-style home with a neatly manicured lawn and an in-ground swimming pool. But after the fire (and the three days of heavy rain that followed), all that was left was a huge black mountain of metal beams, scorched cinder block, and damp, crumbling mortar. The chimney was still standing—sort of—but the entire roof, once a coppery-colored Spanish tile that my dad would pressure wash every other year, had caved in on itself, forming a deep, ash-encrusted V right where the living room used to be.

From our spot on the sidewalk, I could see three windows, and all of them were blown out, every inch of ground in front of them singed black.

I blinked. Hard. Seeing my house this way was like a punch to the gut all over again. The ghosts of fire-engine sirens and my shouting neighbors echoed in my brain like the clanging of a bell, and I had to squeeze my eyes shut just to keep tears from spilling out. But even with my eyes closed, I could still see the policemen and firefighters scrambling around my yard, yelling instructions at one another and trailing fire hoses and foam guns as they tried anything they could to put the fire out, to keep it from spreading. I could even smell the smoke and feel the incredible heat rolling off my house in waves as walls collapsed and windows exploded from the spiking temperatures. I tried to block it all out, to fight back the awful images, but it was impossible.

"*Man*," Violet said as we laid our bikes down on the strip of grass opposite the sidewalk.

I gave my burning eyes a good rub before opening them again. "Yeah . . ."

"Must've been one heck of a fire."

"Biggest one in thirty years, according to the fire chief."

"I believe it." Glancing quickly around, Violet ducked under the strip of yellow crime scene tape (which clearly read DO NOT ENTER) and started around the back, sticking to the shadows like a cat burglar.

"Hey, wait up!" I shouted, but I guess she didn't hear me because she disappeared behind the hedge of soot-stained shrubs without so much as a backward glance.

When I finally caught up with her, she was standing in

the middle of my backyard, turning in slow circles and snapping pictures of the house and the piles of scorched wood and debris that were scattered everywhere.

"*What are you doing?*" I asked, more sharply than I'd meant to.

"I'm photographing the scene for my records. I wanna make sure we don't miss anything." She snapped a couple more pics, the quick flashes throwing bright white triangles across the yard. "This is the same app FBI agents use on their phones. Cost me ninety-nine cents. I found it on sale in the app store."

"Cool."

"It's only going to take me a minute."

"Take your time," I said. Then I turned and walked slowly along the edge of the empty pool, staring silently at the charred remains of the only place I'd ever called home. Closing my eyes, I tried to imagine things the way they used to be, the way *we* used to be—the happy little family in the happy little house with the pink flamingo mailbox.

All of a sudden, a flood of memories came rushing back: my mom tucking me into bed at night, her face lit up by the soft blue-green glow of my Scooby-Doo night lamp; my abuela sitting on one of the tall stools at the kitchen counter, telling her stories while I sat across from her, drinking my mom's famous mango and banana batido right out of the blender; my dad, smiling and breathing hard beneath his Miami Marlins baseball cap as he pushed me down the sidewalk on Christmas morning, teaching me to ride a bike for the very first time.

A lump formed in my throat. Back then everything about my life had seemed so ordinary. So *normal*. But the truth was right now I would give *anything* for that kind of normal. Anything to be with them again. To hear their voices a—

"Charlie, I found something!" Violet shouted, snapping me back to reality. I brushed wetness off my cheeks as she rushed over, holding out her hand. Something glinted on her palm. "It's a key," she said. "Check it out. . . ."

"Where'd you find that?" I asked.

"Behind the shed." She handed it to me. "You've never seen it before?"

I shook my head as I turned the key over in my hand. It looked old. Like something out of a pirate movie—the big iron kind used to open treasure chests or prison doors. The end was in the shape of a pretzel, and the key's teeth reminded me of a shark's, two rows deep and jutting up wildly in every direction; I'd never seen anything like it.

"You said you found it behind the shed?"

"Well, more like *stuck* to the shed," Violet said. "I think it's magnetized."

"*Magnetized?*" Okay, now, *that* was weird.

"And I'm pretty sure it's made of the same metal as your mom's locket. But it's obviously too big to open the locket." She thought for a moment. "Did your parents have a safe, maybe?"

I opened my mouth to say, *I don't think so*—and heard music.

It was faint, but unmistakable.

Mariachi music.

"You hear that . . . ?" I said, tilting my head. I even thought I recognized the song: "Volver, Volver," by Vicente Fernández.

Violet only stared at me. "Hear what?"

"The music. It sounds like—"

Movement to my left caught my eye. I turned to see a figure in a black vaquero jacket and jangling boots snooping around inside what was left of my house.

I didn't think, just grabbed Violet and pulled her down behind one of the piles of charred wood.

"Charlie, what are you doing?" she hissed, swatting my hands away.

"There's someone inside my house!"

Violet peeked over the top of the pile. "Where?"

"¡Ahí!" I whispered, pointing. "Walking through the kitchen!"

She squinted hard, then shook her head. "Charlie, there's no one in there."

Only there *was* . . . Even through the inky darkness, I could make out his round, pale face and the small silver guitar strapped to his back. The dude looked like some sort of mariachi gangster. He definitely wasn't a policeman (not even some funky-dressing detective—nah, not in that crazy getup), which begged the question: What the heck was he doing inside my house . . . ?

Then the trespassing weirdo stepped into a column of moonlight slanting in through one of the huge holes in the roof, and I realized that what I'd mistaken for deep shadow surrounding him was actually a ridiculously oversize sombrero!

Something stirred in the back of my brain. *Who would wear a hat that big?*

Then everything clicked. The hat. The jacket. The exotic silver guitarra.

It was El Sombrerón!

¡El que canta y encanta!

The infamous Central American boogeyman!

But—

How was this possible . . . ?

Before I could even begin to process the craziness of this, the sombrero-wearing supervillain sniffed the air, then turned his dark gaze in our direction.

Yikes!

I quickly ducked back down, yanking Violet with me.

"Charlie! Geez! What is *wrong* with you?"

"It's El Sombrerón!" I rasped. "He's looking this way!"

"El *who?*"

"He's, uh, uh—he's basically a goblin in a big hat and cowboy boots! He likes to ride horses and braid their tails. He also serenades girls with his *guitarra.*"

"He sounds like fun."

"Yeah, except once they fall in love with him, he puts dirt in their food so they can't eat or sleep until they eventually *die.*"

"Not so fun then." She glanced back at the house, concern creeping into her expression. "But Charlie, I don't see anyone...."

"What do you mean you don't see anyone? He's right th—"

Suddenly, the key Violet had found became scorching hot in my hand. I yelped and threw it down with a gasp.

"Charlie, what happened?"

"The key," I said, blowing on the tips of my fingers. "Stupid thing burned me...."

"The key *burned* you?" Violet gave me a skeptical look. Then she touched a finger to it lightly. "But it's not even hot."

"My fingers would strongly disagree...." *Strongly.*

Frowning, she picked it up. "It's as cold as an ice cube. Here. Touch."

"I'll pass," I said. I popped my head back out to check what El Sombrerón was up to, but I didn't see him anywhere. He'd vanished. Goose bumps rose on my skin. "Where'd he go . . . ?"

Violet put her hand on my shoulder. "Charlie, are you okay?"

Feeling dazed, confused—and a little nuts, to be totally honest—I stared back at my house, thinking, *How could he have just disappeared into thin air like that?* It didn't make any sense.

"Charlie, I can call someone. You want me to text my cousin? She's a doctor."

I shook my head. "I'm fine."

"You sure?" Violet didn't sound convinced. "I can text her. It's no biggie."

"I'm fine," I said. "I promise."

But her eyes didn't leave mine; she studied me for a long, quiet moment before finally glancing down at her phone again. "Okay, well, if the coast is clear, then we better get going. It's almost eight o'clock."

She was right. We didn't have time to be seeing mariachi goblins.

CHAPTER EIGHTEEN

The little strip mall on Krome was a knot of low concrete buildings that sat right on the edge of civilization, between a thriving multicultural neighborhood and 734 square miles of marshy swampland known as the Florida Everglades. There was a Quickie Mart, a Sir Galloway Dry Cleaners, a family-owned bodega, and a little body shop. The body shop was closed; it had a sign on the front door that read: REMODELING—BACK REAL SOON! The dry cleaner was open until nine. The Quickie Mart and the bodega were open all night.

We parked our bikes on the side of the mall by the body shop and got to work. Our plan was pretty straightforward: Visit each store, question the employees and shoppers, and see what turned up. Problem was, as soon as we asked anyone if they knew a lady around here who practiced the dark arts, they immediately stopped taking us seriously. Most of them stared at us like they were waiting for a punch line. Others just walked away. The owner of the dry cleaner actually threw us out. But it was the night manager of the Quickie Mart who had the most interesting reaction—he threatened to call the police if either of us tried to slurp slushy directly from the machine. Something told me he didn't *quite* get what we were asking.

Anyway, about thirty minutes later, we were standing in the middle of the mostly empty parking lot, kicking rocks and trying to figure out where we'd gone wrong.

"This doesn't make any sense," Violet said, anxiously rubbing her face. "The numbers added up *perfectly*. And we both saw the articles about the skeletons. So, what are we *missing . . .* ?"

"Maybe we're not missing anything," I said. "Maybe she really does work around here."

"And not *one* person could say, 'Oh, yeah, I've heard of a lady like that'?" She let out a frustrated sigh. "We're going to need a new plan of attack. . . ."

"I'm with you on that," I said. Around us, the wind gusted, blowing through the trees at the edge of the Glades. The tall cypresses bent and creaked. Dried leaves skittered silently along the roadside. In the distance, an animal wailed—a sad, mournful sound that sent a shiver down my spine.

I was about to tell Violet that we probably just needed to ask more people—turn it into a numbers game—when something across the street caught my eye: a swirl of tiny lights glowing luminescent blue just inside the tree line.

The lights seemed to dance and twirl in the darkness, trailing glittery arcs that floated gently on the breeze. For a quick second, all the teeny pinpricks came together to form a single pulsing orb, then scattered almost as quickly, spreading through the trees like the afterglow of fireworks.

I started walking toward the lights without realizing it, like a manatee drawn to warm water.

"Hey, where're you going?" Violet called after me.

"Don't you see that?" I asked, never taking my eyes off the hypnotic glow. The lights were so beautiful I had to get a closer look. Had to.

"See what?" She came up beside me. "What are you—*oh.*"

"Yeah," I agreed in that same dreamy whisper.

"Are those—*fireflies* . . . ?"

"Let's find out."

The lights glowed brighter as we jogged across the street toward them, but then began to retreat slowly into the swamp. Their luminescent glow and the weirdly mesmerizing way they moved—like silky bedsheets rippling in the wind—made it impossible for me to take my eyes off them.

Follow us! they seemed to whisper. *Come, come, right this way!*

So that was exactly what we did. We followed them eagerly into the trees. But every step we took, the lights retreated a tiny bit more. Never too quickly and never too far—just enough to keep us after them.

My feet carried me forward almost automatically. I felt warm all over. It was like I was under some sort of spell—only I didn't care.

In the back of my mind, I could sense something was wrong, but every time I tried to draw the thought forward, the lights grew brighter, more glittery, and I forgot all about it.

Sometime later—I had no idea how long—my foot caught on the edge of a root and I stumbled, momentarily losing eye contact with the lights.

In that split second, the spell broke: The dreamy daze instantly evaporated, and so did my crazy need to follow the lights.

What the heck was that about? I thought, looking around wildly. But I had no more than asked myself that when the answer came, and all the tiny hairs on the back of my neck prickled like the spines on a porcupine.

"Violet, STOP!" I shouted. "It's La Luz Mala!"

I couldn't believe what I was saying—couldn't believe

those words had *actually* come out of my mouth—but I knew it was true all the same. The lights were almost *identical* to how my abuela had described them: the wispy, glowing orbs with mesmerizing powers; the strings of tiny lights that lured unsuspecting people into the dangers of the swamp. Even the color was the same—a brilliant Spanish blue!

It was crazy to think about—insane, even—but this was now the fourth myth we'd encountered—the fourth in just *two* days! The real question was, why did we keep running into things from my abuela's old stories?

"Violet!" I caught up with her, grabbing her by the shoulders. "Violet, snap out of it!" But she wouldn't even look at me, so I shook her. "Hey, wake up!"

Her eyelids fluttered drowsily. "Huh?"

"The lights! They're La Luz Mala!" When she only stared, I shook her some more. "Helloooooo? It's another myth!"

That finally got through to her. She blinked, clarity returning to her eyes, and glanced cautiously back at the glowing spheres, which had paused between the trees maybe ten yards ahead of us, a shimmering blue curtain in the deep dark.

"Charlie, are you sure?" she asked after a moment. When I nodded, a sort of hopeful look entered her eyes and she started toward them again.

"Which *obviously* means we can't follow them!" I said, grabbing her by the tail of her coat. "Haven't you heard the stories?"

"Duh. I read a few of them last night," she said. Surprisingly, she sounded pretty clearheaded, like she wasn't under any kind of spell, which made me even *more* nervous. "It's, like, the most famous myth in Argentina."

"That's right. And if you remember anything else, you'd know that it leads people into *danger*. Specifically, danger in *swamps*. Like the huge one we're currently walking into!"

"Charlie, we *have to* follow it. Don't you get it? Like you said, it's another myth. It means we're on the right track."

I thought about that.

"See what I'm saying . . . ?"

I did, actually. But I *really* didn't like it.

My biggest worry was that La Luz Mala would take us into the heart of the Glades—right into the middle of all that crocodiley goodness—and then suddenly vanish, leaving us stranded. That's usually what happened in the stories. But that wasn't what happened with us. The glowing orbs never dimmed or even flickered as they led us nonstop for close to a mile and a half, through tangles of low-growing vines and fallen logs, their bright pale light casting an eerie glow in the trees. All around us, mangrove roots reached out of the ground like the gnarled, twisted fingers of an old witch. Small red eyes peered out at us from between the loops and knots. The only sounds were the crunching of saw grass beneath our feet and our own steady breathing. Once I thought I saw something ginormous darting through the shadows. I would've bet my life it was a yellowish polar bear, but that didn't make any sense because one, polar bears aren't normally yellow, and two, they sure as heck don't live in the Everglades—not to mention that whatever it was had moved with lightning speed. I told myself to chill, that it was just my imagination, but of course that was easier said than done.

"I hate coming to places like this at night," Violet said a few minutes later. She stuffed her hands into the pockets of her coat and gave a little shiver. "I always feel like someone's watching me. Like they're going to pop out of nowhere, hack me into *itty-bitty* little pieces, then store my mutilated corpse in a portable icebox they keep in their garage."

"Ay, chica. A little graphic, don't you think?"

She shrugged, swatting a mosquito away. "It's the truth."

"How often do you come to places like this, anyway?"

"I go wherever the story takes me, Charlie. Figuratively speaking, of course . . . I've never been out of Florida."

✦ ✦ ✦

La Luz Mala continued to light our way as we trekked deeper into the swamp, glowing between the roots and mangrove trunks, glimmering off the ankle-deep puddles of brackish water. Insects buzzed around us, and with every step, the terrain became muddier and harder to negotiate. My arms were raw from getting lashed by branches. My sneakers kept sinking into the ground and getting sucked off my feet. Twice I went down face-first in the thick mud, giving myself the world's cheapest (and nastiest) facial. Yeah, it was epically embarrassing, but I was honestly too exhausted to care. My legs felt like they were made of Jell-O. My sweat-drenched clothes clung to my skin like wet napkins.

Just when I thought I was about to drop dead of fatigue, we stepped into a small clearing, and La Luz Mala suddenly disappeared, seeming to evaporate into thin air.

"Where'd they go?" Violet asked, turning in a slow circle. Ribbons of sweat streamed down her face. Her hair was matted to her cheeks in soggy clumps. This deep in the Everglades, the humidity was *insane*.

I wiped sweat off my face and looked around. No Luz Mala. But I did see something: a shabby little hut squatting in the middle of the clearing, maybe twenty yards away. It had a thatched roof supporting a huge neon sign, which read—well, mostly *flickered*—THE CRYING PSYCHIC.

And below it, in smaller but equally flickering letters: FREE READINGS FOR KIDS TWELVE AND UNDER! As I stood there, staring up at the sign, the S in READINGS buzzed, darkened, and then exploded in a shower of orange sparks.

I turned to Violet. "The place seems like it's tip-top, huh?"

"Fingers crossed," she said, and we started toward it.

The front door was painted electric pink. An old wooden sign (OPEN—COME ON IN!) hung from the doorknob.

Violet had just raised her fist to knock when the door flew open.

A lady stepped out to greet us. Tall, thin, with shockingly pale skin. She wore a long white dress and stylish Mexican sandals called huaraches. Her hair was jet-black. Her toenails were painted in a sort of Día de los Muertos theme with marigold flowers and big ol' smiling calaca heads. I didn't even bother asking if she was the crying psychic because her wet, shining eyes and puffy cheeks practically shouted it.

"Hola. My name is Señora L," she said in a low, sniffly voice. "Welcome to the Crying Shack." Then, as if to drive home the point, her face crumpled like an empty bag of potato chips and she burst into tears.

Violet and I looked at each other.

Wow, I mouthed. Violet was speechless.

After almost thirty seconds of full-on, snot-snorting bawling, the crying psychic finally pulled herself together and welcomed us into the hut.

I'll admit it—from the outside, I thought the hut looked kind of cool in a laid-back, islandy sort of way. But inside, it was a total *freak show*. Every nook, every cranny, *every square inch* of the place was packed with stuff—and when I say stuff, I mean *weird stuff*. Dead bats and birds dangled from the ceiling on strings. Spooky black wax candles burned in ancient-looking sconces. Along the walls were fur-covered shelves (at least it *looked* like fur) crammed with dusty bottles and old glass jars of all shapes and sizes. Some were filled with dark powders, others with gelatinous globs bobbing around in murky liquid.

A curtain of yellow and purple beads hung down the center of the back wall. Around the curtain, arranged on the moldy corkboard like some spooky teenage shrine, were dozens and dozens of unframed photographs. All of them had been taken at night, and all of them featured a smiling Señora L standing in front of some river with her arm around a young kid. Every photo had a different kid in it—six boys, six girls—and they all looked about as happy as a turkey on Thanksgiving to be posing with her.

"Por favor," she said, pointing us to a small round table in the middle of the room. It was covered by a black velvet cloth and surrounded by three cushy-looking chairs. A crystal ball on a glass stand sat in the center of the table. "Make yourselves at home," she said. "Mi casa es tu casa."

Violet and I dropped gratefully into the chairs. And as we did, I heard some banging and muffled sounds coming from behind the beaded curtain.

"What the heck is that?" I said, looking around.

Señora L slid a couple of locks (there must've been at least ten different ones on the doorframe alone—a few dead bolts, about twice as many night latches, and a couple of childproof sliding locks) and then joined us at the table.

"Oh, it's just the rats," she said dismissively. "I have a bit of a vermin issue being all the way out here in the middle of the Everglades and all. But don't mind them. They're harmless. Now, before we begin, I need to learn a little bit about the two of you. Do either of you enjoy breakfast croquetas?"

I frowned, not sure I'd heard her right. "Excuse me?"

"You know, eggs, chicken, and jamón breaded and fried to a beautiful golden crisp."

"Uh, yeah, I love croquetas. . . ."

Violet was nodding. "Sounds good to me."

The psychic lady's lips pulled back in a broad, almost cheerful smile. "Good, because breakfast is the most important meal of the day. By the way, what sizes are you?"

"What do you mean?" I asked.

"Pajama sizes."

Pajama sizes? Why in the world would she need to know our *pajama sizes*? I shook my head. "I'm a medium, I guess."

Violet shrugged. "Yeah, I'm a medium too."

"Ah, okay." There was an old-fashioned trunk under the table. Señora L undid the flat metal latch, opened it, and pulled out two striped onesies—one blue, the other pink. "These should fit snugly, then." She handed them to us. "Compliments of the house."

"Um, gracias." I honestly didn't know what else to say.

"Go ahead," she urged us. "Try them on."

"Actually, I'd rather not," I said. "I'm kinda sweaty right now."

The psychic's lower lip began to tremble, and she suddenly burst out crying again. Big, loud, gasping sobs that shook her whole body. "You don't like my gift!" she bellowed between sobs. "You hate it!—¡Lo odias!"

"No, no, no," Violet said, raising her hands and patting the air, trying to calm her. "He doesn't hate it. He *loves* it. We both do. We just don't want to put them on quite yet. Later, for sure, though."

"For sure?" Señora L sounded hopeful.

"For sure, for sure."

"Absolutamente," I agreed with a firm nod. Had to say something, right?

"They're made in Guatemala," the crazy psychic lady informed us as she dabbed the corners of her eyes. "One hundred percent cotton. Very comfortable."

I rubbed the blue fabric between my thumb and index finger, trying to seem like I was into it. "Yeah, feels great."

Señora L smiled at me. "You two remind me so much of my children. . . . You're going to make absolutely *lovely* additions to the family!"

"What family?"

She gestured at the wall behind her. At the pictures.

"Oh. Yeah, sure, we'd love to take a picture when we're done."

"Maravilloso. So, then, let me tell you about today's specials. We have tea leaf readings for five dollars, tarot card poker for two. I interpret dreams for a flat fee of fifteen US dollars an hour—but no nightmares. Oh, and I should mention that I've recently discovered a method for bottling my tears, which gives them up to a forty-day shelf life." She pointed to a row of amber-colored bottles sitting side by side and three rows deep on the wooden cabinet in the corner of the room. The taped-on labels read: TEARS OF FATE. "I sell them by the ounce, and luckily for you two, they're twenty percent off today. Just four easy payments of $249.99."

"*A thousand dollars for your tears?*" I burst out. Couldn't help myself. "What do they do? Cure *zits?*" Geez, talk about a snake-oil salesman—or in this case, snake-oil sales*woman*.

"Actually, they lead you wherever the universe wants you to go," she explained. "I discovered my gift completely by accident. One day I was crying near a river"—*No surprise there*, I thought—"and a lost camper a few miles downstream unwittingly scooped up some of my tears into his canteen. Yada, yada, yada, long story short, he found his way back to civilization safe and sound." She wiped one cheek with the cuff of her sleeve. "I accept cash, credit, and Bitcoin if either of you are interested."

"Uh, sorry, we don't have any money on us," Violet said, and the lady made a face like she was going to start the waterworks again. "But hold on! See, the thing is, we came here for a very specific reason. . . ."

Señora L perked up a bit. "And what would that be?"

"Well, my friend here is experiencing some strange manifestations, and we'd like you to take a look, tell us what you think."

"Manifestations, huh?" Her shiny red eyes narrowed on me. "What kind of manifestations . . . ?"

"Uh, well, a month ago I grew a pair of horns," I said casually. Like it happened to everyone. "Then, like, three days ago, I got these." When I pulled back my sleeve to show her the feathers, one came off, floating lazily across the table toward her.

The psychic snatched it out of the air and held it directly between her eyes. "Hmmm," she said, examining it from pointy end to fluffy tip.

I didn't take my eyes off her face. "Do you have any idea what's happening to me?" I asked after a couple of seconds.

She thought for another long moment, then shook her head. Her dozen or so necklaces jingled like bells. "I can't say that I do, though it certainly reminds me of something."

"Of what?" Violet asked quickly.

Señora L picked up the crystal ball. "Perhaps you've seen this symbol before." The long black nail of her index finger clicked against the smooth underside of the ball, where a *very* familiar symbol had been stamped into the glass.

"That's the same symbol that was on the map!" I said, nearly leaping out of my seat. The horns and feathers!

"Sí, it appears on many items in this world. . . . It's a picto-prophecy. About El Cambiador."

My skin sprang up with goose bumps. "Wait. You're talking about that old myth . . . ? The *Morphling?*"

"It's no myth, mi hijo." Señora L's eyes glittered as she spoke. They reminded me of my abuela's—dark and full of mysteries. "Anyway, years ago, you could find that symbol on almost anything—even common household items like this glass ball. It was a symbol of hope."

"What does the prophecy say?" Violet asked.

"The five feathers represent the fifth Morphling born into our world. The two horns speak of the two distinct manifestations—horns and feathers. The five feathers combined with the two horns yields the number seven, which, being the perfect number, speaks of the child's perfect work: bringing the long-sought peace between the Land of the Living and the Land of the Dead. The prophecy was given so that we would be able to recognize the child when it came. And there are those among us who have been looking for the one who would come manifesting horns and feathers for many, *many* years now." She let out a low sigh. "Of course, the prophecy itself is more than *nine hundred* years old, and the child has never been seen, much less heard from. Most believe La Mano Peluda managed to kill the poor thing before it could even be born into our world. And without a Morphling to oppose them, La Mano Peluda has grown even more powerful. It's why you don't see the symbol too much anymore. . . ."

My pulse was racing. I felt the same swirly sort of panic I did before a pop quiz, but I forced myself to sound calm as I asked the most important question in our conversation, maybe the most important question of my life:

"Señora L, is it possible that *I* could be the Morphling . . . ?"

Just hearing myself speak the words made my heart pound so hard I thought it was going to burst through my chest. It was one thing to accept the fact that mythical beings existed, that they lived among us. But to consider the possibility that I, Charlie Hernández, might *actually* be one? That was a whole 'nother level of crazy.

The psychic stared at me for a moment. "I—I don't know . . . ," she stammered. "*Are you?*"

I shrugged. "How should I know? That's why we came *here*. We were looking for a lady who deals in the dark arts. Someone who could explain what's happening to me."

Her gaze narrowed suspiciously. "Who told you there was a lady around here who dealt in the dark arts?"

"The calaca. The one in La Rosa."

"You mean *Gregory?*"

"I don't know. We're not *exactly* on a first-name basis. The freak was a trade away from bashing our heads in with a shovel."

Señora L grinned. It was a happy sort of grin. "He does have a terrible temper, doesn't he?"

"So, you're her, right?" Violet said. "The lady he was talking about?"

"Sí, sí, that's me. But I'm sorry. . . . I really can't help you in this."

"Then who can?"

"Any member of La Liga de Sombras, probably. Queen Joanna, for sure."

I shook my head. The League of Shadows? "What's La Liga de Sombras? And who's Queen Joanna?" I wasn't exactly up to date on the monarchs of the world, but the name didn't ring any bells.

"Olvídalo," Señora L said, waving a dismissive hand. "That information won't be of any use to you anyway. I think we should do your complimentary palm reading now."

She didn't give me a chance to say no, just snatched my hand and cradled it between both of hers. Her touch was cool, her fingers surprisingly gentle as they traced invisible lines across my palm. "Hmmm."

"Is that a good 'hmmm'?" I asked. "Or a not-so-good 'hmmm'?"

Her lips pressed into a thin line as she lifted her gaze to mine. Her pupils were huge, bottomless. I could see my own worried face reflected in them; it was all bloated and cartoonish like the images in fun house mirrors. "It is as I feared," she said ominously. "Both of you are in *grave* danger. . . ."

Violet and I both sat up. "*What?*" we said in unison.

"Sí, sí . . . many different people are after you. *Bad* people. *Dangerous* people!"

Violet was shaking her head. "Like *who?*"

"Doesn't matter. But I know how to keep you safe."

"You do?"

"I most certainly do," Señora L announced happily. "You can stay here with me! Here en mi casa!"

Frowning, I said, "You mean, like, for the night?"

"No, tonto, not just for the night," she corrected. "*Forever.*"

Just then there came more banging sounds from behind the curtain. This time, though, I thought I heard voices, too.

Suddenly, I got a really bad feeling in the pit of my stomach.

CHAPTER NINETEEN

Señora L clapped her hands together, smiling widely, crazily, and I realized with a jolt of alarm that the psycho psychic was looking at us with the same sort of hungry intensity you might see in the eyes of a hunting lioness. "So how about you two slip into those pajamas now and get off to bed," she said in a motherly sort of tone. "It's getting late, you know."

"I think it's time to go," Violet whispered in my ear.

We both stood up. "So, uh, we're gonna get going now . . . ," I said to Señora L. "You're right. It's pretty late. But we'll drop by next week for some tarot card poker, maybe. I'm also a big Go Fish guy. . . . How about Tuesday? ¿Está bien?"

"Oh, no, no, no," she said, scrunching her thick brows together as she shook her head vigorously from side to side. "I'm not letting you back outside. What kind of mother would I be if I just let my children wander through the Everglades at this time of night? ¿Estás loco o qué te pasa?" She fixed us with another loony smile. "Now, come give your mother a hug, slip into your pj's, and then off to bed. ¡Vamos!"

When she spread her arms, the sleeve of her dress pulled back to reveal a large black tattoo done in fancy cursive letters. It read: *Maria.*

All of a sudden, everything made sense. The random bouts of crying. The photos with the kids. Her overprotective, bordering-on-psychotic maternal instincts.

She even called herself Señora L, for crying out loud.

¡Si fuera perro te muerde! said a little voice in my head. It was one of my abuela's favorite phrases—basically, *If it had been a dog, it would've bitten you!*

And it would have bitten me, all right. Bitten me *hard.*

"You're La Llorona, aren't you?" I breathed.

"Don't you call me that!" she snapped. "¡No te atrevas! In this house, you will refer to me only as *Mamá. . . .*"

Violet had already started to backpedal toward the door. "Uh, Charlie, what's going on . . . ?"

"She's the Crying Woman," I whispered, inching away from the table. "The one from the legends."

"You mean the lady who lurks by rivers and kidnaps children?"

"That would be her."

More pounding from behind the curtain, and this time I clearly heard: "Help! Somebody help us! We're trapped!"

"In fact, it looks like she's already kidnapped a few," I pointed out.

La Llorona snarled. "Why are both of you so afraid of me . . . ? What makes you think I'm such a *bad* person?"

"For one, you tried to use a phony palm reading to scare us into *living* with you!" I shouted. A trick I was pretty sure she'd used on more than one occasion. Probably explained the trunk full of kid-size pajamas in her living room.

She shrugged. "That's not *that* bad."

"Okay, well, and two—*you killed your kids*! Your REAL kids!"

"That was my husband's fault!" she shot back. "He cheated on me. It drove me *insane*! I was having a really, *really* bad day! Everyone has them!"

"True. Everyone does. But only *crazy* people KILL THEIR KIDS!"

Her furious gaze sharpened on me. "You keep talking to me like that and I'm going to wash your mouth out with soap, niño malagradecido. . . . Now, obey your mamá! Get into your pajamas and get ready for bed!"

Just then a cold fist pressed into my back—the doorknob. This was our chance.

"Go, Violet, go!" I shouted as I whirled to start undoing the locks. I guesstimated it would take me ten seconds to undo all of them. Plenty of time.

Or so I thought.

Because that was when La Llorona began to scream.

CHAPTER TWENTY

I t started low, a bloodcurdling moan that quickly rose in volume until it filled the entire bungalow.

I clamped my hands over my ears as a crushing wave of sadness swept over me, filling me with the deepest, darkest grief I'd ever known. Suddenly, I didn't care about escaping anymore. Didn't care about figuring out what was happening to me, didn't even care about finding my parents. It was as if a storm cloud had settled over me. A churning, whirling funnel so thick and black I couldn't see any way out of it.

Next to me, Violet had collapsed to the wooden floor and was now curled into a small ball under La Llorona's table, weeping loudly. Tears were streaming down her face like someone had opened a faucet behind her eyes. They pooled on the floor around her head, sort of like a watery crown. I dropped to my knees beside her, burying my face in my hands, feeling big, fat tears rolling down my own cheeks. It was the strangest thing I'd ever felt. I couldn't explain why I was so sad, why I was crying so hard—I just *was*. And it was the only thing I wanted to do. The ONLY thing.

I can't go on, I thought bitterly. (The words seemed to have bubbled up out of nowhere.) *No, I won't go on without my children! Not without my little ones!*

Wait—*little ones?*

I didn't have little ones.

I didn't have big ones, either.

Just then, it hit me. This wasn't me! La Llorona was somehow filling us with her thoughts, her emotions, somehow using her awful wailing sobs as a sort of mental link.

I had to fight her. I had to block her out. But how could I do that when my entire world felt like it was crumbling around me?

This isn't real, I told myself. *Snap out of it, dude!*

Beside me, Violet began to shriek, "He cheated on me! He CHEATED on me! *HE'S A CHEATER!*" Clutching desperately at her tear-streaked face, she began flailing around on her back like an overturned turtle, and I realized (even through another tidal wave of grief) that her mind was snapping. If I didn't do something—and do it *quick*—we were both goners.

But what?

Suddenly the answer slammed into me like a Mack truck: Maybe I couldn't block La Llorona out of our minds, but I *could* stop the wailing at its source.

So that's exactly what I did.

Jumping to my feet, I snatched the crystal ball from its stand on the table and shoved it into La Llorona's open, screaming mouth.

It was like I'd hit the mute button on her vocal cords. Abruptly, her horrible wailing cut off, and what felt like a heavy blanket lifted off my mind. A heartbeat later, Violet stopped crying too. She pushed to her knees, looking dazed, confused.

"What the heck was that?" she breathed.

"No time to explain." I didn't waste a second. I darted past the choking psychic (who now looked like a cat trying to cough up a hair ball—back arched, her entire body rolling in spastic little fits) and searched for a hidden door behind the curtain.

"Charlie, what are you *doing?*" Violet shouted, undoing the locks and flinging open the front door.

And just as she did, I spotted a shiny silver knob poking through beads.

"One sec!" I twisted it. Yanked open the door. And nearly got trampled as a dozen little kids—the exact same ones from the photos—came stampeding out.

They pounded across the bungalow like a herd of buffalo and burst out the front door and into the night.

A moment later, a pair of huge gray rats fell through the roof of the tiny room and scurried out the door after the kids, chittering angrily. Apparently, the Crying Shack really did have a vermin problem.

"Hey, I just put them to bed!" La Llorona yelled at me—well, more like *squeaked*. The crystal ball was lodged halfway down her throat and now bulged there like a giant, glowing Adam's apple. "Do you have any idea how hard it is to get twelve eight-year-olds to bed on time on a school night?!"

On the other side of the room, Violet was in full-on cheerleader mode, jumping up and down on her toes, frantically waving me over like I was a wide receiver sprinting down the sideline for the game-winning touchdown. "Charlie, *c'mon*!"

I started toward her—then stopped. One more thing. I hustled over to the wooden dresser and snagged a jar of tears. Hey, if the lady charged a thousand dollars a bottle, it had to be good for something, right?

As I pounded out the door after Violet, I heard La Llorona yell, "¡Hasta luego, mis niños! I'll be thinking of you!"

◆ ◆ ◆

"Now, *that* was a close call," I said as we started back through the musty swamp. "Dang, and I forgot my complimentary pj's."

Violet gave me a funny look.

"What? Those things looked comfy as heck."

She laughed. "Yeah, and I'm already missing those breakfast croquetas. . . ."

"Oh man, those sounded good, didn't they?"

"*Really good.*" Violet slowed down a little, then hopped over a large puddle of black water. I went around it, walking over a bridge of mangrove roots. "But you know what's even tastier than croquetas?" she said.

"What?"

"All that juicy info Señora L was spilling."

"What are you talking about? Like what?"

"Well, now we know about La Liga de Sombras. And we have a name—Queen Joanna."

"And what are we supposed to do with that? I really don't think anyone she knows is going to be on Facebook."

Violet turned to smile at me. "Probably not. But I'll run it through the AMM later tonight."

"The *what?*"

"It's the database the FBI runs names and phrases through." When I made a face, she said, "My uncle works for the Bureau. I hacked his password—silly man uses the same seven letters and two numbers for every single log-in. Even his Netflix account."

Twenty minutes later we emerged from the swamp and started along the tree-choked shoulder of the road, heading south on Krome. Considering the fact that we had found our way back pretty much by feel, we'd actually come out impressively close to where we'd first spotted La Luz Mala—the little shopping mall was only fifteen blocks or so down the narrow two-lane street, a brightly lit square sitting on the edge of nowhere.

"So, when do you wanna try the tears out?" Violet asked, taking the jar and swirling the clear liquid. "I hope it's not something dangerous. . . ."

"I could try them tonight," I said. "Any idea how they might work?"

"Not really. But nothing a little trial and error shouldn't be able to solve."

"We should probably do it back at your house, though. You know, just in case it *is* dangerous." Like if it turned out to be pure, unfiltered acid and started burning through my fingers the instant it touched my skin.

"Good idea," Violet agreed.

"And you should probably hold on to them too," I said with a smirk, "for safety reasons."

She gave me a sideways grin. "Nice to hear you're so concerned with my well-being."

When we got within half a block of the strip mall, I saw two older-looking kids on bicycles ride out from behind the body shop. They wore tank tops and flip-flops, and even though they were pretty far away and getting farther, I could clearly see they were way too big for the bikes they rode, and I had a moment of panic, thinking they'd jacked us.

Heart pounding, I ran out wide to get an angle on the spot where we'd left our bikes—

And that was when I saw her.

That was when I saw my mom.

CHAPTER TWENTY-ONE

She was standing by the body shop, right next to our bikes (which hadn't been stolen, after all). Her back was to me, but I instantly recognized her brown, sun-kissed skin and the small butterfly tattoo near her ankle. Her hair, just like always, was a dark red color that made me think of dried chilies.

It would be impossible to describe what I felt right then, because I'd never felt anything like it before. It was like a volcano was erupting inside me—a hot liquid explosion of shock, relief, and joy all mixed into one. There was no way I could keep it in.

"Mom!" I burst out. "¡Mami!"

"Your mom's *here?*" Violet asked, sounding shocked. "Where?"

"That's her—by the car place!" I broke into an automatic sprint. "Mami, over here! *Mom!*"

At that point, I expected her to turn around. I expected her to see me coming, shout my name, and start running toward me with her arms flung open, crying hysterically. Only that didn't happen. Instead she wandered into the alley behind the mall like she hadn't even heard me.

I'm going to lose her! The horrifying thought swept through my mind like a whirlwind as my sneakers furiously pounded the pavement. *I'm going to lose her all over again!*

But the second I turned the corner, I let out a huge sigh of relief. My mom had stopped between the buildings and now stood facing the back wall of the alley, by a dumpster. Weird, sure, but I figured she must've been waiting for me or something.

"Mom!"

My voice echoed in the dimly lit alley. Nearby, I could hear the fuzzy sound of static as someone flipped through radio stations; it sounded like it was coming from the bodega.

"Mom!" I ran up behind her. "Mom, it's me—Charlie!"

This time she heard me. And this time she turned. But the instant she did, my relief turned to horror.

She wasn't my mom.

She wasn't even human.

CHAPTER TWENTY-TWO

A monster. That was the only way to describe this thing. From the neck down, it looked human enough (though I now saw that it didn't look *anything* like my mom). Its skin was pasty white, its hands withered and ancient. But from the neck up was where things got really bad. It had the face of a horse. And not your average handsome Thoroughbred, either— more like a dead horse . . . a *long*-dead horse. Its muzzle was broad and bony, covered with lumps, bumps, knobs, and pus-gushing bruises. Its bulging black eyes seemed to look everywhere and nowhere all at once. A steeply slant-ing forehead stretched down to where there should've been a nose but wasn't. Instead, I could see tufts of ratty black hair growing out of the gaping cavity, as well as everywhere else on this hideous thing's head—under its chin, along its jaw, behind the pointy cones of its ears. Its lipless mouth formed a permanent scowl. A scowl overrun with jagged, razor-sharp teeth.

The creature was so ugly, so mind-numbingly *repulsive*, that the mere sight of it had paralyzed me somehow. I couldn't look away—couldn't even close my eyes to block out its hideous face!

"Charlie!" Violet's voice blurred in my ears, seeming to come from far away. "Charlie, where'd you go?"

It took everything in me, every ounce of my willpower, but I managed to blink out of the trance just as the monster lunged for me. She swiped one of her talon-tipped hands at my face with blinding speed. I staggered back, stumbled on a soda bottle. Her nails whizzed by my cheeks, missing by centimeters.

"Don't be shhhy now, niño," the horse-lady said, circling to her left. Her voice was a serpent's hiss. It echoed off the walls of the alley, making it sound like she was all around me. "Thisss can all be over quickly. You sssimply have to ssstand ssstill!" And she lunged again.

I dodged, nearly tripping over my own feet, and slammed up against the side of the body shop. A stab of pain went through my ribs, but I hardly felt it. I didn't have time for pain; all my focus was simply on staying alive!

"What *are* you?" I shouted as I scrambled off the wall and away from her. "And what do you *want*?"

"Doesssn't matter," the horse-lady hissed. "All you need to know isss that mine will be the lassst face you *ever* sssee." Her awful smell washed over me then—the stench of rotting meat and zoo exhibits just after feeding time. It rushed up my nostrils like a flood, making my head spin, as footsteps echoed in my ears.

A second later Violet came into view, panting.

"Charlie—"

"Violet, stay back!" I warned. "This thing isn't human!"

"What do you mean it's *not human*? What is it, then?"

"No idea!"

The horse-faced lady sneered in disgust. "Never *heard* of me . . . ? You shhhould be BOWING before me, for I am the rightful ruler of the Azzztec Empire!" At my confused—and most definitely *terrified*—expression, she added, "Perhapsss you've heard my legend. . . . It'sss been told all over Cccentral America for agesss: the legend of Sssihuehuet."

Sihuehuet? It didn't ring any bells. Which was sort of weird, because I was pretty sure my abuela had taught me nearly every legend ever told across the Spanish-speaking world. Was it possible she'd left this thing's story out?

"Or perhapsss you know me by another name," the monster said, once again reading my face. "Cccigua."

Cigua? Hmmm. Still didn't ring any bells. "Uh . . ."

The creature's forehead creased with concern, its

ancient pasty skin so flabby that it almost looked like a frowning bulldog. "¿Nada? Nothing?"

"Not really . . . ," I admitted.

"Are you posssitive?"

"I, uh, think so. . . ." I felt like I was back in school, being pressed by one of my teachers to come up with an answer that I should've known but didn't. Wasn't much fun in class with teachers I liked, definitely wasn't any fun with some horse-faced abomination that was trying to rip my face off.

The thing went quiet for a second, then asked, "How about Cccegua?"

I bit my lip, trying to think. "Eh . . ."

"What?" she burst out. "You don't know that one *either?"*

"Sorry?" If I weren't so terrified, I would've felt embarrassed for her. Maybe. Okay, probably not. "Uh, maybe you have, like, one or two more?"

"¡*Cállate!*" she snapped. "I'll lead thisss converssssation!" Then the walking horror show went into deep thought for a second or two before finally saying, "Ah, perhapsss you know me by the oldessst of my namesss . . . *Sssihuanaba.*"

La Sihuanaba—of course! "You're the peasant girl who became a queen but cheated on the king and got cursed!" I couldn't believe I hadn't realized it on my own! As if her hideous horse face wasn't a dead giveaway, the fact that she'd been able to take the form of my mother—even if only from behind—should've made it as obvious as a slap in the face.

"Ah, ssso you *have* heard of me. . . ." The monster wreathed its muzzle in a brutal-looking grin. "In thisss you are quite fortunate, boy."

"Really? And how is that exactly?"

"Becaussse I will now extend to you the sssame offer I extend to all my victimsss who are wissse enough to recognizzze me," she said.

I highly doubted that I was going to like her offer, but at least it was something, right? "Which is?"

"Tell me where Cipitío isss, and I'll ssspare your life."

Cipitío . . . *Cipitío*. I'd definitely heard the name, but in my frantic state I couldn't seem to remember exactly who—

Oh! It was her son! The child born from one of her extramarital affairs. He'd also been cursed, if I remembered correctly; poor kid had been given backward feet.

I frowned, confused. "How the heck should I know where your son is?"

La Sihuanaba sighed. "Alwaysss the sssame boring anssswer . . ."

"But I don't know! Honest!"

"Oh, I believe you," the monster replied, the flabby curtains of her cheeks pulling back in a ghastly half smirk. "And now you *die*. . . ." Her mouth opened wide, and she bared her fangs at me. They were long and pointed, dripping yellowish liquid.

I had a moment to think, *Aw, man, nasty!* and then she flung herself at me again.

I ducked and rolled along the wall. La Sihuanaba danced to her left, cornering me between the side of the building and the dumpster. The venom ran down the sides of her muzzle like drool, dripping to the ground around her bare feet. Sizzling into the cement.

She's a walking poison factory! I thought with a fresh surge of panic.

An instant later something small flew through the air, smacking the creature on the back of the head.

"Yoo-hoooo!" Violet yelled. "Over here!"

The hideous horse head swiveled in her direction. "Leave usss!" she hissed. "Thisss doesssn't conccccern you!"

"You'd be *sssssurprised* what concerns me!" Violet shot back mockingly. She threw another rock. This one hit La Sihuanaba right on the nose, and the monster let out a horrible sound—something between a shriek and a dying horse's last neigh. "Come get me!" Violet taunted her. "I got a big ol' sugar cube waitin' for you in my back pocket!"

But the horse-lady didn't go for it. Instead, she spun back around with a murderous look in her eyes. The message was crystal clear: She wanted *me*.

"Why are you doing this?" I shouted at her. "What'd I ever do to you?"

"Jussst sssettling an old sssscore," the monster replied matter-of-factly.

"But I don't even know you!"

"Not with you, boy! With La Cuca. Shhhe took sssomething from me, and now I'm going to take *you* from *her*."

Was she talking about the evil witch from those old legends? "I don't even know a Cuca! I swear!"

Those horrible black eyes fixed on me. "And how well do you know my sssstory . . . ?"

I shrugged. "Pretty well, I guess."

"Do you remember the wretched, two-faced bruja in it?"

I racked my frantic brain. "The witch . . . oh, sure! She's the one who gave you the potion so you could trick the king into marrying you. Then she gave you another potion so you could kill him. But I don't think that one worked out too good. . . ."

"No, as a matter of fact, it *didn't*! Becaussse inssstead of *killing* the king, the potion turned Yeisssun into a *giant* sssavage monsssster, and he ruined everything! I wasss cursssed and cassst out of the empire—*my* empire! And it isss for thisss treachery, thisss *purposssseful* betrayal, that I will now exact my vengeancccce."

"Charlie, how do you beat that thing?" I heard Violet

shout from the other end of the alley. She was down on her hands and knees now, searching for more rocks.

"How should I know?" I shouted back.

"I mean, like, in the *myths*! How do people survive when they run into her?"

How *did* people survive . . . ? I tried to think, but I couldn't focus on anything past the pounding in my head and La Sihuanaba's gruesome face staring right at me. My brain was so fuzzy it felt like I was swimming through a bowl of sancocho soup.

But somehow, like a flash of lightning, my abuela's words came back to me: *The few who have seen La Sihuanaba face-to-face and lived to tell the story claimed that she fled from them when they reached for their crucifix or bit down on a machete.*

A machete. Wouldn't mind having one of those right about now.

My eyes desperately scanned the alley. Nope, no machete. But I *did* spot something—a pair of car antennas sticking out of the half-open dumpster.

La Sihuanaba must've seen a plan forming behind my eyes, because she charged me just as I was about to make my move, forcing me away from the dumpster.

She slashed. I stumbled. She hissed. I screamed.

"Charlie!" Violet shouted, flinging another rock. This

one bounced harmlessly off La Sihuanaba's head as her deformed jaws parted in a horrible sideways grin.

"Ssslippery little one," she murmured. "But you do realize you have no chance of essscape, don't you?"

She was trying to intimidate me. Trying to keep me scared, on the defensive. I wasn't going to let it work. This time when she charged, I held my ground until the very last moment, then slipped through her arms and dove for the dumpster.

La Sihuanaba might've had the face of an old, dead horse, but she was quick as a viper. She was on me in a blink, her talons slashing at my back, her wild hissing filling the air around me. Had I been half a second slower, her claws would've sliced ribbons down my back, carving me up worse than a Thanksgiving turkey. Too bad for her— and so, *so* good for me—I hadn't been.

Antennas in hand, I whipped around just as she closed the distance and raised them in the shape of a cross. Instantly, the horse-faced demon shrank back, shrieking in pain and surprise. I saw the skin along her bony muzzle begin to sizzle like someone had poured hot acid on it. I know it sounds weird or whatever, but that had to be the most beautifully repulsive thing I'd ever seen!

I lifted the makeshift cross high. The antennas caught the moonlight and reflected the cross shape back at the demon. It was too much for her. She let out another blood-curdling shriek and began to melt into her dress. Right before my eyes, she dissolved until she was nothing more than a steaming blob of bubbling yellow goop surrounded by about four yards' worth of cottony fabric.

For a long moment, I just stood there, stunned, hardly believing my eyes.

Then Violet rushed over, shouting, "Charlie! Charlie, are you hurt?" She ran right up to me, her eyes huge, her breaths coming in big, heaving gasps. Her fingers closed around my arm like mini vises, and I winced. "Charlie, did she get you? Are you okay?"

I shook my head. "Nah, she didn't get me. . . ." But the truth was I didn't feel too great either. My legs were rubber. My heart was whamming so hard I was sure it would pop like a piñata any second now. "Close but no ciga—"

Suddenly, the ground shifted underneath me, and my knees unhinged. I would've smacked my head on the pavement if Violet hadn't caught me.

"Whoa, whoa, careful . . ." She hefted my weight, easing me back against the wall. "What's wrong?"

I closed my eyes. I had no clue. "Dizzy," I whispered.

Violet took my wrist, checking my pulse. Finally she said, "You're fine. It's only shock. Put your head between your knees and breathe."

I let myself slide to my butt on the cold alley floor. I wasn't buying the whole head-between-the-knees thing, but once I tried it, I started feeling better. My muscles loosened up, breathing became a lot easier, and pretty soon the world stopped spinning. Apparently, on top of her *many* other talents, Violet would also make a pretty good EMT.

"Better?" she asked when I finally looked up. I smiled—tried to, anyway. "You had me worried there for a sec," she said. "I was about to give you mouth-to-mouth."

I'm not sure what kind of face I made, but it must've been pretty funny, because Violet burst out laughing.

"Relax, Charlie. I'm just messing with you . . . ," she said.

I tried another smile. "Yeah, thanks for that."

"You're welcome. Oh, and by the way, was that thing another one of the myths your grandma taught you?"

I nodded.

"And the Crying Woman, too, right?"

"Yep."

Violet bit her lip in concentration. "That's—*interesting. . . .*"

It *was* interesting. In fact, I was starting to wonder *exactly* how much my abuela had known about these myths and why she'd told me all those stories in the first place. Had she known that these things *actually* existed? Was there any conceivable way she could have predicted that one day I would run into some of them? Had she been trying to protect me with her stories—maybe even *prepare* me?

And if so, then maybe it wasn't just my manifestations and my parents' disappearance that were linked—maybe the myths were somehow connected too.

A moment later, a soft breeze blew through the alley, swirling Violet's hair as she nodded toward the blob of sizzling yellow goop formerly known as La Sihuanaba. "Caught a whiff of that yet?" she asked.

I had. The smell sort of reminded me of my third-grade lunch box—and that wasn't a compliment. "Smells like moldy fish sticks," I said, pulling my shirt over my nose.

"Probably time to go."

"Yep." I pushed slowly to my feet, using the wall for support, and Violet hooked an arm through mine to steady me as we started walking.

Maybe it was just my imagination, but about halfway down the alley, I thought I saw movement out of the corner of my eye—a massive yellowish blur dashing across the rooftop of the little bodega. I turned, squinting against the harsh white glare of a nearby lamppost, but didn't see anything. No birds. No cats. Nada.

Great, I thought, shaking my head. *I'm on my way to becoming the world's most paranoid middle schooler.*

And probably for good reason . . .

Violet put a hand on my shoulder. "What's up?"

"Nah, nothing."

"You're looking better already," she said with a smile.

I smiled back. "Gracias." My head was still throbbing, though. I rubbed my aching temples. "So, you wanna head back to your house and try the tears?"

"Actually, I think we should hold off on that," she said. "It's been a long day. We should get some rest first . . . try the tears tomorrow. Remember, the mystery at Lilac Inn wasn't solved in a day."

I didn't get the reference, but I knew she was probably right.

She usually was.

CHAPTER TWENTY-THREE

The following morning my alarm clock went off about ten hours earlier than I would've liked. Groaning, I reached down to pull the covers over my face and immediately realized two things. One, my feathers had finally, *finally* come out—I could feel their tickly edges and pointy ends spread all over my pillows and bedsheets. And two, something was very, *very* wrong with my left arm. From the elbow down, it felt all stiff and cold, and the entire wrist area was throbbing like I'd pulled an all-nighter on Xbox Live. As a lifelong gamer and guitar player, the possibility that I might be developing some form of carpal tunnel had me bugging, but it wasn't until I blinked the sleep out of my eyes and got a good look at my aching left hand that my anxiety *really* kicked into high gear.

My hand looked like a giant lobster claw—er, my hand

was a giant lobster claw! Thick and red and narrowing to a pair of sharp pincers.

I tried flexing it and then almost peed my pants when the thing actually opened and closed at my command!

How can this be happening to me again? I screamed on the inside. *And so soon!*

Next thing I knew I was down the stairs and in the painfully bright kitchen, rummaging through the drawers and cabinets, searching frantically for something—*anything!*—to cover up this monstrosity. In less than twenty minutes, I'd have to be at school, and Halloween wasn't anywhere close enough for me to stroll into first period looking like a walking advertisement for Red Lobster.

Unfortunately, skipping school wasn't an option. Any unexcused absences or strange behavior (which probably included manifesting bizarre crustacean appendages) and child services would send one of their psychologists to the house to check up on me. And an investigation by a huge, powerful government-run agency was just about the *last* thing I needed right now.

Dropping to my knees, I flung open another cabinet, pushed aside what looked like a pair of big black cauldrons (yeah, Mrs. Wilson has weird taste in stuff), reached in a little deeper, and *yes!* I found one of her old oven mitts sandwiched between a pair of dusty dolls she'd stored under the sink for some reason. It was a ratty-looking thing with a faded picture of Minnie Mouse on the front, but it also happened to be the *perfect* size. I'd just slipped it on when a large shadow fell over me. At first I didn't bother turning around. I was pretty sure there was no way Mrs. Wilson could've come down those creaky old stairs without me hearing; I figured the shadow must've been cast by a bird landing on the windowsill or something. But then someone cleared their throat behind me, and I jumped to my feet so quickly that I nearly split my head on the edge of the counter.

Mrs. Wilson was standing at the foot of the stairs, arms crossed over the front of her silky nightgown. Her sharp green eyes held a mixture of curiosity and something else . . . concern, maybe. "Is that my oven mitt you're wearing?" she asked, raising a brow.

For a moment I just stood there, staring at her blankly, wondering how in the world she'd managed to sneak up on me like that. The only thing I could come up with was that I'd been so distracted searching through the drawers that I simply hadn't noticed the sound of her footsteps. Had to be it. That, or Mrs. Wilson was a part-time ninja.

When I finally opened my mouth (intending to lie to her, of course), nothing came out, so I decided honesty would probably be the best policy.

"I, uh—yes . . . this is your oven mitt I'm wearing," I admitted.

"Would you like to explain *why?*"

I nodded, then said the only thing I could think of that made even a lick of sense. "Research purposes."

"Research purposes?" She shook her head, looking confused, and I couldn't really blame her. "Are you studying home economics in school?"

"Yes! Exactly!" *Thank you, Mrs. Wilson!*

"Oh, that's wonderful! I had no idea."

Me neither. Surprise! "Uh-huh. Been waiting for a spot to open for a while now, and wouldn't you know it, one finally did. So, yeah . . ." All I could feel was the pounding of my heart and the hammering of my pulse in my neck; it made it almost impossible to think.

"In that case, you can use my better one." Crossing to the pantry, she opened a drawer and brought out another oven mitt. "Here." She held it out to me. This one was crisp and white, practically brand-new. "Give me that raggedy old thing and you can take this one to school. It's a bit more *masculine*," she added in a quiet voice.

"Oh, no, no, no. This one's fine. Really." I stepped out from behind the counter, patting my Minnie Mouse claw cover with a big, stupid (and completely fake) grin on my face. "And I'm a newbie in the kitchen, anyway. . . . I wouldn't want to mess that one up. It's so . . . nice and clean and all."

Her eyes narrowed. "Charlie?"

"Yes?" I squeaked.

"Are you feeling all right?"

"Uh, absolutely." I stood up straighter, squared my shoulders. *Good posture shows good spirits!* as my first grade teacher used to tell the class. "W-why do you ask?"

She pointed—but did not look—down at my legs. "Well, because you're not wearing any pants, dear. . . ."

"Looking good," Alvin said when I walked into fourth period social studies later that day. "I see you've gone from ski-resort casual to *Top Chef* chic."

Sighing, I dropped into the desk behind him. "Don't you have anything better to do than worry about what I'm wearing?"

He thought about that for a sec. "Not really . . ."

Sam was sitting to my right, and I could feel his gaze burning a hole in the side of my face. "¿Qué quieres, Sam?" I asked. "What is it?"

"I was just wondering if my grandpa's tobacco smoke was making me hallucinate again, or if you were *actually* wearing an oven mitt to school. You're not crying out for help, are you, Charlie?"

"Nah, he's just given up all hope of ever being popular."

Alvin twisted around to face us. "I saw an episode about it on *Ellen* once. I think it was called 'When Preteens Give Up.'"

"I haven't *given up*," I grumbled, quietly slipping the mitt under my desk. "I'm just . . . trying to find myself. I mean, isn't that what middle school is all about? Trying new things?"

Alvin's face screwed up. "That's college, man. Middle school is about surviving long enough *to get to* high school."

Sam said, "I thought high school was about surviving long enough to get to college."

Alvin put a hand on his shoulder. "We've got a long road ahead of us, buddy." Then he turned to me, eyes bright. "So, you ready for tonight?"

"What's tonight?" I asked, and he gave me a look like, *Are you kidding me?*

"Dude, it's *Thursday*. Last week we all agreed that we were going to sleep over at my house today so we could get up early tomorrow before school and be the first ones at the mall to register for auditions. Which are *Saturday*." He frowned. "You didn't forget, did you?"

Actually, I did forget. Because I was busy morphing into *a scum-sucking crustacean!* "No, I didn't *forget*. . . . I just—I can't make it."

"*What?*" Sam shrieked. "You're messing with us, right?"

"Sam, relax. I'm sure they'll let you register without me."

"No, they won't!" he practically shouted in my face. "The FAQ page *clearly* states that all the members of the band must be present for registration. ¿No sabes leer, o qué?"

"Of course I know how to read—"

"I must be having a nightmare...." Alvin faced forward, rubbing his temples. "That has to be it, because there's no way this is happening right now. Not with auditions less than *two days away!*"

A few heads turned in our direction; people were starting to stare. Perfecto. Just what I needed.

"Guys, listen, I'll be there, okay? I can't sleep over because I got something else I got to do. But I'll be at the mall. Now, can both of you please just chill?" *And stop drawing attention to me!*

"All right, everyone, settle down," Mrs. Grant said, walking into the room. "Get out a sheet of paper and a pencil. We're having a pop quiz." When about half the class moaned at that, she quickly added, "No worries. It's not going to be graded." As she set her handbag down, her gaze went to the back of the room, and she let out a low sigh. Then I saw why: Behind me, in her usual back-row seat, Alice Coulter was waving a meaty paw over her head. "The answer is *no*, Ms. Coulter. No, you may not go to the bathroom. No, you may not check something in your locker really quick. No, you may not go see a nurse. And no, you may not, under any circumstances, take a nap during my class."

"But Mrs. Grant, I just wanted to let you know that Charlie's in violation of the school dress code," Alice said, and I felt my insides shrivel like bacon in a frying pan. "I mean, unless he's trying out to be our new lunch lady!"

Most of the class laughed at that. Alice and one of her dingbat friends smacked hands.

I hate middle school.

"Quiet!" Mrs. Grant snapped. Then she looked at me and frowned. "As much as it pains me to say this, Charlie, she has a point. The dress code doesn't permit any"—her eyes went to my oven mitt—"*accessories. . . .* Please take it off so we can get started."

"I, uh, bruised my hand really bad," I said, thinking quick. "I'm using the mitt for a little extra protection. . . ."

"Well, if Charlie can wear that *nasty* old oven mitt, then I can wear my ball cap," Alice said, pulling it out of her stinky gym bag.

Mrs. Grant sighed. "Put that away, Alice. . . . You know the rules."

"But that's so not fair!"

"I *said* put it away," Mrs. Grant told her sternly. Then to me: "Charlie, I understand you hurt your hand, but please take the mitt off so we can begin. . . ."

I hesitated. My heart was pounding so hard I figured the rest of the class could probably hear it. *Oh man, oh man, oh man! What do I do?*

"Charlie?" Mrs. Grant said.

I stared at her helplessly. "Yeah?"

"Take off the mitt."

"Dude, just take it off," Alvin hissed at me. He had twisted back around in his seat and was staring at me with a look that said, *Bro, have you lost your freakin' marbles?*

"What are you waiting for?" Sam asked, kicking my foot under the desk.

Mrs. Grant was still watching me. Crossing her arms now the way teachers do when they want to let you know that you're getting on their last nerve. "Charlie?"

From behind me came the soft wet snap of someone popping bubble gum. Closer and to my left, I heard someone say my name again—Sam, probably—but the sound seemed far away now, buried beneath the weight of a couple dozen or so curious eyes.

Prickly sweat broke out on my forehead and on the back of my neck. My pulse was beating like war drums in my ears. It was quickly becoming the only thing I could hear.

Keep it together, dude. . . . Just keep it together.

Feeling like I was on the witness stand for a trial that

would decide the rest of my life, I opened my mouth to say something, but my tongue felt like it had been glued in place. For a moment, I just sat there, imagining how the class would react if I actually took off the mitt, if I *actually* showed everyone my claw. I imagined their slack-jawed faces. Imagined the awful silence that would sweep through the room, louder than any nuclear bomb. Imagined the pandemonium that would no doubt follow. The screams and shouts of surprise. The kids scrambling out of their desks, scrambling away from me. The pointing, the gasps. The only thing I didn't imagine was how Alvin and Sam would react, and that was because I honestly didn't *know* how they would react. Deep down inside, I wanted to believe that they *wouldn't* totally panic, that they wouldn't run away from me like all the other kids. But something even deeper down was telling me that there was no way they could accept me. And how could they? How could they accept a freak?

"I . . . can't," I finally managed.

Mrs. Grant looked confused. Confused and disappointed. Which sort of sucked because she was one of my favorite teachers. "Then I'm going to have to ask you to leave my classroom."

"But Mrs.—"

"Charlie, it's your choice. Get rid of the mitt or you're off to detention."

Not really much of a choice, I thought. Defeated, I dropped my head. "Yes, ma'am . . ."

As I gathered my things and started slowly out of the room, I heard Alice shout, "Hope you win lunch lady of the month, Charlie!"

CHAPTER TWENTY-FOUR

One thing was for sure: I couldn't go to study hall. Even if the hall monitor in charge didn't ask me to take off the mitt, Alice was still in every single one of my upcoming classes (thank you very much, scheduling people), and knowing her, she would *definitely* bring up the whole dress-code thing to those teachers too. Thing was, I couldn't go straight home, either. It was still before noon, which meant that Mrs. Wilson hadn't left for her daily trip to the local flea market. She had all these boxes and boxes of little kids' toys that she was always trying to get rid of down there; I guess she'd been expecting child services to pair her with a younger kid when she'd gotten me. At least that's what it seemed like. Anyway, if I came home now, she'd have a bunch of questions I wasn't in any mood to try to talk my way around. So I decided my best move—now that I'd shown up for homeroom and wouldn't be marked absent for the day—would be to get out of here. Take a nice little stroll up to Miracle Mile and just hang out for a while. The shopping strip wasn't too far from school, a mile, maybe a mile and a half. Plus, it was on the way home. So that's exactly what I did.

The tail end of the morning rush was just beginning to wind down by the time I got there; there were only a handful of moms pushing strollers and a few groups of older guys playing dominoes beneath the row of pastel-colored umbrellas on the sidewalk in front of one of the trendy cafés.

I walked slowly along the glittering storefronts, taking my time, hoping no one would notice an unaccompanied minor strolling aimlessly around. Fortunately, no one did. Probably because there weren't that many people to notice in the first place. It seemed like my biggest problem was going to be killing time, and I was thinking about heading over to the local bookstore (my plan was to hide out toward the back somewhere, maybe find myself a comfy beanbag chair and flip through some of the new releases) when I came around the corner and something in the display window of O'Hara's Pawn stopped me in my tracks. It was a bike, old and thin-framed, with two seats and two pairs of handlebars. The sign on the window read: POPULAR 1930S TWO-SEATER!

It was a tandem bike. Like the one Violet had mentioned wanting as a kid.

And just like that I had a great idea.

It was almost seven o'clock when I made it to Violet's house later that night, and the moon was a huge silver disk in the sky. After hiding her surprise behind the tall leafy palm that stood at the edge of her neighbor's yard, I sprinted up the porch steps, hoping she wouldn't be too upset with me for being a little late. Even if she was, though, I figured I had the ultimate get-out-of-jail-free card. Man, I couldn't wait to see the look on her face!

I had just raised my fist to knock when a voice said, "Hey."

I turned to see Violet sitting on the long, built-in bench on the far side of the porch. The moment I laid eyes on her my mind blanked. I forgot where I was, what I was doing here—even how rude it was to stare. She was wearing a long, silky dress the color of a wintry sky, and her hair, which was done up in a French twist, glittered like diamond dust. Her lips were a glossy pink, her lashes dark and impossibly long, and her skin glowed as if backlit by the sun. She looked, in a word, *amazing.*

"You're late," she said, getting up.

"And you're—*wow . . .*"

Her cheeks turned tomato red, and she looked down at

her dress, smoothing a hand over the shimmering fabric. "Too much, right? I was just telling myself I went totally overboard."

"No. Not too much." I stepped forward—tried to anyway. I wasn't sure my legs were receiving any commands from my brain at the moment. "You look *beautiful*. . . ."

And you can chalk that up as the understatement of the century.

"I've never met a queen before, so I thought, why not dress up, you know?" Her dazzling blue eyes rose to meet mine, and I was stupid enough to look directly into them; I had to catch myself on the banister or I would've tumbled backward down the steps. "I see you're not wearing your jacket," she said, giving my outfit a once-over. Jeans, Miami Heat T-shirt (Dwyane Wade—who else?), oven mitt. Doubt she was impressed.

"Yeah, I got *other* problems now. . . ." I raised my left hand. Er, *claw*.

Her eyes went briefly to it. "So?"

"So . . . ?"

"Can I see it?"

"Oh. Yeah, sure." The instant I slipped off the ratty old mitt, her face lit up like Downtown Miami on the Fourth of July.

"That's *insane!*" She touched one hand lightly to my

claw. "That's gotta be the most amazing thing *I've ever seen!*"

I couldn't help smiling. Somehow, the weirder I got, the cooler she seemed to find me. It made me feel halfway normal. "I have a surprise for you," I said.

"Really?"

"C'mon." I led her down the steps and past the palm tree where I'd hidden the bike, but she didn't notice it right away, so I sort of stared in its general direction until she finally got the hint.

"Oh my gosh, Charlie!" She raced over to the bike and crouched down beside it. "A 1939 Rally's tandem three-speed! Where in the world did you find this?"

I grinned, feeling my heart thump against my rib cage. "I have my ways. . . . You like it?"

"I *love* it!"

Well, that's a relief, I thought, because I'd had to pawn my mother's locket to buy it for her. I figured I could work some odd jobs over the summer—cut a few lawns, work weekends at the local car wash—to pay the money back.

Her fingers glided along the glossy red frame. "Did you know that this is, like, one out of thirty-five that were ever made? Most collectors don't even know that. They think the tandem three-speed was an extension of Rally's tandem *two*-speed line, which would then make it a Twoie 300—you know, a standard production run that they made around 1952. But it wasn't. It was *its own* luxury line of bikes subcontracted by the Rally Cycle Company to this tiny parts producer out in Wisconsin."

Wow, she seemed to know as much about old bikes as I knew about myths. Pretty impressive. "Huh. I did not know that."

"Yeah, and the interesting thing is that that little Wisconsin-based company switched over from making bike parts to cheese curds to try to keep from going bankrupt. Funny thing was, at the time, Rally had no clue. So, after they received the first shipment of parts, all of which were handmade because the company had sold off most of its parts-making machinery to pay off creditors, Rally called them to ask when the rest were coming and found out they weren't because the company was now a cheese-making outfit. RCC obviously had to cancel the line, and the few bikes that had been assembled with the first batch of parts were sold off to recoup some of the money they'd lost in R and D."

"Really?"

"Yep. And maybe the coolest part is that the spokes for the wheels"—she pointed at them—"were molded after tractor parts because that's what the company made before switching over to bike parts and eventually Wisconsin cheddar."

"Man, you sure know your Rally stuff." Coming from anyone else, the lesson in bicycle history would've probably caused me to die of boredom. But for some reason, when she told the story, I just wanted to hear more.

"It's what makes this bike such an oddity," she said with a smile. "And you know how much I like oddities. . . ." She smoothed a lock of hair behind one ear, her smile widening, glowing. "Maybe that's why I like you so much, Charlie Hernández."

Yeah, I was smiling again. Couldn't help it. "Are you saying I'm odd?"

She crinkled her nose. "Maybe just a little."

A moment of silence. Then I said, "Anyway, you got yourself a pedal partner now."

Violet nodded slowly, her eyes locked on mine. "Yeah, I think I do. . . ."

I held the bike as she flipped up the kickstand with her foot. "So, where are we gonna try the tears?"

"I know just the place," she said, hopping on.

CHAPTER TWENTY-FIVE

It took us fifteen minutes to ride over to the little park by Vizcaya, and by the time we got there it was so dark I couldn't see the swing set, the slide, or even the gazebos and pine trees by the seawall. We leaned the bike up against one of the concrete benches and got to work.

"All right, let's do this," Violet said, bringing the jar out of her purse. The wooden cork made a nice, satisfying *POP!* as she yanked it out of the bottle. I didn't smell any noxious fumes, which I figured was a pretty good start. "Ready?"

"Yeah, but how do you think it works?"

"Well, La Llorona said that her tears lead people to where the universe wants to take them, right? But I don't think she meant that in the literal sense." She held up the jar. "I mean, tears can't lead people. . . . They're just tears. So, what I'm thinking is that they might give you a vision or something."

I wasn't quite sure where she was going with this. "So you're saying I should . . . ?"

"Splash them in your eyes."

"*Splash them in my eyes?*"

She nodded and offered me the jar.

"Kinda gross, no?"

"Sure, but you got any better ideas?"

I sighed. I didn't. "Perfecto." Slipping off the oven mitt, I traded it to Violet for the jar. Then I dipped a couple fingers into the cold, murky liquid (hoping to still have them when I pulled them back out—which, thankfully, I did), tipped my head back, and hovered my now dripping fingers over my eyes, trying to score a hit.

The first few drops were total air balls. (I got myself on the bridge of the nose once and sent the others streaking down my temples.) But the fifth one splashed directly onto my pupil—and with it came a burst of stinging pain.

I flinched, hard, rubbing at my eye with the back of my hand, and the stupid jar slipped right out of my claw. I didn't need to see what happened next because I heard it shatter as it hit the sidewalk and felt the splash against my sneakers.

"You okay?" I heard Violet ask.

"No."

A second later, I realized it wasn't the tear that had stung me; it was some kind of bug. A gnat, probably. I could feel it in there—the hump of its tiny exoskeleton stuck to the under-side of my eyelid. The little sucker must've flown into my eye at the exact same moment the tear had gone in.

"Got a bug in there," I said, still rubbing.

"Hopefully, you got a tear in there too," she said, "because we're going to have to make another visit to the Crying Shack to get any more."

My heart sank as I glanced down to see the puddle of La Llorona's tears glittering dully on the gray cement.

"Well, did you?" she asked.

"Yeah, I got one."

"And does anything look different to you?"

I closed my other eye to check. "Everything looks a bit—*watery*. . . ."

"Maybe we need to give it a sec," she said.

So we did; we waited. A few seconds went by. Then a minute. I watched an old beat-up minivan trundle past. The traffic light at the corner changed from green to yellow to red and then back again. Violet stared at her watch, tapping her foot impatiently.

After about another thirty seconds or so, I threw my hands up. "Nothing's happening," I said. "The tears don't do anything." Honestly, it was frustrating; I'd kind of risked life and limb for that jar. But, really, what did I expect? They were just tears.

"It's okay," Violet said, but she looked a little disappointed herself. "Doesn't matter. Yesterday when I ran La Liga de Sombras through the FBI's database, I got some interesting returns. We should be good to go." She frowned.

"What's wrong?"

"Well, I have the addresses on my phone, but unfortunately, we're going to have to take the tandem back to my house."

"Why?"

"Because both places are pretty far. I'll call us an Uber or something."

Just then I became aware of a strange sound . . . like water sloshing inside a half-filled balloon. At first I thought it was coming from the little pond. But then I looked down and my eyeballs nearly popped out of their sockets.

La Llorona's tears—which had been splattered all over the place just a second ago—had formed into two long quivering streaks on the sidewalk. They looked like a pair of fat, liquid caterpillars. And the craziest part? They were *moving* . . . sort of wriggling their way up the sidewalk, along the edge of the grassy path.

"Uh, are you seeing this . . . ?" I asked Violet.

"Seeing w—" She broke off, her eyes growing to the size of Frisbees. "Oh my God . . ."

We both looked at each other, sly grins beginning to creep across our faces.

I said, "I guess she really meant it when she said the tears lead you, huh?"

La Llorona might've been one crazy mamá, but her tears were without a doubt some of the most useful ever shed on planet Earth. They led us clear across town, past two busy shopping malls, through an endless, tree-lined maze of high-rises that sat on the edge of Biscayne Bay, and across a wide, eight-lane intersection, all without evaporating or being absorbed by the concrete. Fifteen minutes later, when they halted at the bus stop right across from Bay-front Park, we were pretty sure our liquid GPS had gassed out. But then a bus pulled up, and they climbed aboard using a sort of liquidy Slinky-like maneuver that had the toy company's catchy little jingle playing in my head: "It's Slinky, it's Slinky, the favorite of girls and boys." For a second Violet and I just stood there, too stunned to do anything but stare. I mean, we'd seen a lot of crazy stuff in the last few days—*a lot*—but this was right at the top of that list. Fortunately, we managed to snap out of it pretty quick, squeeze our two-seater onto the bus's one-size-too-small bicycle rack, and then squeeze *ourselves* through the closing accordion doors before our not-so-friendly Haitian driver yelled something in Creole (or maybe it was French) and put pedal to metal.

The bus wasn't too full—maybe five or six people spread out over the thirty or so benches. We took a seat near the front, directly behind the tears, which had paused, not so inconspicuously, in the center of the aisle, just on the other side of the white DO NOT CROSS line. Surprisingly, none of the passengers seemed to notice them—well, no one except for a dazed-looking homeless dude who stared at them from under the bill of his grimy Dolphins cap for almost a full minute before shaking his head and dozing off. Apparently, he'd seen weirder things in Miami.

Maybe twenty stops later (honestly, I lost count after, like, *twelve*), the twin salty streaks slinked their way silently off the bus, and we hopped on our bike and followed their glittery, snail-like trail around a corner and up a nice quiet street lined with tall palm trees and short black mangroves. There were apartment complexes to our left, large, freshly mowed fields to our right. At the end of the block, the tears turned right, and we eventually wound up in a small parking lot with a churchy-looking building on one side and a huge, rectangular archway guarded by a wrought-iron gate on the other. Through the archway, beyond a vast garden dotted with trees and large stone statues, I could see what appeared to be another building—some sort of old Spanish monastery.

"I think we're here," I said, glancing around. "Wherever *here* is ..."

Sitting on a folding chair in front of the archway was a rent-a-cop in a dark blue uniform. He rose as we approached, completely unaware that close to a thousand bucks' worth of magical tears had just slipped soundlessly between his legs and through the fence.

"Hi. Can we go in?" Violet asked.

The rent-a-cop limped over, shaking his head like he hadn't heard her. Up close, I could see he had big, almost bulging eyes set a little too far apart and papery-pale skin, probably from working late nights and sleeping through most of the day. Dude needed a tan. *Badly.* "What was that?"

"Um, we just wanted to visit," I explained, trying to sound friendly.

"Do you have an invitation?" he asked. When we shook our heads, he crossed his arms over his barrel of a chest. "Then you can't come in. The monastery's closed anyway. Come back during regular visiting hours."

"But we just wanted to take a quick look around," Violet said. "It's for, uh, a school project. . . ."

The guard's eyes narrowed. "I don't care if it's for the *FIFA World Cup.* I told you *we're closed.* Now, I'm gonna give you two exactly *three* seconds to split before things get ugly." Then he barked at us. Yeah, *barked*. Like a dog. I guess he thought that might intimidate us.

"Olvídalo," I whispered to Violet. "Forget it. He's not gonna let us in. Let's roll."

So we showed him our rear reflectors and pedaled into the grassy field that sat to the left of the monastery, cruising along a chain-link fence like a couple of Depression-era kids on our state-of-the-art 1930s tandem.

When we'd gone a little ways, I hopped off the bike and peered into the lot, trying to find another way in.

"So, what do you want to do?" Violet asked.

"Looks like we're gonna have to jump the fence," I said. It really was the only way; the monastery was surrounded on all sides—far away by a low cement wall, closer by this fence.

She gave me a funny look. "You've obviously never worn a gown before."

"Does look a little constricting, now that you mention it. . . ."

"Yeah, and in all the *wrong* places." Violet slapped a hand to her forehead. "Can't believe I forgot to pack my trusty pair of wire cutters!"

"Wait. You have a *trusty pair* of wire cutters . . . ?"

She nodded. "I usually keep them in my backpack. You won't believe how handy those things are."

"Yo tengo una mejor idea," I said. I slipped off the oven mitt and clacked my claw together a few times. "Who needs wire cutters when you got these bad boys?"

The chain link was tougher than it looked—I had to really put some muscle into each snip—but less than five minutes later, I had cut us a medium-size opening at the bottom of the fence. Pleased with my work, I glanced up at Violet. "Whatd'ya think?"

"You're a natural, Charlie. What can I say?"

"I'll go first to make sure there's nothing to mess up your dress or whatever."

"Muchas gracias."

I was about to start crawling when I heard someone shout behind me. "Hey, you two! Get away from the fence!"

I turned and saw the guard racing up the sidewalk toward us, his walkie-talkie in one hand, a long black flashlight in the other.

"I'll handle him," Violet said, bringing a can of pepper spray out of her purse.

"Um . . . he's a pretty big guy, V."

"I've sprayed bigger."

As if taking offense to that, the guard gave a hellish shriek and leapt forward, diving headfirst into the empty air. There was a loud, tearing sound as his uniform exploded—like, *literally* exploded—and a mass of mangled black fur shot out from his body. Something between a canine and a demented Thoroughbred (I couldn't really see it as a man anymore—not after it nearly tripled in size and its once-human face elongated into a thick, furry muzzle), it flew through the air with the grace of a ballerina, then hit the ground in full stride, sending tremors through the pavement and slinging ribbons of foam from between its rows of razor-sharp teeth.

"Still sprayed bigger?" I asked. As I gaped wide-eyed at the beast, a creepy feeling of déjà vu settled over me. There was something so familiar about the dark, hungry eyes, the flying drool, the massive fur-covered body. I'd seen this thing before. . . . But where?

Then the creature looked straight at me, its red eyes glowing, and my heart skipped a beat. It was a nahual! My abuela must've told me twenty different stories about these things. The most famous one involved a band of travelers who were attacked one night on a dark country road by an enormous black dog that robbed them of their possessions. As legend had it, one of the travelers shot the animal during the scuffle, but when they tried to track it, following the trail of its blood, they came upon a richly appointed hut, where they found a peasant tending to a leg wound. The travelers eventually gave up on the search for the dog and returned to the nearest village, where they were told that the man they had seen in the hut was actually a nahual—a shape-shifting sorcerer.

"Let me guess," Violet said. "You recognize him too?"

"Uh-huh."

"Another creature from Hispanic mythology?"

"Uh-huh."

"Any idea why we would keep running into things like this?"

"Nuh-uh. But we should probably run."

Without another word, Violet dove for the opening in the fence and started to shimmy her way through. I waited my turn, heart flopping around in my chest, but couldn't stop myself from looking back at the creature. It was less than fifty yards away now and closing fast, glowing red eyes wild, silver moonlight flashing off its mangled coat as it charged up the sidewalk. Dang, that thing was fast!

"Charlie!"

Violet's scream snapped my head back around.

"What's wrong?" I started to say. Then I saw the problem: The hem of her dress had gotten caught on the chain link; she was yanking on it desperately with both hands, but it wouldn't come free.

"It's stuck!" she cried.

Crud, crud, crud. Not good. NOT good.

"On it!" With frantic fingers, I attacked the dress—picking, plucking, pulling (I even tried bending the chain link), but nothing worked. Fear squirmed through me like something alive and slimy. My eyes flew back to the nahual. Only thirty yards away now, looming closer and closer. In less than three seconds, we were gonna become monster chow.

"Charlie, do something!" Violet screamed. So I did the only thing I could: I snipped off the piece of her dress that had gotten caught in the fence with my claw. (Yeah, yeah, I know. You never—never, ever, *ever*—mess with a girl's fancy party dress. But I really didn't think she would mind in this case.)

Now free, Violet scrambled the rest of the way through the hole. Then she whirled, shot a hand toward me, and shouted, "Take it!"

But I never got a chance. Because just as I reached for her, something rough and slimy wrapped itself around my ankle with a loud, wet slurp—and pulled.

My legs were suddenly swept out from under me. I belly flopped onto the pavement, the breath exploding out of my lungs in a big *whoosh*. The world lurched around me, and next thing I knew, I was being dragged rapidly down the sidewalk, my arms and legs flailing, fingers scrabbling madly at the cracks between the slabs of concrete. Then I threw a terrified look over my shoulder and finally realized what was going on: The creature had me lassoed with its nasty purple tongue!

"GRRRRROOOSSSSS!" I screamed, kicking and struggling, but the thing's floppy wet flavor-taster was ridiculously strong *and* ridiculously grippy. Like an octopus tentacle. No way I could fight myself free. Not even close.

Behind me, I could hear Violet rattling the fence like a crazy woman. "*Let go!*" she shouted. "*Let him go!*"

I saw her drop to her knees like she was going to crawl back to my side and screamed, "VIOLET, NO!"

"THEN HOW DO YOU EXPECT ME TO HELP?" she screamed back, and in that same instant the shape-shifter's tongue tightened painfully around my ankle. Numbness blossomed up my leg, and I cried out, twisting my body and stomping on its tongue with the heel of my other foot, but it didn't do anything; the creature just kept reeling me in, faster and faster, toward its gaping, razor-lined jaws.

This close, I could feel the intense heat pouring off the thing, could hear a low, almost rattlesnake-like hiss coming from deep inside the dark wet tunnel of its throat. The horrible stink of its breath washed over me—something between a pair of three-week-stale gym shorts and spoiled milk.

I can't believe I'm going to die like this, I thought. *Eaten alive on some sidewalk in North Miami Beach by a creature that shouldn't even exist!*

"Violet, run!" I shouted. "¡Vete! Get out of he—"

The walkie-talkie the nahual had dropped on the sidewalk suddenly crackled to life. There was a sharp, high-pitched squeal, followed by a furious female voice:

"WHAT ARE YOU DOING, PERRO CALLE-JERO?" the voice raged. "YOU'RE SUPPOSED TO LET THE CHILDREN INTO THE MONASTERY, NOT INTO YOUR BELLY! HAVE YOU ONCE AGAIN FORGOTTEN WHAT SIDE YOU FIGHT FOR?"

The nahual abruptly released my leg. Backing fearfully away from the walkie-talkie, it covered its face with one of its great black paws and whined deep in its throat, as if trying to apologize to whoever was on the other end.

But the lady was having none of it. "¡ALÉJATE! GET AWAY FROM THE CHILD!" she roared, and suddenly the ferocious beast (once ferocious, anyway) tucked its long fuzzy tail between its legs in terror and bounded off into the night, vanishing from sight.

For a moment I was too stunned to blink, much less get up and run. But I definitely wasn't about to just lie there and wait for that thing to change its mind about making me dinner. Scrambling to my feet, I hustled back over to the fence, scuttled through the opening, then nearly got leveled as Violet slammed into me, wrapping me up in a huge hug.

"Oh my God!" she shouted, crushing me with that trademark cheerleader strength. "You're okay!"

"Barely," I said sheepishly. And it was right about then that I realized I'd lost my mitt at some point in the scramble. I looked around for it but didn't see Minnie anywhere. The nahual must've eaten her. Gobbled her up like a half-priced doggie treat at PetSmart. Better her than me, I guess.

Violet was shaking her head. "But what happened? Who was that on the walkie-talkie?"

"No idea. But I don't think we wanna be here when Lassie's man-eating cousin gets back." I grabbed her hand. "C'mon!"

CHAPTER TWENTY-SIX

The ancient wooden doors of the monastery swung open at our approach (though it didn't look like anyone had opened them), and a flood of white light spilled out, swallowing us up in its dazzling brightness. Instinctively, I raised my arm to shield my face, but the light began to fade almost as suddenly as it had appeared.

Beside me, I heard Violet say, "Interesting . . ."

"Very," I agreed, blinking sunspots out of my vision.

Then I looked around—and gasped. Not because the room was so incredibly massive or because the walls were seamless slabs of white marble or even because the ceiling was made entirely of glass—a gigantic, translucent bubble through which I could see a blue-black canopy of stars twinkling almost close enough to touch.

No, it was the people, or should I say the *beings* . . . that made my breath catch, that got my heart thumping crazily against my ribs.

The tallest of the three was leaning against a great oak table in the middle of the room—a basajaun, no doubt about it. The dude was simply *ginormous*, easily over twelve feet tall, with long, whitish-yellow fur and a hard leathery face that looked almost human from certain angles. (Not many, but definitely a few.) An assortment of crude tools hung in its scraggly mane—a small rusty pick, the head of a hammer, a few smooth stones. . . . I even thought I saw a makeshift screwdriver dangling deep inside the matted strands of its bushy blond beard.

I remembered hearing how basajauns were extremely industrious creatures—how they learned to build tools, cultivate crops, and how they taught those skills to early settlers. Now, judging from the smart brown eyes that stared back at me from within the folds of its thickly fleshed face, I had no doubt this creature was just as intelligent as the legends made it out to be. If not *more*.

On the opposite end of the table, arms crossed in a watchful pose, stood the undisputed king of Salvadoran folklore: El Justo Juez, or the Just Judge. Dressed in dark flowing robes and high black leather boots, he looked like a mix between a Supreme Court justice and Batman. His shoulders were broad, his long, lean body fiercely upright, seemingly carved out of the hardest, driest stone. To top it all off, where his head should've been was a column of wispy gray smoke, which flickered every now and then with the sharp crackle of an ember. The fact that I couldn't tell which way he was looking—or if he was even *looking* in the first place—somehow made him all the *more* terrifying.

Over to our left, there was a massive fireplace where purple flames licked and popped. Sprawled out before it was a large and unbelievably beautiful dog. But not just any dog—El Cadejo. A being said to have taken the form of a canine after God created it to look after and protect man. Its glowing blue eyes smoldered like hot coals, and its fur, the color of freshly fallen snow, glistened as though it had been painted with sunlight.

As I stood there gawking at the three legendary figures—I was pretty sure my tongue was dangling somewhere down around my ankles—someone spoke up from behind the cluster of plants in the corner. At first I saw no one. Then my eyes adjusted, and I realized there wasn't anyone behind the plants; the plants *were* someone . . . a lady, curvy and barefoot, with huge anime eyes and hands so big they looked like they belonged on an NBA power forward. Her hair was a tangled mess of vines and leaves, and her skin was dark green, covered with lily pads and other small blooming flowers. She wore no clothes—only strips of fuzzy gray moss, which grew on her like lichen on a log.

"Madremonte," I breathed. *Mother Mountain.* "I can't believe you actually exist. . . ."

"And yet she does," said a voice.

I looked around and saw someone else—a woman in a fancy tiered gown standing at the window on the far side of the room. She was tall and slender, her long, pale arms glittering with an assortment of bracelets and jeweled armbands. A golden crown, studded with square-cut emeralds, sat atop layers of thick auburn hair, which coiled at the nape of her neck.

When she turned to face us, I saw she had eyes so bright and green there was no way they could possibly be human. In fact, I knew exactly what she was—a bruja. My abuela had described *many* of them.

"I must beg your perdón for such a terrifying greeting," she said, and this time I recognized her voice—which had a distinct air of royalty to it—almost immediately: She was the lady from the walkie-talkie. The one who had saved me. "Our night watchman happens to be a Nahual of the Forgotten Foothills, and they are without a doubt some of the most unruly creatures walking our planet."

I didn't think "unruly" was the right word (more like psychopathic or savage or maybe even bloodthirsty), but I wasn't going to argue.

"However, their loyalty is without question," she continued casually, "and thus they are indispensable. Do try to forgive him. And you have my word that it will *never* happen again." Then her lips split into a mesmerizing smile as her brilliant emerald eyes locked onto mine. "In any event, Charlie, Violet, it is my pleasure to finally meet you face-to-face. . . . My name is Joanna. I am the Witch Queen of Toledo. And *we* are the League of Shadows."

CHAPTER TWENTY-SEVEN

At first all I could think was, *We found them! We found them, we found them, we found them!* And it felt amazing. Like, *incredible!* But then I realized something was weird....

"Wait. How the heck do you know our names?" I started to say. And that's when something even *weirder* happened: What felt like a tidal wave of information slammed into me with enough force to knock me back a step.

Suddenly, I knew the answer to my question. But not only that—I knew the answer to *every* question I could *possibly* come up with. I knew this place wasn't just a monastery; it was also what was known as a Provencia—an ancient, warded structure of which there were dozens spread throughout the Americas and the Iberian Peninsula.

I knew that these Provencias served as regional

strongholds for the League and their allies. I knew that the first had been built more than twelve hundred years ago, during the time of the Spanish Kingdom of Asturias, and that the one we were currently standing in had had its bricks blessed by Pope Alexander III and a Cistercian monk in AD 1174. Over the last nine hundred years, it had survived two different all-out attacks from a horde of Oókempán ogres and a raging wildfire started by some naughty duendes.

Somehow I also knew that all the mythological beings standing before me referred to themselves as "sombras," or shadows. I knew there were good sombras and bad sombras. I knew La Liga was a coalition of good sombras and that they had been engaged in a millennia-long struggle against La Mano Peluda—or the Hairy Hand—a cabal of evil sombras intent on expanding their dominion from the Land of the Dead into the Land of the Living. I knew that the Land of the Living—or, our side of things—was teeming with all sorts of supernatural races and beings, everything from clans of tiny, spear-wielding pixies called zips to tribes of Basque giants known as jentilak. I knew that over the years most of these races had entirely segregated themselves from one another, because all they'd ever end up doing was warring over land or resources or power, and that it was La Liga's function to bring as many of them together as possible in order to form a unified front against La Mano Peluda.

I also knew that the big hairy basajaun dude had been following Violet and me for a couple of days now. Images of us biking around Miami, trekking through the Everglades, even facing off against Sihuanaba flitted through my mind like an old-fashioned film reel on fast-forward. There I was, tripping over the mangroves, my hair matted to my forehead, sweat pouring down my face. And there was Violet, slinging a rock at the horse-faced demon. I knew that it was Queen Joanna who had ordered the basajaun to follow us and that she'd been preparing to contact me before she found out we were on our way over.

An instant later (or at least what felt like an instant later—in reality I had no clue how much time had passed) a flash of bright light streaked across my vision, and I came back to myself with a gasp, looking around dazedly. "What. Just. Happened . . . ?" I whispered.

"El Cadejo touched your mind," the Witch Queen of Toledo said casually, like it was the most natural thing in the world. "Now you know all that you need to. Again, I apologize, but there isn't much time for questions."

"El Cadejo is an ancient being," El Justo Juez explained. His voice crackled like a hearth. "He existed long before modern languages were invented; he is unbound by them. He can speak directly to a person's soul."

The fate of this world hangs by a thread, pequeño. Even the slightest misstep on our part could spell the end of mankind. Words once again bounced around inside my brain as if I had thought them up myself, but this time I knew who it was. El Cadejo continued: *A darkness has begun to slither out of the old and forgotten places of the earth, an ancient evil whose thirst for domination cannot be quenched.*

"Ay, sí, let's just tell the children *everything!*" Madremonte snapped. A flurry of purple leaves tumbled out of her hair. The vines looping around her arms seemed to twist tighter, turning from a bright green to a deep dark brown.

"We've already discussed this, Señorita Monte," the witch queen said firmly. "The child represents our best chance to win this war."

"Sí, *the* child does," she agreed in an exasperated tone. "But *that* is not the child!"

"If you have your doubts, speak them now," said El Justo Juez. "No espere."

"My doubts? Bueno, para empezar . . . how old is he? Eight? Nine?"

"I'm twelve," I said, and Madremonte raised one mossy eyebrow in mock surprise.

"Oh, twelve. Is that so? Well, you are just all grown up, aren't you?" Then, to the others: "Which would *still* make him the youngest Cambiador in history."

"Youth is not a disqualifier," Joanna said.

"Nor is it a guarantee of ability," Madremonte shot back. "And let us not forget the prophecy or the meaning of the two horns. They represent a double portion of power, no? Meaning that the fifth Morphling will be the most powerful yet. And we all know that *two* manifestations for a Morphling with absolutely no training is already unheard of. Now consider this child. . . ."

What about him? asked El Cadejo.

"Ay, just look at that thing on his arm, for the love of the mountains! ¡Mira!" Her eyes, a swirling storm of yellows and browns, zeroed in on my claw. "Correct me if I am wrong, but from where I am rooted, that would certainly count as a *third* manifestation. Such ability is beyond even what was foretold in the prophecy. And let us not forget that the prophecy makes no mention of a claw in the first place! *That child* is *not* a Morphling. This has been brutally clear from the moment we began watching him. What more evidence do any of you need? This is not photosynthesis, mis compadres. . . ."

"I do not believe it is that simple this time," the queen said in a low, thoughtful voice. "I sense something in him . . . algo diferente."

"That is because your hope has blinded you! It has caused you to lose sight of the truly important tasks such as using what influence we have left to rally our allies and instead go searching the globe for *child heroes!*"

That is not fair, El Cadejo said, fixing her with his glowing gaze.

"¿Cómo no? It is merely the truth! The lobisomem clans have begun infighting again. The mukis of Cajamarca have stopped arming anyone but their own kin, which, need I remind you, violates the treaty of 1496, a treaty ratified in the halls of Castile by Joanna's own ancestors! And the Nacaome comelenguas, those wretched tongue-eating birds, have begun feeding on cattle and livestock in full view of villagers, which effectively violates *every other* treaty that's ever been agreed upon! The sombras are leaderless. They are all doing what is right in their own eyes. We must show *strength,* not desperation!"

As if to emphasize her point, a faint shudder shook the room. No one—except Violet and me, that is—seemed to notice.

"Can you not feel the darkness creeping into this world?" Madremonte whispered, touching a hand lightly to Joanna's arm. "Can you not feel its hungry jaws tightening around our throats? The influence of La Liga is already diminishing. Our alliances are collapsing all around us. Tell me that you do not hear the whispers of war on the winter winds."

La bruja's beautiful green eyes shifted first to me, then

back to Señorita Monte. "Indeed I do, for its awful song haunts me both day and night." She looked around at the others. "Juez, your best judgment. Is my course righteous, or does my heart deceive me?"

There was a brief moment of silence during which the column of wispy smoke above his shoulders wavered. When he finally spoke, his voice was like the sizzling of hot coals. "I do not pass judgment on issues of the heart, mi reina. I only judge between right and wrong."

"Muy bien," Joanna said. "Then this matter shall be resolved tonight. I will take the boy to see the oracle."

Juez stepped forward. "Perhaps that may not be the wisest course. We have not received any communications from our Provencia in La Roja in more than three days. I suspect treachery within our ranks. There have also been sightings of an Oókempán hunting pack in the region. It is far too dangerous."

At the queen's shocked look, Juez asked, "What's wrong, mi reina?"

She did not know of the fall of Toledo, El Cadejo answered.

Joanna squeezed her eyes shut for a brief moment. Her cheeks had suddenly turned deathly pale. "Ojos que no ven, corazón que no siente," she whispered after several seconds. She sounded completely heartbroken, and I was pretty sure she was fighting back tears.

Violet nudged me. "What does that mean?"

"Eyes that do not see, heart that does not feel," I said into her ear.

It was almost a whole minute before the queen spoke again, and when she did, her voice was little more than a rasp. "It seems the hour of judgment is upon us. I pray our courage does not fail us now."

"And I pray our good sense does not either," Madremonte said. With that, she started toward the back of the monastery, trailing a tangled mass of vines and purple weeds. I finally got why they called her Mother Mountain—because that's exactly what she looked like: a forest-covered mountain on two legs.

El Justo Juez spun in her direction. "Señorita Monte, ¿a dónde vas?"

"My forests need me," she said as she disappeared through a golden door below the wall of windows. "I don't have time for babysitting!"

El Cadejo turned the fuzzy white dome of his head toward Juez and must've communicated something, because they both abruptly started toward the same door.

"They're leaving?" Violet asked Joanna.

"They have many matters to attend to," the queen replied calmly.

Suddenly, about seven or eight itty-bitty little guys in

Spanish breeches, pointy hats, and what looked like clogs made of rocks came bumbling out of the hallway to our left. They had bloated purple eyes the size of plums and skin so pale you could almost see through it to the cords of wiry muscles flexing beneath. Between them, they were hefting a large wooden chest loaded with all sorts of ancient-looking weapons—swords, battle-axes, maces, and leather slings. They made it about halfway across the room before one of them saw Violet, shrieked like a terrified billy goat, then tripped over his own two feet, taking a few of his buddies down with him. The heavy chest clattered loudly to the marble floor, and when Joanna turned to glare at them, they all immediately dropped to one knee, bowing their little heads in reverence. The layers of dark hair snaking out from under their hats hung over their faces like silky curtains.

"¡Perdone, mi reina!" one of them cried.

"¡Sí, perdone!" shouted another.

"¡Perdone, perdone!" the rest of them began to chant.

Then they quickly surrounded the chest, picked it back up with a collective grunt, and disappeared down another long hallway, chattering noisily among themselves like a flock of excited geese.

Joanna sighed. "Duendes can be a little skittish around humans." She glanced down at my claw, her expression still tight. "Charlie, let me take a closer look at that. . . ."

"Uh, sure." I held up my big red lobster claw, feeling sort of embarrassed, and after a moment's study, she began to wrap it in a thin white cloth (to me, it looked like the stuff doctors use to make casts) that she seemed to have materialized out of thin air. As she worked, I was struck by how familiar she looked; I'd seen this lady before—there was no doubt in my mind—and maybe even more than once. The only question was, where . . . ?

When she finished, I flexed my claw, testing it. The material fit pretty snugly but still let me work the pincers. It looked just like a regular old cast.

"Cool," I said.

"Sí, *cool.*" La bruja's lips smiled, but her eyes still held a look of concern. "This way you won't attract any unwanted attention."

Just then, the huge hairy hominid to her left let out a deafening roar. The sudden explosion of sound washed over me like a meatball-scented tsunami, and I almost colored my undies.

"*Geez* . . . ," I said. "What's up with him?"

"He would like both of you to know that he'll be joining us tonight," answered Joanna.

"Really? All that *grrrrrr* just to say, 'I'm coming with'?"

"Juan is a very passionate individual."

Huh. A basajaun named Juan. I kinda liked it.

"He once saved an entire Spanish military infantry unit," Joanna continued. "Juan single-handedly fended off more than two hundred vampire dogs with only the jawbone of a dead mule. He then gave one of his more impassioned speeches at the foothills of the Pyrenees, rallying the soldiers to help him drive the rest of the marauding Dips out of the country."

Violet was shaking her head. "Wait. So he can actually *speak?*"

Joanna made an amused face. "¿Cómo no? To say basajauns are extremely intelligent would be like saying the sun is hot; you simply have to get used to their thick gallego accents."

"Hold up," I said. "You're telling me that Bigfoot's big brother is coming with us and you were worried about *my claw* attracting attention . . . ?"

"Basajauns are quite skilled at remaining inconspicuous," the queen said. "None more so than those of the tribes of Gibraltar from whence Juan hails. How do you think they've gone so long without being properly photographed?"

She had a point there. "Gotcha."

Another rumble—this one much stronger—shook the room. The fancy long-stemmed candles set along the walls in silver holders flickered. In another room, something fell to the ground and shattered.

Violet's wide eyes found the queen's. "What's going on? Why does this keep happening?"

"It's the chasm," she replied. "We believe it may be disintegrating."

"*The chasm?*"

"The invisible wall that separates the Land of the Living from that of the dead. Many believe that La Mano Peluda has found a way to erode it, that they've been working at it for eons. We are now beginning to feel its effects in this world."

"What happens if the chasm is destroyed?" I asked hesitantly, not sure I really wanted to hear the answer.

"The pasillos between the two worlds would become unnecessary—our enemy could unleash a large-scale invasion anywhere on the planet, donde quieran."

Yep, didn't want to hear that. I thought about all the people who could be hurt—or *worse*—if an invasion of things like La Sihuanaba came pouring in from another dimension and felt my chest go numb as the leg the nahual had tongue-strangled.

"So, how are you going to stop that from happening?" Violet asked.

"We can't," Joanna replied matter-of-factly.

"*You can't?* What do you mean, *you can't?*"

"I mean, it is impossible. If the chasm is truly disintegrating, there is no power on earth that can repair it. Our only concern now must be in stopping La Mano Peluda."

I shook my head. "And how are you going to do that?"

"Not *I*, mi niño, but *you*. See, La Mano Peluda's army grows because of fear—the fear that they will soon rule both worlds and that all who oppose them will be forced to pay with their very souls. If you are indeed the Morphling, then you are living proof that the ancient scriptures are true, that there truly is one who can stand against them. The light of your coming will slow their recruiting and cause all of those who have joined their number out of fear to fall away. It will also cause many of our allies who have cowered in fear to once again take up arms.

"Sadly, mi niño, the fate of the living has been reduced to a mathematical proposition. If we can reduce the number of La Mano Peluda's forces, we may yet stand the slimmest of chances. If we cannot, or they manage to convert La Sociedad de las Calacas—which would give them control over virtually every pasillo between the worlds, control that they do not yet possess—*or* if the chasm does indeed collapse, then their armies will sweep over the face of this world like a dark, unquenchable fire."

Violet said, "So your plan is basically to . . . ?"

"Find the Morphling. Then do everything in our power to keep him or her alive."

"I'm no math whiz or anything," I said, "but that mathematical proposition thingy you just laid out? It doesn't really sound like it's in our favor. . . ."

"That's because it's not," the witch queen replied simply.

I rubbed the center of my forehead. My brain had started to spin. There was so much to process. So many questions. So much *pressure* . . . "Do you really think I could be the Morphling?" I asked finally. "Like, *for real?*"

La bruja's expression did not change. "That is what I intend to find out."

"So, where's this oracle?" Violet asked. "Is she nearby?"

"Actually, it's a *he*—and he's quite a ways from here. But fortunately, there's brinco."

I frowned, confused. "*Jump?* What is that?"

"A form of metaphysical travel. Hopefully neither of you has inner-ear issues." Joanna turned to the huge desk in the middle of the room, brought a small silver dish from one of the drawers, and held it out to us. On it, fat slimy maggots wriggled and writhed. "Take. Eat."

Eat? She had to be messing with us. "What the heck are those things?" I blurted out, feeling my stomach churn.

"Tequila worms. But don't worry. They haven't been soaked in alcohol. Y están bien frescas."

Actually, their alcohol content and freshness was *the least* of my worries. "You don't really expect us to put those things in our mouths, do you? I mean, they're *alive!*"

The Witch Queen of Toledo wagged a long, jeweled finger at me. Her many rings glittered brightly in the candlelight. "Not just put them in your mouth, but eat them. And eat them *quickly.*" She dropped one into each of our palms. The nasty little things were cold as ice cubes and coated with a slimy film of mucus. Just the *thought* of chewing one up made me wanna blow chunks. "As I mentioned earlier, we haven't much time."

Violet didn't hesitate. She tossed the ugly little sucker back like it was a gummy bear. The girl obviously didn't have a gag reflex—like, *none.* That, or she might've been related to Andrew Zimmern. "Go ahead, Charlie," she said in between crunchy (and gag-inducing) chews. "They're actually not bad. . . . A little sweet, but not bad."

Can't believe I'm doing this, I thought, forcing my mouth to open. Then, before I could think better of it, I pinched my nose, tossed the slimy, squirming, disgustingly *alive* invertebrate down the old hatch—and, of course, instantly regretted it.

The flavor was like old shoe leather. Or spoiled nuts. And the texture was somehow even worse; it was basically like chewing wet sand.

I glared at Violet. "Not bad, huh . . . ?"

She giggled. "I thought you liked sweet."

"It *isn't* sweet," I grumbled, which made her giggle even more. "You're so gonna pay for this. . . ."

"Bueno, now, gather around, children," Joanna said, motioning us closer. "And close your eyes so you don't get nauseous."

Yeah, a little late for that.

Then the Witch Queen of Toledo spoke a single word: "¡Vámonos!" And the ground seemed to slip out from beneath my feet.

CHAPTER TWENTY-EIGHT

I'm not sure what I expected brinco to be like, but it was probably the weirdest thing I'd ever experienced. In my entire life. And *that* was saying something. It felt as though we were flying . . . and at the same time *falling* somehow. Being stretched and simultaneously compacted. Pulled apart and squeezed. A gust of icy wind (I'm talking *arctic* cold) blew across my face, swirling my hair into a spiky mess as the world around us—or what I *sensed* as the world around us—began to wobble and bounce like a drunken top. My ears popped with the sudden change in pressure. My insides squirmed. I could feel that nasty little tequila worm trying to crawl its way back up my throat, and I had to swallow hard just to keep it down. Dark shapes and bursts of flickering green light began to whip across my closed eyelids, and then everything seemed to blur into a single dizzying stream of motion, and it felt like we were picking up *even more* speed, though I still couldn't tell if we were traveling up or down, much less forward or backward. Instinctively, I wrapped my arms around Violet as she wrapped hers around me, and then, just when I was about to yell at Joanna to make it stop (*for the love of God, para ya!*)—

Everything went still. Completely, absolutely, *perfectly* still.

When I opened my eyes again, we were standing in the middle of a large cobblestone square surrounded by low, red-roofed buildings. Narrow streets ran off in all directions. To our left was a manicured garden. To our right, maybe fifty yards away, a massive cathedral rose out of the gray stones. With its old-school baroque facade and pointy steeples, it looked like something straight out of the Middle Ages.

"Where are we?" I asked, rubbing my eyes. Something about it all was vaguely familiar—the narrow streets, the gray cobblestones, the old-world architecture—but for several seconds I couldn't put it together.; my head was still spinning a little.

Then it clicked.

"We're in the Santiago de Compostela Cathedral square . . . ," I said, turning to gape at the queen. "We're *in* Spain! In *Galicia*—la tierra de meigas!" *The land of witches!*

Honestly, I expected her to have some pretty cool powers (you know, being a witch queen and all), but teleporting us across four thousand miles of open ocean in the blink of an eye? Now, *that* was seriously impressive.

"Muy bien," Queen Joanna said, and grinned at me. She sounded impressed. "You're certainly a very cultured boy. . . ."

As I looked around, my mouth dropped open in amazement. So many of my abuela's stories had taken place *right here*—right in these very streets! Huge battles between warring basajaun tribes, a bloody showdown between a pack of Dips and a lobisomem (that's a werewolf) who had become a priest—even an epic family throwdown between two insanely powerful sister witches that almost ended the world as we know it. According to an old legend, the Santiago de Compostela Cathedral had been built as a sort of outpost in the eleventh century, a forward operating base to support Spanish troops as they battled the clans of one-eyed giants called tartalos that were threatening to overrun Spain. Over the years I must've pictured myself running around this place, like, *a zillion* times. Fighting monsters. Brujas. But to actually *be* here? Smack-dab in the middle of all this history and myth? *That* was truly mind-blowing.

"Perhaps one day I'll give both of you a tour," Joanna said. "But today we must move quickly. El Tucano-yúa rules these skies. Plus, my sister can be anywhere."

I frowned at her. "Your sister?"

"The black sheep of the family, you could say. In any event, it is not safe here."

As if to make her point, darkness began to spread over the square like a heavy blanket. The wind suddenly picked up, and the temperature dropped almost ten degrees in the span of a few seconds. A heartbeat later, dozens of winged creatures appeared out of nowhere, hovering over the rooftops. They were small, maybe three feet tall, with bony arms and even bonier legs. They wore simple tunics made of dried leaves, animal skins, and scraps of tattered cloth. Their eyes were too big for their faces. Their heads were too big for their bodies. They sort of looked like shriveled old men. Only I knew what they really were and just how dangerous they could be.

"Acalicas," the queen whispered, her expression darkening. "And of the Haunted Valley, no less."

"I've never heard of that kind," I admitted.

"That's because few have ever seen one and even fewer have lived to tell the tale."

Well, that was nice to know.

"Charlie, what are those things?" Violet asked, spinning to look at me.

"Weather fairies," I explained. "Mean little suckers too."

Beside me, Juan began to growl low in his throat. He pinned his large humanish ears back against the sides of his massive skull and bared his teeth in a terrifying snarl. Dude was obviously getting ready to rumble.

"Oye, hey, there's no reason to get all worked up . . . ," said a deep, melodic voice. Then a figure in a ridiculously oversize hat melted out of the shadows near the steps of the cathedral, and the breath caught in my throat. It was El Sombrerón! His silver guitarra glinted in a strip of pale moonlight, and the black metal spurs on his black leather boots clinked with his every step.

"That's the guy I saw at my house!" I whispered to Violet. "That's *him*!"

"I just wanna have a little chat with el niño," said the legendary sombrero-wearing goblin, casually strumming his guitarra. "Le's not make a big deal about it, okay?" His dark eyes peered out at me from beneath the impossibly broad rim of his black hat. "Oye, muchacho, why don't you start walking, eh? I don't got all day, you know. . . ."

"Sorry, señor," the queen replied, stepping in front of me. "But el niño is busy at the moment. Perhaps some other time."

"Oye, no, I don't think so, lady. . . . Me and the kid gonna talk. And right now!" His nimble fingers danced across the strings of his guitar, and the sound they produced was utterly mesmerizing—a slow melody filled with sadness and longing.

I had time to think, *Dang, this guy can play!* And then the army of acalicas rose higher into the air, as if responding to the music, their leather wings blurring in the growing darkness as they began to chitter among themselves.

Suddenly the wind began to blow harder. Thunder rumbled. Above us, angry-looking clouds gathered and churned (they looked like a fleet of huge black warships gathering for battle), but the rest of the sky in every direction was completely clear. I didn't need to be a meteorologist to know something was *very* wrong with this picture.

Joanna pointed to our left. "Go that way," she said as leaves and bits of trash began to swirl above the cobblestones. "Use the side streets. Find another way into the cathedral. Go. ¡Dale!"

Violet and I nodded, then took off running with Juan leading the way, his mass of yellowish fur rippling like a golden waterfall. Around us, the wind whipped and howled, and huge bolts of lightning exploded overhead, sizzling through the sky. The clouds broke. Rain began to pour down, fat, slow drops at first, then getting fatter and faster until they pounded down from the sky like millions of angry little liquid fists. My shirt instantly stuck to my skin. My sneakers squished like soaked sponges. Muddy puddles had formed everywhere, and the cobbles, worn smooth by centuries of foot traffic, had become dangerously slick. My feet kept slipping and sliding all over the place, and I nearly ate it, like, five different times. Once, Juan grabbed my arm just before I cracked my head on the edge of one of the benches scattered everywhere. I would've thanked him, but there wasn't any time.

"*DEETH WAY!*" the basajaun roared.

We dashed into the narrow side street lined with shops. Tables and chairs crowded us on both sides. Dim display windows blurred by. Above us, along the pointy ledges of the roofs, I caught glimpses of dark shapes flitting in and out of view. I hoped it was just a bunch of curious pigeons, but then lightning flashed, turning the world white, and my worst fear was confirmed—acalicas. Dozens of them. Racing along the rooftops, spinning and whirling and twirling in some sort of festive-looking rain dance. Their bright pale eyes stared down at us; mischievous smirks twisted their tiny lipless mouths.

"¡Ahí!" I shouted, pointing wildly. "Up there! A bunch of them on the roof!"

Juan heard me loud and clear. He dug a pickax out of his bushy beard and flung it at the edge of the roof like a Frisbee. It exploded through the concrete like a bomb, sending a handful of weather fairies flying. Their itty-bitty bodies spun end over end as they hurtled, screaming and flailing, into the swirling sky.

Abruptly, the rain slowed to a drizzle. The wind stopped. Even the sky seemed to lighten a bit.

"Nice shot!" Violet yelled. "That'll show them!"

Only it didn't. The storm picked back up just as suddenly as it had died down and with even more ferocity this time. An icy gust of wind howled down from the sky and tore through the alleyway, tugging viciously at our clothes, pulling at our hair, and making my eyes water. Violet's gown billowed out behind her like a sail. Debris began pelting us from every direction, and anything that weighed less than a couple of pounds went flying.

As we neared the end of the street, the wind picked up even more, blowing hard enough to rattle the windows of the little shops. Banners began to rip. Signboards advertising yesterday's specials were caught up in swirling drafts. A huge wooden table rolled past me as if guided by an invisible hand and crashed through a café's front window, spraying glass everywhere. And even though Juan shielded us with his massive body as we dashed past, I still felt a blast of shards against my legs and sneakers.

"*FASTHUR!*" he roared, urging us on.

Up ahead, the narrow cobblestone path veered right, and we followed it, our feet scrabbling for traction on the wet stone. My heart was a runaway train in my chest. My throat burned. My sides ached. I wasn't sure how much longer I could keep going like this—my lungs felt like they were on the verge of bursting—but I didn't stop.

We came out in a wide backstreet, flanked by old brick buildings. The one to our left had small balconies with wrought-iron rails; a couple of the rails had been partially ripped out of the walls and now dangled at the mercy of the raging winds. One suddenly came free as I ran underneath it, torn off the wall by a sudden gust.

I didn't have time to avoid it. The railing would've split me in two if the basajaun hadn't swatted it away with the back of one enormous fist. There was a squeal of metal as the railing met Juan's knuckles and then a deafening clatter as it crashed to the ground somewhere behind us. Juan, meanwhile, didn't even flinch. Guy was unbelievable!

"Those things are everywhere!" Violet shouted, looking up at the buildings, her eyes huge and full of panic. "What are we gonna do?"

"Just keep running!" I shouted as we pounded down a short set of concrete steps. "We're almost there!"

Thunder crashed and forks of blue lightning crackled across the sky. I could feel the buzzing tingle of electricity as it skipped over my skin like a thousand tiny tentacles. The rain turned to hail. The pebble-size hunks of ice stung our arms and ricocheted off the sides of the buildings, sending bits of icy shrapnel whizzing by our faces. They slashed at us as we dashed between a couple of newer buildings and spilled out into another plaza, this one larger and wider than the last.

Ahead of us, in its center, stood an elaborate stone statue: four horses with webbed feet supporting a coffin (I think it was supposed to be the coffin of Saint James) on top of which sat an angel with a bright star in its upraised hand. Hailstones pounded the statue mercilessly, but water still spewed from the horses' stony mouths, the streams whipping this way and that in the gusty wind. And just beyond it, flanked on one side by the iconic Torre del Reloj (or clocktower), loomed the cathedral.

Almost there, I told myself. Casi casi.

"Quickly now!" shouted a familiar voice, and I glanced back to see Queen Joanna charging up the path behind us, her long tiered gown fluttering out behind her like wings. Her hands and feet were moving so fast they blurred, and she caught up with us almost immediately. "Eyes straight ahead, children!" she ordered. "No looking back!"

But, of course, when someone tells you not to look back . . . well, you can't really help it. My gaze drifted past her, toward the narrow tile-lined alley, and what I saw froze my blood: Swelling up behind us like a massive foaming tidal wave of blackness was an army of acalicas. There must've been thousands of them—no, tens of thousands of those skinny, bald-headed faeries with their pale eyes, toothless grins, and bony skeletal wings that looked like they belonged in some sort of fossil exhibit. The sound of their wings beat in my ears like thunder.

And as if that weren't bad enough, El Sombrerón suddenly emerged from the shadows to our left. "Oye, hey, I jus' wanna talk, okay?" he said, gently strumming his guitarra.

For some reason, his freakishly calm demeanor made my pulse kick up another notch, and I swung my head around, running even harder now.

"Do not stop!" Joanna instructed us. "No matter what you see, do not stop until we are through the cathedral doors!"

"OYE, LADY, YOU THINK I'M MESSIN' AROUND HERE?" El Sombrerón yelled. "OKAY, THEN—LE'S PLAY!"

No sooner had he spoken those words than jagged bolts of angry red lightning began spitting down from the sky like artillery fire, hammering into the ground and throwing up huge chunks of scorched stone. Some struck so close I could feel my hair crackle with static. One sizzled into the cobbles directly in our path, leaving my ears buzzing and my eyes burning with the afterimage. It happened so fast I didn't even have time to scream (honestly, I didn't even have time to *flinch*), but I knew it was only a matter of seconds before one of us got deep-fried to a tender crisp.

With a wild cry, Queen Joanna threw up a hand. Her fingers spread wide and shafts of blinding light shot from between them, forming a bubble of blue energy above us that sparked and flared as it deflected lightning bolt after lightning bolt. Thunder boomed everywhere. The plaza rumbled with its incredible power.

I ran on blindly. Violet was right on my hip, her hair whipping across my face, her breath rasping in and out, in and out. The queen, meanwhile, was still leading the way, with Juan only a stride or two behind. We were so close now I could see the intricate carvings above the two doors that faced the Platería Square and on the great pillars that both flanked and separated them. In the fiery flickering light of the death bolts, the designs were breathtaking. Not that I had much breath left in me, though.

"Into the cathedral, niños!" Joanna cried. She flicked her wrist, and the massive iron doors flew open as if punched by an invisible giant fist.

The instant we stepped inside, the basajaun slammed the doors shut behind us with a reverberating *boom!* almost as loud as the thunder itself. Then he looped a rusty iron chain around the giant doorknobs, sealing us in. My ears rang in the sudden silence.

"That's it?" Violet rasped, hands on her knees, chest heaving. "I mean, you don't expect that to keep them out, do you?"

But Joanna had already disappeared into the shadows of the sanctuary. "The cathedral is warded," she called back. "It'll buy us some time, though perhaps not enough. Vamos!"

Santiago de Compostela Cathedral was arguably my grandmother's favorite place in the whole wide world. I could remember her describing it to me in painstaking detail even back when I was still in diapers. She'd go on and on about the soaring vaulted ceilings, the Gothic cloisters, the Pórtico de la Gloria—and especially the high altar with its gold-leaf canopy that covered the crypt and the massive Solomonic columns twined with grape leaves.

Ever since I was little, I'd always dreamed of coming here myself one day. I'd imagined walking down the narrow aisles and taking in all the amazing artistry, the history. You know, just sort of hanging out. But today was *definitely* not that day.

Joanna led us through the cathedral at a breakneck pace, flying around corners and under archways, pounding down long hallways and zigzagging her way through forests of stone columns. Honestly, I had no idea how she could tell where she was going. It was so dark in here I couldn't see so much as a sliver of light. Twice I almost ran headfirst into Juan's hairy, rock-hard butt cheeks, and once I actually did, smacking my head on a gluteus maximus so dense and muscular it might as well been a hunk of rock. Finally, we came to a tiny room somewhere toward the back of the cathedral, with cobwebs dangling from the ceiling and not a single piece of furniture anywhere on the lumpy stone floors. There was only a basement door, which was crisscrossed with chains and padlocked.

I thought Juan would have to go all beast-mode to bust through, but then Joanna raised a hand, and suddenly the chains came to life, grinding and clinking until they undid themselves and the padlock snapped off. Juan quickly took hold of a slim metal handle and lifted the door, which groaned like a giant waking from a two-hundred-year nap, then motioned for us to follow. Inside, a narrow stone staircase led down many flights of steps. The walls were made of porous rock, and it was pitch-dark, but I thought I could hear water bubbling close by. The whole place felt ancient and undisturbed.

When we reached the bottom, we found ourselves in a square-shaped room with low earthen ceilings and a large, square-shaped pool in the middle. The pool itself couldn't have been more than three feet deep, but the water was such a deep azure color that it looked almost black. And it shimmered . . . as if it had been sprinkled with millions of tiny diamonds. Rippling patterns danced across the walls, making the room feel like it was in constant motion. The pool was the only light down here, but it was more than enough.

"Welcome to the Basin of Youth," Joanna said proudly.

"The *what?*" I was pretty sure I hadn't heard that right.

"The Basin of Youth," she repeated. "It was built in the early fifteen hundreds by the famed explorer who discovered the legendary fountain in St. Augustine, Florida. He wanted a place where he could bathe in the life-giving waters whenever he returned to Spain." She knelt at the edge of the pool, skimming her hand along its glassy surface. "As I heard it, more than ten thousand gallons were loaded into huge wooden crates and shipped back across the Atlantic on el *San Cristóbal* to fill this very pool."

"That's *nuts*," Violet murmured. Her gaze was fixed on the pool, her eyes impossibly blue in the glittery play of lights.

"Actually, it proved to be a most wise decision. Within a few years of its discovery, the limestone walls that encased the Fountain of Youth began to crack, and other sources of water from various subterranean tributaries mingled with the fountain's water, contaminating it. These waters, how-ever, remain pure to this day."

Wow. Now, *that* was some interesting history. Maybe if stories like that actually found their way into textbooks, my third period wouldn't be such a snoozefest.

"But where's the oracle?" I asked, squinting into the semi-darkness. There didn't seem to be anyone in here but us.

Joanna's lips broke into a cunning smile. "Come and see. . . ."

I wasn't sure where this was going, but I knelt beside her anyway. As I peered over the edge, I saw my reflection staring back at me, my face rippling in the glassy blue water. This close, the pool looked way deeper, maybe as many as twenty feet deep. I half expected to see a school of small fish swim by.

"Okay, so where is he?"

The witch queen's eyes shone in the pool. They gleamed like the square-cut emeralds in her crown. "First you must go for a swim."

A swim? Was she crazy? The water was probably, like, fifty degrees—if that. And I didn't see a wet suit lying around anywhere. But just as I opened my mouth to tell that I wasn't a big fan of hypothermia—or going swim-ming in jeans, for that matter—I felt one of her hands clamp painfully around the back of my neck. I barely had time to register what was happening before she thrust my head down, dunking me face-first into the pool.

Instantly, a surge of icy water rushed up my nose, stinging my eyes. Bubbles swirled around me. For half a second, I was too stunned to do anything but just sort of float there, my head and shoulders bobbing in the freezing water.

Then I realized that the witch had lost her mind, that she was trying to drown me, and my brain kicked into survival mode: I flailed and thrashed, slapping at her hands, prying at her fingers, trying desperately to make her let go—but nothing worked. The witch was viciously strong and viciously determined to hold me under. Her grip tightened. She forced my head down deeper. More water shot up my nose and down the back of my throat. My lungs filled with liquid. I started to choke.

Somewhere behind me—it sounded like a heck of a ways away—I could hear Violet screaming at the top of her lungs. Screaming, *You're going to kill him!* Joanna, however, didn't seem to care; she wouldn't let me come up for air.

My panic turned to terror as black spots began to dance before my vision. The pressure on my chest was agonizing; I couldn't hold my breath any longer. I had to breathe!

Just when I thought I was about to pass out, something strange happened: The world around me began to rumble, and suddenly the floor of the pool fell away in a swirl of white tile and black stone. A circular chasm opened before my eyes—a spinning, twisting vortex of blackness and water. I felt myself being pulled toward it. Felt Joanna's hands let go. And then I was sucked headfirst into the darkness.

Lightning flashed around me. Thunder rolled. Powerful currents tore at my body, slapping at me with their icy fingers. Desperate, I tried to suck in a breath . . . and was surprised to find that I could. My lungs instantly filled with air, with fresh oxygen, and I can't even begin to describe how great that felt.

The world began to harmonize around me—sights, sounds, and smells all melting back together. I realized I wasn't falling anymore. No, I was actually *standing*. On solid ground. On my own two feet.

What the—?

I looked around and saw with a jolt of surprise that I was standing in the middle of a lush tropical jungle. Tall trees rose around me, their trunks fuzzy with moss, their branches draped with vines. A woodcreeper chirped nearby. Dozens of blue-and-green butterflies flitted through the bushes. I heard whooping and gibbering above me and glanced up to see a large gray monkey clinging to the underside of a branch, watching me with its little silver-ringed eyes.

Coolest. Thing. Ever. My dad would have *loved* it here.

I smiled, inhaling deeply for the first time. The air was damp and hot, but ridiculously pure; I couldn't have been within thirty miles of a city.

This wasn't just jungle. . . . This was *deep* jungle.

But how the heck had I gotten here?

"¡¿Oye, quién va ahí?!" shouted a voice. Spanish. Male. "Announce yourself at once, or meet your fate at the point of mi espada!"

I whirled toward the sound of the voice. Behind me stood a man about my height, with tightly cropped reddish hair and an impeccably styled mustache/goatee combo. He had lean, aristocratic features. Sharp brown eyes. He wore a snug-fitting, waist-length jacket (I think it was called a doublet), loose-fitting hose, and tall black boots. An old-fashioned pistola hung loosely from his belt, and his long, curved sword flashed brilliantly in the fierce tropical sun as he lifted it, grazing the side of my Adam's apple.

Dude looked like a fancy pirate. A *dangerous* fancy pirate.

"¡Habla!" he commanded. "Speak!"

I was still a little dazed, but I managed to pick my name out of my brain. "I'm Charlie. Charlie Hernández."

"Hmm . . . *Charlie.*"

He stretched out my name, so it sounded like "Chh-haaaarrrlieee."

"Should I know you?" he asked, making a funny face.

"I—I don't think so. . . ."

Slowly, my gaze drifted past him to a small lake, where a trio of miniature wooden ships floated and bobbed on the turquoise water. They looked like old sailing ships from the 1500s, equipped with everything from solid wood masts to huge white sails with red crosses on them. Whoever built them had obviously taken the time to get every last detail perfect. "Did you make all those yourself?" I asked, pointing past him.

"Ay, sí, sí, of course!" A big grin split his deeply tanned face, and the pressure suddenly lifted off my throat as he lowered the sword. "They're my pride and joy. The exact replicas of la *Santa María*, el *Santiago*, y el *San Cristóbal*. ¿Te gustan?"

Those names definitely rang a bell. "Yeah, they're awesome. . . ."

He stuck out a hand. "Ponce. Nice to meet you!"

"Wait. *Ponce?* Like, of the de León fame?"

"Correcta-mundo, muchacho."

"Oh snap! I actually go to your middle school!" I said. And when he only stared, I quickly added, "Well, not *your* school, of course . . . but, uh, the one they named after you. It's a middle school. Ponce de Leon Middle. It's in Coral

Gables. That's in *Miami*. Miami, Florida . . . Oh, and they named a street after you too. Also in Miami."

Ponce was giving me a funny look.

"What?" I asked.

"Ay, nada. I'm jus' thinking. . . . So I leave my beautiful home in España, traverse a treacherous and violent sea, overcome starvation, a general lack of supplies, establish the first European settlement in Puerto Rico, and then, as if *all that* isn't impressive enough, I discover *Florida*, and *still* all you people could think to do in my honor was to name a middle school and *a street* . . . ?"

Was I *actually* being scolded by a five-hundred-year-old explorer? "Well, it's a pretty nice school, though . . . and a nice street. As far as streets go, anyway."

"I'll have to take your word for it, I suppose." He rubbed his chin with one hairy-knuckled hand, then started mumbling to himself. "A middle school and *a street*. No lo creo . . . no lo creo para nada."

This was obviously a touchy subject for him. But I didn't have time to try to help him through it. I had *my own problems* at the moment. "Uh, by the way, I have an itty-bitty question—where *the heck* am I . . . ? And what are *you* doing here?"

"What am *I* doing here? This is *my* island. I'm el gobernador. The question is, what are *you* doing here?"

"I . . . uh, I'm looking for the oracle."

"Well, in that case, I have some good news for you, muchacho—you have found him!"

My eyes bugged. "*You're* the oracle?"

"Don't sound so surprised. I was an explorer, a sailor, a governor—I named Florida, for the love of the sea! You don't think I can handle being a part-time *diviner?*"

"But . . . wasn't the only reason you ended up in Florida because you got lost looking for Bimini?"

He frowned. "What's your point?"

"No, nothing. I just didn't think *an oracle* would make such a silly mistake. . . ."

"Ay, sí, so silly. I'd like to see *you* try to survive thirty long days out at sea with nothing but a map, a compass, and your steely Spanish intuition to guide you. Oh, and a little información for you, amigo: I was looking for *the Fountain of Youth*—*not* Bimini—and I *found* it. All my other missions were simply covers for my life's one great obsession."

Interesting. "So, the fountain actually gave you eternal life, huh?"

"Sí, but not exactly how I imagined it would."

A flock of blackbirds flew overhead, chirping loudly. I looked up. The sky was crazy bright and cloudless. "Where are we?" I asked.

"Puerto Rico. Well, *spirit* Puerto Rico, to be more precise . . . The most *beautiful* place in all the Land of the Dead!"

His words took a few seconds to sink in. But when they finally did, my heart slammed against my ribs so hard, I wouldn't have been surprised if it had actually burst out of my chest and gone running off into the trees. "*¿La Tierra de los MUERTOS?*" I shrieked.

"Sí. And to think Columbus's snot-nosed brat of a son—Señor Diego Colón—muscled me out of the governorship all those years ago. Ah, but now we're both dead, and only *one of us* is governor of la Isla de Encantamiento. Would you like to guess who?"

"Espérate," I said. "Hold up. So I'm *currently in* the Land of the Dead . . . ?"

"Sí, señor, you most certainly are."

"Are *you* dead?"

"Sí, señor, I most certainly am."

"Am *I?*"

"No, señor, you most certainly are not." He glanced down at his Spanish longsword, which glinted brilliantly in his hand. "Would you like to be?"

"Most certainly not. But wait—doesn't La Mano Peluda control the Land of the Dead?"

"Much of it, sí. All around my island, beyond the great

seas, evil plots and schemes and the fires of war are constantly stoked. But not here . . ."

I looked around. It was hard to imagine evil being anywhere *near* a place like this. "Looks like we're in paradise. . . ."

"If you look hard enough, muchacho, you can find paradise even in the darkest places."

"Wait up. You just told me that the Fountain of Youth gave you eternal life."

"And?"

"And you're *dead.*"

"Ay, sí, gracias for pointing that out, *Capitán Obvious.* However, if my troops had not been ambushed by the Calusa Indians near Punta Gorda and I myself not been shot in the thigh with a poisoned arrow, I would never have died of natural causes—hence, *eternal life. . . .*" He got a faraway look in his eyes. "In fact, I'd still be sailing my beautiful *Maria* around the Caribbean even to this day. . . ."

I felt my hand ball into a fist at my side. I couldn't believe this, couldn't believe Joanna hadn't told me *up front* I'd have to travel to the *Land of the Dead* to meet the oracle. How shady was that? Whatever. I didn't have time to think about that right now. I just had to find a way out of here. But first . . .

"The queen wanted you to check me out," I told Ponce. "To see if I might be El Cambiador . . . the Morphling."

"*The Morphling?*" Ponce's gaze narrowed; he looked completely caught off guard. "What do you know about the *Morphling* . . . ?"

"Just what's in the stories," I admitted. "How the hero manifests animal traits and uses them and the witch's own vanity to defeat her and save the village."

Those were actually some of my favorite stories, though like most myths, the details usually changed depending on where you heard it. A fisherman in Andalucía would tell you that the Morphling defeated the witch by manifesting fins and gills and then challenging her to a race through the Mediterranean, where she drowned in her own tempest. A farmer in the Sonoran Desert in Mexico would say the Morphling beat her by manifesting an armadillo's shell and challenging her to a contest to see who could withstand the fierce heat of the desert sun the longest. There were even a few versions of the myth where the witch kills the Morphling—actually cuts out its heart and eats it, becoming even more powerful. Those had always freaked me out when I was little.

"¡Ah, muy bien!" The world-famous explorer smiled proudly at me. "But did you also know that all Cambiadors have a chullachaqui in their family tree?"

I shook my head. I mean, I knew what chullachaquis were (they were these cool forest-dwelling dwarf dudes with the ability to transform into pretty much any animal—they could take the form of humans, too; some myths even considered them the protectors of the rain forest), but I had no idea that they had anything to do with Morphlings.

"Sí, they are related, you might say. But because Morphlings do not completely morph into an animal, they can manifest multiple animal traits *simultaneously*, making them much more powerful than any shape-shifter."

"Makes sense."

Ponce just stared at me for a moment. "Well, do you?"

"Do I what? Have a chullachaqui in my family tree?" When he nodded, I gave a little shrug. "I—I don't think so. . . ."

"Let me ask you something. How did you even come to hear the tale of the Morphling?"

"Isn't it, like, super famous?"

Ponce's dark eyes narrowed. "Actually, it's one of the most closely guarded secrets in either of the worlds."

I frowned. How could that be? My abuela had basically told me the complete *opposite*.

"Pregunta, who told you this tale?"

"My grandma. She taught me all sorts of myths."

"Interesante . . ." He paused, staring off into the leafy tangles of trees like he was pondering something complicated. A tricky crossword puzzle maybe. After a moment he said, "Who sent you to me again?"

"Queen Joanna."

A deep frown creased his face. "The Witch Queen of Toledo still lives, eh? I've never trusted esa bruja. . . ."

I can understand why, I thought.

Ponce sighed. "Anyway, let me have a look at you." He motioned for me to move closer, and when I did, his stubby little fingers immediately went to work, picking through my hair, feeling behind my ears, even flicking me on the tip of the nose. Not once, but *three times.*

I looked at him, annoyed. "Was that necessary?"

"Nope. Just thought you had a boogie." He pawed through my hair one last time, and something flashed in his eyes—surprise maybe?—but it was gone so fast that I thought I must've imagined it. Finally, he stepped back, shaking his head. "Bueno. I'm sorry, mi hijo. . . . You are not the Morphling."

"I'm not?" The disappointment in my voice surprised me. I guess I hadn't realized just how badly I'd been hoping to be the Morphling. To have an answer (as crazy an answer as that would have been) to what was happening to me.

"Unfortunately, no."

I shrugged, staring down at my wrapped-up claw. I could almost see the bright red color of the shell through the gauze. "So what am I, then?"

"Un equivocado," Ponce replied quickly.

"*¿Un equivocado?* What are you talking about?" I knew the meaning of the word—in Spanish, it meant "wrong" or "mistaken"—but I'd never heard it used like that.

"Don't worry about it, muchacho. Just make sure to let Joanna know so she'll leave you alone, ¿está bien?"

"So that's it, then? Just one quick look and you can tell for sure?"

He put a slim brown hand on my shoulder. "Muchacho, when you've seen as much as I have, one look is usually all it takes." Then he glanced up at the sky and shouted, "Not the Morphling. So sorry, señorita!"

Following his gaze, I squinted against the blinding glare of the sun. "Who are you talking to . . . ?"

"Never mind that. Oye, looks like you might've dropped this. . . ." Ponce squatted in the grass, pointing at something.

"Huh?"

"In the mud," he said. "You gonna pick it up, or what?"

"Pick *what* up . . . ?" I bent down to see what he was talking about. And just as I did, Ponce suddenly hooked an arm around my neck, pulling me in close.

His breath was hot on my face as he whispered, "See, my uñas?" He showed me his nails—they were longish, sort of clipped square at the ends, and crusted with fresh mud.

"They look pretty dangerous, no? I've used them to whittle spears out of wood, to slay a three-hundred-pound boar on the beautiful western shores of South Florida. Which, let me tell you, was no walk in the park. But you should know that there are *far more* dangerous uñas on your side of the world—and *one* in particular. If I were you, I'd go home—home sweet home, as you kids might say—and do everything in my power to get rid of it . . . might even save your life."

Get rid of a *fingernail?* What in the world was this nutjob blabbering about?

Before I could ask, Ponce jumped to his feet, wiping his dirt-smudged hands on the stuff wrapped around my claw. "And if I were you, I wouldn't ask any more questions," he said, aiming a warning finger at me. "Spend another minute on this side and you just might find yourself trapped here . . . *por toda la eternidad.*"

"TRAPPED HERE FOR ETERNITY?" I shrieked. "Well, how do I get back?"

"The witch didn't tell you?" When I shook my head, he gave me an apologetic look. "You're not going to like this part, amigo. . . ."

Then he drew his pistola and thumbed back the hammer.

"Wait. You're not going to *shoot* me, are you?"

He shrugged. "It's the fastest way back."

Oh, c'mon! "Wait!" I shouted. "What's the slow way? I wanna do the slow way!"

But apparently the world-famous explorer, governor, sailor—*whatever*—didn't; he simply took aim at the center of my chest and pulled the trigger.

CHAPTER TWENTY-NINE

BAAANNNGGG! That was the last thing I heard.
And then—

I jerked back, breaking the surface of the water with a gasp, and landed hard on my butt. Shapes and shadows crowded in around me. I squinted, trying to focus. Slowly, the shapes resolved themselves into faces, familiar ones—Violet, Queen Joanna, and the basajaun named Juan. They were standing over me, Violet on my right, Queen Joanna and Juan on my left. Their faces were tight, their eyes big and full of concern as they silently watched me push to my feet, dripping water.

"My apologies," Joanna said. "It was the only way to get you across—one must be scared half to death."

Violet looked terrified; her lower lip quivered as she wrapped her fingers tightly around my upper arm. "Charlie, are you okay?"

I nodded, blinking water out of my eyes. "Yeah, I'm fine."

"We saw and heard everything," the witch queen said.

"In the pool," Violet explained, pointing. "Like it was a movie or something."

"All right, so then what's that thing he called me?" I asked Joanna. "An *equivo*—"

There was a great crashing sound above us. The entire underground cavern shuddered and shook. Loosely packed earth rained down from the ceiling.

The witch's eyes flicked to the basajaun. "They've pierced the veil."

"Then give us some more of those worms and brinco us out of here!" Violet said.

The queen frowned. "I'm sorry, but I don't have any more on me. . . ."

"*What?* So, we're *stuck* here?"

"*Stuck?*" Joanna echoed. "Of course not. Close your eyes." The moment we did, the world seemed to wobble around us, and the next thing I knew, we were back in the Provincia, a galaxy of stars floating overhead so close it looked like I could reach out and pluck one out of the sky.

"Better this time, no?" the queen asked. "You get more and more used to it."

"Wait, so we don't actually have to *eat* anything to do the brinco thing?" I said, glaring up at her.

"Of course not," she replied with a curious expression. "What in the lands do *tequila worms* have to do with brinco?"

"Natha," said Juan, shaking his massive furry cranium. "Nothing."

"Then why the heck did you make us *eat* those disgusting things?" I shouted at her.

La bruja's eyes flashed. She didn't like being yelled at. "First of all, I did not *make* you do anything. Secondly, one should never engage in any form of sombra travel on an empty stomach. And tequila worms just so happen to be an *excellent* source of protein and dietary fiber."

"I'm sure." Feeling sick, I wandered over to the red leather couch near the window and plopped myself down on it. As I rolled onto my side, trying to focus on keeping this morning's breakfast down (not to mention that nasty little worm she'd made me eat), I noticed that the dirt Ponce had smeared on my cast was somehow still there. And it looked exactly like it had in the Land of the Dead—dark brown and impossibly rich. "How is this even possible . . . ?" I said, holding up my arm for Joanna to see. "There's dirt on me . . . dirt from *over there.*"

"Why would that surprise you?" she asked. "The Land of the Dead is just as real as this world. Some say it's even *more* real."

I sighed. Whatever. I wasn't even going to try to wrap my mind around that.

"So, what's an equivocado?" Violet asked. "You never told us."

"Un equivocado is a general term for someone whose physical abnormalities cannot be easily explained," the queen replied with a sigh of her own. "Most of the time it is used to refer to someone who has been mistakenly cursed."

Of course. Because why not, right?

"Which, unfortunately, seems to be the cause of Charlie's manifestations. The good news is that it will likely go away in time. Maybe by high school." With another sigh, Joanna slumped into the tall wingback chair behind her desk. "Now, if you two would please excuse me, I have impending calamities and the end of the known world to attend to."

"But what about my parents?" I said, sitting up quickly. "Okay, so I'm not the Morphling; but you *are* still gonna help me find them, aren't you?"

"Tens of thousands of people go missing in the United States alone every year," the queen said in a tired voice. "Many more tens of thousands on a global level. I suggest you contact the local police department. Hasta luego, niños."

"No, c'mon, please ayúdame," I started to say, but as I got to my feet, I quickly learned that helping me wasn't on Joanna's top ten list of things to do—it probably wasn't even on her top hundred. How did I know? Because half a second later, Violet and I were back outside the monastery again, standing on the wrong side of the fence, a yard or two from where we'd left the bike.

"Great." Slumping my shoulders, I kicked a rock into a bush, feeling *totally* defeated. What the heck was I supposed to do now? "*Perfect!*"

"Charlie, we *are* going to find them," Violet said, putting a hand on my shoulder. "This is just a small bump in the road." When I gave her a *you've got to be kidding me* sort of look, she quickly added, "Okay, fine. More like a small mountain in the road. But every tough case has one. In fact, I don't think I've ever written a single piece where something didn't go wrong at first. Stuff just . . . *happens.*"

As much as I appreciated her optimism, I wasn't in the mood for a pep talk. "Let's just get out of here," I grumbled. "I wanna go home."

CHAPTER THIRTY

The following morning I walked into school to find Alice Coulter engaged in her favorite pastime: She had Alvin pinned up against the wall of lockers with her gang of bully clones gathered around them in a loose semicircle, laughing and knuckle-bumping each other like the brain-dead Neanderthals they were. It was a minute or two before the first bell, so the halls were virtually empty—just a few stragglers wandering around, trying to buy themselves a few more seconds of freedom before first period. I didn't see any teachers.

"Man, I said I'll get you ten bucks *tomorrow*," Alvin was pleading. "I don't bring lunch money to school anymore. I stopped in third grade. Because of *you*! Don't you remember?"

Alice's grip tightened on the collar of his shirt. "I remember you peeing your pants every other day in third grade, but that's about it."

"That was *one* time!" he shot back. "And my doctor said it could have been a bout of excessive lower-body perspiration, so it's still up for debate!"

"Debate this," she said before yanking open a locker and tossing Alvin inside. "Now, you make any noise in there before we let you out, and I'll *personally* make sure you wear your underwear as suspenders for the rest of your natural-born life." Then she slammed the locker shut, clipped on a combination lock, and her squad of stooges started banging on the flimsy dented aluminum and laughing their heads off.

The sight of someone being abused like that, of a bunch of morons taking pleasure in the suffering of others—taking pleasure in the suffering of my *best friend*, no less—sent a surge of anger through me, and I charged up the hall, pushing my way through the clique of idiots and getting right in the chief idiot's face.

"Let him out," I growled. "*Right. Now.* Or else."

Alice looked genuinely shocked. "Was that, like, a threat?"

"Exactly like one." And next thing I knew, I'd grabbed Alice by the collar of her crisp white jersey and pinned her up against the wall, her feet dangling an inch or two off the ground. Behind me, I heard several gasps as most of her posse backed away.

"*Let me go!*" Alice rasped, looking disbelievingly down

at what she must've assumed was just a regular old cast covering my regular old hand. "*Now!*"

"Apologize," I said, tightening my grip. "And *then* I'll think about it."

"*I apologize,*" she choked out quickly.

"What?"

"*I said I apologize.*"

"*¿Qué?* I still didn't hear you." I turned my head. "Try saying it into my good ear. . . ."

"*I said I freaking apologize, you nut! I apologize!*"

"Good choice," I said sarcastically. Then I let go, and she crumpled to the ground in a heap.

Panting, her angry red eyes boring into me like lasers, Alice rubbed at the bottom of her throat with one of her meaty mitts. "You're going to pay for that, punk. . . ."

"Do you take cash or credit?" I said. When I made like I was going to grab her again, she flinched, reddened with sudden embarrassment, then scrambled to her feet and ran away down the hall. Most of her crew went after her, but a few of the denser ones just stood there for a moment, staring at me with looks of utter bewilderment. It wasn't until they were all gone that I realized how crazy what I had just done was.

I stared down at my claw, stunned. Where had all that power come from?

"Someone there?" Alvin squeaked. "Kind of dark in here . . . and stinky."

I glanced around to make sure no one was watching, then snipped the lock with my claw and swung open the locker. Inside, a defeated-looking Alvin was curled into a tiny ball, his arms crushed up against his body, glasses dangling precariously from the tops of his ears. "Comfy?" I asked.

His eyes opened slowly, and a confused look passed over his face. "Oh." For some reason, he didn't look—or sound—very excited to see me. Not exactly the response I was expecting.

"*Oh?* Is that all I get for busting you out?"

"Thanks," he said in a flat voice.

"That's what amigos are for, right?"

"Amigos." He laughed, a low, bitter sound, then climbed out of the locker and started up the hall.

"Hey, where are you going?"

"Class."

"You're not gonna wait for me?"

"Why should I?"

Confused (and a little insulted, to be completely honest), I jogged after him. "Alvin, bro, what's wrong?"

He whirled on me. His eyes were huge and red-rimmed. "You, dude. *You're* what's wrong!"

"Me?"

"Yes. *You!* You've been a ghost, dude. You're never online. You don't return any of my calls. You act like you don't see my texts." He frowned, looking disappointed. Disgusted, even. "You missed registration, man. . . ."

Oh, snap. Registration! I'd forgotten all about that.

His voice shook as he said, "We were supposed to be a band, man. A team. How could you sell us out like that?"

"I—I've been really busy lately, Al. . . . I told you that."

"Yeah, I know. Busy running around with little Miss What's-Her-Face." His eyes went to my cast, and he shook his head. "Look at that. You even went and busted up your arm and didn't think to gimme a call." His lower lip trembled. "You've been totally ignoring us, man . . . totally ignoring *me.*"

"Dude, Alvin, it's not like that," I started to say, but he cut me off.

"No, dude. I'll tell *you* what it's not like! It's not like we were Facebook friends. We've been best friends since kindergarten. *Kindergarten.* But the second some pretty girl smiled at you, you forgot all about that. You sold us out for a girl, Charlie. And for Violet Rey, of all people."

"She's not that bad, Al."

"Not that bad? She's a Mattel, dude. A plastic. The girl probably has M.I.C. stamped on the back of her neck!"

"What's that supposed to mean?"

"Made in China!"

"All right, bro, chill. . . . Now you're being a little rude."

"Funny part is, you're so blinded by her glossy lips and shiny nails that you don't even see what she's doing."

I frowned. "What are you talking about? You don't even know her."

"Think about it, Charlie. You've been going to school with this girl for, like, six years. That's half your life. And all this time she hasn't looked your way once. But then all of a sudden she becomes head of the student newspaper and you start acting all weird and stuff and now she's all over you." His eyes narrowed to angry little slits. "You honestly don't see what's going on . . . ?"

"No, I honestly don't."

"That's because you've got stars in your eyes, kid! But you're her next project. You're her next front-page story."

"*Please,*" I said, rolling my eyes at him. "Gimme a break." But what if he was right? I felt stupid even considering the possibility, but how well did I *really* know Violet . . . ? I mean, yeah, she seemed genuine. She seemed *amazing.* But what if it *was* all an act? Just a twisted little game to get close to me. To get her front-page story.

"She doesn't care about you, dude," Alvin said. "Never has."

"Bro, look, I know you think you're protecting me and

all, and I respect that—I *appreciate* that. But that's not what's going on here. *Believe me.*"

"Okay, then, what's going on? Clear this *whole thing* up for me, because obviously I have no clue." He crossed his arms, waiting. "Go ahead. . . . I'm listening."

I hesitated, not sure how much to say. I mean, how much could I even *tell* him? This whole thing was insane! And if I told him *everything*, told him about how much of a freak I was becoming, could I honestly expect him to accept me when I couldn't even accept *myself*? But before I could decide, he said, "That's what I thought," then turned and started walking away.

"Dude, hold up! Give me a freakin' second to *think*!"

I was about to go after him when the sound of music— was that . . . *mariachi music?*—filled the hall. I had time to wonder, *But isn't band class on the* other *side of the school?* Then something hard (and completely invisible) nailed me right in my gut.

I gasped as the force of it lifted me off my feet and slammed me to the ground with a bone-crunching *thud*. Everything happened so suddenly that at first I didn't even feel any pain, only shock. But when the music stopped, I got an even bigger shock: All at once a figure materialized in the hallway before my very eyes.

And not just any figure—it was El Sombrerón!

CHAPTER THIRTY-ONE

His surprisingly human-looking face—sharp Hispanic features, olive skin, a few days' worth of
beard stubble—swam in and out of focus as I
rolled onto my side, trying to suck air back into
my pancaked lungs.

"Ay, muchacho, muchacho," he said in a low, laughing
voice. "You're a hard one to get ahold of." I felt hands patting me down, going through my pockets. "Don't have it on
you, eh? Where did you hide it? ¡Habla!"

"I don't know what you're talking about," I managed to
choke out.

El Sombrerón gave a frustrated groan. Then he dropped
a heavy knee across my chest, pinning me to the ground.
Next thing I knew he grabbed a handful of my hair and
began to braid it so tightly that a cry of pain tore from my
throat.

"Just tell me where it is and I let you go," he whispered into my ear as I squirmed and kicked, trying to fight him off.

"I. Don't know. What. You're talking about." I could barely force the words past the pain. "¡No sé!"

"Don't lie to me!" He twisted the knot of my hair tighter, and I cried out again. The enormous black brim of his hat stretched from one corner of my vision to the other, seeming to block out the entire world. There was only me, him, and the burning, shooting pain on my scalp. "Don't you lie to me, or my face is the last you ever gonna see, ¿me entiendes?"

"I'm not lying!"

"Cross your heart, hope to die, stick a needle in your eye?"

"Yes!" I screamed.

"Hmmm." The crazy hair-braiding goblin thought for a second, then stood up, shaking his head. "Why do I believe you?"

"Oh, I don't know . . . maybe because I'm telling *the truth!*" I stared up at him, rubbing my aching head, my breath still wheezing in and out of my lungs. "Dude, what do you want?"

He made a face. "*What do I want?* What do you *think* I want. . . ?* I want La Uña de la Bruja!"

"*The Nail of the Witch?*" I had no idea what he was talking about.

"Never heard of it?" he asked, and laughed quietly. It was a low, melodic sound. Almost soothing. "No one's ever told you about the cursed dagger that was born in the fiery depths of Cerro Azul, forged by the Cherufe warlords themselves, and cursed by a brujo so wicked that just the mere sight of the blade has been known to drive the weak-minded *insane?*" I knew the Cherufe were evil volcano-dwelling magma monsters, but I'd never heard of any cursed dagger, and when I shook my head, the guitar-playing super freak grinned and said, "Well, rumor has it that someone in your family's got sticky fingers, compadre. Know what I mean?"

"You're saying someone in my family *stole* that . . . that *thing?*"

He laughed again, louder this time and more genuinely. "Ay, amigo, I just can't make my mind up about you. . . . You're either the world's greatest liar or a *very* clueless little chico."

"I think we should go with option two," I said.

His grin widened, revealing rows of tiny, pointed teeth. He reminded me of a panther with his hungry smile and that wild, untamed look in his eye. "You don't know me very well, do you, amigo? See, I *always* get what I want, ¿sabes?"

"But what about the girl in the legend?" I blurted out

without thinking. "The one whose parents had a priest bless her hair so you couldn't go near her anymore."

"Ay, sí, Sophia"—he smiled, a dreamy look in his eyes—"my great love . . ." Half a second later, his eyes suddenly cleared, and a sort of angry snarl twisted his lips. "Why you gotta go digging up old wounds like that, eh? ¿Qué te pasa?"

Maybe I'd been hanging around Violet too much, but I got the sudden instinct to flip the script on him, to start asking the questions myself. At the very least it would buy me some time to figure out how I was going to get away from him.

"You work for La Mano Peluda, don't you?" I said (mostly because it was the first question that popped into my brain). "You know, the Hairy Hand?"

"Yes, *I know*. But I don't work for *nobody*, mocoso. I only work for *me*. And for your información, I'm not the only treasure hunter after La Uña." Off my surprised look, he said, "What? A man can't have a legitimate profession? You expect me to just braid horses' tails all day?" He *tsk*ed me. "Anyway, once word got out that La Cuca and La Mano Peluda were looking for La Uña, well, *everyone* started looking for it. That particular bruja has been known to pay a *great many quetzals* for enchanted items."

La Cuca. There was that name again—the one Sihuanaba had mentioned. "Are you talking about that witch from all those scary myths?"

"*Myths . . . ?*" El Sombrerón laughed. "You of all people should know better by now, no?"

Guess he had a point there.

"Oye, but what I'm trying to say is, it will be far better for you to deal with me than with one of my competitors; and you can trust me on that one. Some of them can be a little rough, ¿sabes?" He thought for a second. "Bueno. This is what we are going to do. You're going to take me to your house and we're going to look for La Uña. If we can't find it there, then I'll let you pick the next place we go looking. If it's not there, either, then I'm going to play the last song you'll ever hear, if you know what I—"

The ground began to rumble. From behind us came a distant whinny and the thunderous pounding of hooves. El Sombrerón's gaze narrowed, focusing up the hall.

"¡Contra!" he cursed.

"What's happening?"

"Sounds like *Johnny Law* is nipping at my spurs again, primo. I gotta go . . . *for now*. Vaya con Dios, niño."

Taking a step back, he raised his silver guitarra and began to play, strumming a slow, haunting melody. Immediately his form began to shimmer and shift with the vibration of the chords. I sat up, rubbing my eyes, but when I blinked them again, he was gone.

A split second later, the deafening clatter of hooves

filled my ears and a rush of wind swirled my hair as a massive shadow fell over me.

I looked up to see a great black horse rearing high on its back legs. Scales of black armor glinted along its sides, and its eyes glowed like a pair of burning coals. Front legs the size of tree trunks pawed wildly at the air. When it finally came down, I got my first look at the rider: flowing dark robes blacker than the night itself and a head made of pure smoke. It could only be one man.

El Justo Juez stretched one huge black-gloved hand in my direction. His voice crackled off the walls like exploding fire logs as he said, "Which way did he go?"

I started to point, then realized it was point*less*. "He— vanished. . . ."

The column of smoke above his shoulders momentarily blazed fiery red. "¡Madre!"

His huge sable steed let out its own wild cry. Twin pillars of hellfire shot from its nostrils, singeing the cheapo linoleum floors.

"I've been tracking El Sombrerón since he ambushed you at the cathedral," Juez said. "We believe he may have información that could prove useful in our struggle against La Mano Peluda."

"But he told me that he didn't work for them," I said.

"He doesn't . . . as far as we know. But someone like

him often hears much of what is spoken in darkness."

I shook my head. There was so much going on, so much I didn't understand. What wasn't La Liga telling me? Why did I keep getting dragged back into all of this?

"Juez, what's really going on here?" I said. "I mean, El Sombrerón thinks I have some sort of treasure—La Uña de la Bruja or something."

The headless rider jerked back in his saddle so abruptly that his horse whinnied and reared, its black-as-night hooves rising so high they crashed through the ceiling, obliterating a couple of the overhead panels. Hunks of foam rained down around us.

"¡No puede ser!" Juez cried in a thunderous voice. "It can't be!" The sound of his words echoed up the hall loud enough to make the whole building rumble. I was surprised no one had stuck their head out into the hall yet. A moment later, he seemed to compose himself and said, "Then it is worse than I feared."

A finger of fear skittered down my back. "What? What is?"

"Charlie, La Uña de la Bruja is a cursed weapon, a thing wrought of pure evil. And the fact that a sombra like El Sombrerón is hunting for it means La Mano Peluda is now poised to begin their slaughter."

"Their slaughter of *who?*"

"Charlie, I'm going to speak openly with you. You are in *great* danger. Through the millennia that weapon has been used exclusively—*¡exclusivamente!*—for a single purpose: to kill Morphlings."

And the finger of fear turned into icy claws clamped around my throat. "But, Juez, what does any of that have to do with *me*? I'm *not* the Morphling. . . ."

"Pequeño, don't you understand? Simply because *we* know you are not the Morphling doesn't mean La Mano Peluda does. And they believe their hour has come. They are going to kill everyone and *anyone* who they believe might have even the *slightest* chance of being the Morphling. See, the Morphling represents hope, and they cannot allow hope to spread, hence, they cannot allow the Morphling to live."

"So you're saying they're going to kill me *just in case* . . . ?"

"I'm afraid so. And not just you. Any child they believe might be the Morphling is now in the greatest peril. La Mano Peluda is absolute evil and will stop at nothing to achieve their ends. They place no value on human life. In fact, they only see value in *destroying* it."

Magnífico. So basically I was being hunted for *possibly* being something that I *knew* I wasn't. Things just kept getting better and better, didn't they?

Juez's horse pawed impatiently at the ground. Its massive hooves carved deep, curving ridges in the soft tiles. Some poor unsuspecting kid was going to take a nasty fall here. "Charlie, I have to go," the judge said, "but I do hope to see you again one day. You are a courageous boy with a wonderful and selfless spirit."

I stared up at him, grateful for his words but also feeling utterly helpless. "Thanks for that, Juez. I think you're awesome too. . . . You've always been a hero of mine. But, like, what am I supposed to do now?"

"My advice is simple," he said softly. "Do everything within your power to stay alive."

CHAPTER THIRTY-TWO

Hope you're ready to get your hands dirty," Violet said as she marched into my bedroom later that afternoon. "We have *a ton* of research to do." She dropped her book bag onto my bed. "I brought my laptop. Got a bunch of links that, as Cap McCaw might say, 'Might just be *pivotal* to our current dilemma, my dear.'"

When I didn't say anything, she frowned.

"What's wrong? Did something happen?"

Yes, I thought, but shook my head. "Don't really wanna talk about it."

"Not a problem." She took out her laptop and set it on my bed. "We're going to be reading mostly. Nice braid you got there, by the way. Very Pippi Longstocking-esque."

I sighed, rubbing my face.

"Charlie, are you feeling okay?"

"I'm fine, Violet. . . . I mean, there's nothing wrong with

me. Besides, of course, for the fact that I haven't seen my parents in forever, I'm turning into some kind of *mutant crustacean freak,* and, oh, that's right, the maniac in the ridiculously enormous black hat decided today would be a good day to play bongo drums on my small intestine."

"You were *attacked?* Where?"

"At school. He wanted me to find something for him. If I don't, he said he'd kill me. No biggie."

"Charlie, this was *today?*"

"Just before first period. Oh, and my best friend now hates my guts. Forgot to mention that one. That's the cherry on top."

Violet frowned. "Why would your best friend hate your guts?"

Because of you, I thought bitterly. *He hates me because of* you. "Look, I don't wanna talk about it. In fact, there's nothing I want to talk about *less.* In the *world.*"

"Okay, so we won't talk about it. Let's get to work." She took a seat on the edge of my bed, motioning for me to do the same. I didn't, but she continued anyway. "All right, I'm going to need to know the whole story if we're going to get to the bottom of this. Tell me about the night before your parents disappeared." She brought out a notepad and pen. "Did you notice anything out of the ordinary? Anything at all?"

"Will this help you finish your story?" I mumbled.

"What?"

"Nothing." I ran a hand roughly through my hair. "I don't wanna talk right now, okay?"

A long moment passed before she spoke again. "Charlie, it's going to be hard to piece together what happened without your cooperation. You're going to have to let me in."

I shrugged.

"Why are you being like this?" she said. "What's wrong?"

"What's wrong with *you*?" I snapped.

"Excuse me?"

I let out another sigh, and the next thing I knew, my frustration boiled over. "Why are you even here, Violet? Huh? Why don't you just go back to hanging out with the cool kids and doing whatever it is you *cool* kids do and just leave me alone? Because you sure as heck didn't give a crap about me before you saw that map."

Violet looked stunned. "Did you seriously just say that?"

"Deny it. Deny the fact that you haven't so much as looked my way in *six years*. How come you never talked to me before? How come you never even said hi?"

"How come you never said hi to *me*?" she shot back. "That street runs both ways, Charlie." She stared at me, her chest rising and falling like a restless sea. "What's gotten into you?"

"Guess it just took me a while to realize why you're really hanging out with me, that's all."

"Oh, yeah? And why is that, Charlie? Enlighten me. Because last time I checked, I was trying to help a *friend*."

"Doesn't matter," I mumbled, and looked away.

"Doesn't matter, or you just ran out of dumb things to say?" She jammed her notepad into her back pocket and started to put away her things. "Sorry I ever tried to help."

"Yeah, well, I'm sorry I ever let you. And I'm sorry that I pawned my mother's locket to buy you that ugly old bike!"

Violet flinched. That had hurt her. "You're acting like a total jackass, Charlie . . . a mean, *stupid* jackass!" Tears welled up in her eyes—big, wet drops that I could almost make out my reflection in—but still I couldn't stop myself.

"And you're as plastic as a Mattel doll!" I shouted.

Violet stepped forward, getting right in my face. "Don't you dare talk to me like that!" she shouted back. "Who do you think you are?" Then she snatched her bag off the bed. "I'm leaving."

"Good."

"Good!" At the door, she turned back to say, "I don't know who you are anymore, Charlie Hernández. . . . I have no *freakin'* clue!"

"Yeah, well, welcome to the club!"

Shouldering her book bag, she turned to leave, but then froze, staring down at her hands. *She must've hurt herself somehow,* I thought with a stab of fear. Cut a finger or something.

"What happened?" I breathed. I peered over her shoulder. Saw that her fingertips were sparkling with what looked like millions of tiny black diamonds. "What is that stuff . . . ?"

"Some kind of sparkly dirt." She touched her fingers to the strap of her bag, and when she pulled them away, I could see little designs glittering against the black of the strap. Then I realized they were words:

ENCUENTRA LA UÑA.

DESTRÚYELO ANTE QUE SEA MUY TARDE.

"It's some kind of message," I said. "It says to find the Nail. To destroy it . . . before it's too late."

Violet began touching things—her shirt, the table, my arm—and everywhere she touched, the same message appeared. "Freaky cool," she whispered, looking down at the tips of her fingers. A second later, understanding lit her eyes. "Charlie, it's the stuff on your cast! The dirt from the Land of the Dead!"

I glanced down. Realized she was right. The smudges from Ponce's dirty fingers were sparkling on my cast.

"The message has to be from the oracle," Violet said. "But what do you think it means?"

"He did mention something about nails. . . ." I scratched my head, trying to remember. "He said that there was a really dangerous one on our—" Then it hit me. "Oh, the dagger!"

"Huh?"

"It's the weapon El Sombrerón is after! ¡La Uña de la Bruja! The Nail of the Witch! Ponce must want us to find it and destroy it!" I thought back to the conversation, and the words just spilled out of my mouth: "And it might even save my life."

"*Save your life . . . ?* Charlie, you're not making any sense."

"No, listen. It's used to kill Morphlings. El Justo Juez told me that. And that's why the Hairy Hand wants it. That's why Ponce thinks destroying it might save my life."

"But Charlie, news flash—you're *not* the Morphling. . . ."

"Yeah, *we* know that. But the Hairy Hand probably doesn't."

Violet nodded. She understood.

"And by getting rid of it, we might not just be saving my life—" I began to say.

"But the Morphling's, too," Violet finished.

"Exactly."

She thought for a moment, then shrugged. "Fine. Let's say you're right. About all of it. Let's say destroying the dagger will save everyone, the whole world. How are we supposed to go about finding it in the first place?"

"Because Ponce told me just where to look," I said as it dawned on me.

CHAPTER THIRTY-THREE

The yellow crime scene tape was still up when we got to my old house, but the piles of scorched wood and ash that had littered the backyard were gone.

As I followed Violet around back, I could only hope that La Uña hadn't been accidentally trashed by whatever county cleanup crew had cleared the place out.

"Hope you're right," Violet said as we walked through the side gate. The grass hadn't been cut in so long that it brushed our ankles as we walked across it to the center of the yard. "You sure he said that it was here?"

"Positive." Ponce had told me to go back home, hadn't he? Home sweet home. Where else could he have meant?

"Where do you want to look first?"

"Inside the house, I guess." It was a huge mess, but what choice did we have?

"Well, before we start digging around in there, we

should probably check your parents' shed first, no? I mean, that's where I found this. . . ." She pulled out that old pirate's key from her pocket. It winked brilliantly in the afternoon sun.

"'Kay."

As we approached the shed, I noticed my dad's bulky padlock was missing. "Someone's been inside," I said.

"Watch out." Violet raised one jean-clad leg and gently nudged the corner of the door with her foot. It swung inward easily but didn't open all the way; something was blocking it.

"I'll go," I said. I squeezed my way through the narrow gap and into the darkness of the shed.

"How's it look?" Violet asked.

"Not good."

The shed was a certified disaster area. All the drawers and cabinets were hanging open. The row of mason jars my dad kept on his workbench had been swept off and dumped onto the floor. Jagged hunks of glass littered the ground. Even the box labeled CHRISTMAS STUFF had been sliced open, string lights spilling out like electric guts.

"Someone's *definitely* been here," Violet said, joining me inside.

"They were after La Uña."

"Unless it was a random looting."

Possible, but I didn't think so. It didn't *feel* random. Whoever did this was after something, something *spec*—

Suddenly, the big antique key Violet was holding shot out of her hand. It flew straight across the shed and stuck, teeth-up, to a cardboard box labeled BOOKS, ETC.

Violet's wide eyes found mine. "What the—?"

"Freaky." I could feel my heart clobbering against my ribs as we went over to the box and knelt beside it. Our eyes met through the dusty dark. I nodded.

Violet tore back the flaps of the box to reveal a handful of books (hardcovers with faded spines) and, beneath them, some sort of metal chest.

"A safe?" she guessed.

"Probably." Only it looked more like a plain old hunk of metal. There were no markings on it, just a big old keyhole on the top.

"You don't think . . ."

Except I did. Pulling the key free, I slid it into the lock and turned—

I might as well have stuck a fork in a toaster: A jolt of electricity raced through my hand and up my arm, zapping me.

"PAH!" I yanked my hand away, fingertips buzzing, and watched with growing panic as shafts of reddish light spilled out of the safe, glowing fiercely in the dim shed.

Instinctively, I had raised my hands to shield my face. Now I lowered them and looked around, wondering if I'd lost my frijoles. Snow had begun to fall inside the shed— yeah, *snow*—tiny flakes that drifted down from the ceiling like slowly falling confetti. Having lived in Miami my entire life, I'd never seen snow (not in person, anyway) and never knew what the big deal was. I finally got it.

"*It's amazing . . . ,*" I murmured.

Violet reached up to touch one of the falling flakes, and for a second it rested lightly in her palm before melting away. "*Awesome.*"

"And there's *that,* too."

The safe had disappeared. Like, *literally.* In its place, peeking out from under a velvet jeweler's cloth, was a jagged hunk of crystal. Dark red and radiating a faint yet dazzling light, it was about as long as a TV remote and shaped sort of like a bear claw, with tendrils of smoke roiling around just beneath its glassy surface.

"That's gotta be it," Violet whispered, leaning forward.

I picked it up, and the air around me began to crackle—a deep, steady hum. I could feel this thing's power radiating in my hand. It throbbed with energy, throbbed like a beating heart, and I knew (not so much in my head, but deep down inside me somewhere) that this was something dark and dangerous and very, *very* much alive.

"We have to destroy it," I said, looking up at Violet. "Like, *now*. Right now. We have to—"

From behind us came the buzzing whir of wings. I turned and instantly felt my mouth go dry: An acalica stood in the doorway, its pale eyes gleaming, its teeny, lipless mouth twisted in a mischievous smirk.

Dios mío . . .

It raised its bony little hands, and twin miniature black funnel clouds snaked out of thin air to touch down in the center of its tiny, wrinkled palms. The air inside the shed began to stir. Bits of debris rose around us. Overhead, the steel rafters were vibrating like plucked strings. In about five seconds, this entire plane was going to come crashing down on us.

Right as I opened my mouth to say, *Now, hold on there, dude,* there was a flash of white as something absolutely *ginormous* leapt through the doorway with a roar, swallowing the acalica in a single bite.

¡El Cadejo!

The mighty canine's tail caught the door, slamming it shut as he spun to face us. His glowing blue eyes burned into mine.

More are coming, he said as he slinked past us. He went to the corner of the shed and immediately began to nose about. *Stand back.*

Pointy shards of wood and hunks of concrete went air-borne as he started to dig through floorboards. His huge padded paws were a blur, and soon streams of dark earth were spraying over our heads in wide arcs.

An instant later, El Cadejo disappeared into the freshly dug hole and stayed down there exactly three seconds. When he emerged, a clump of grass was dangling from his chest, and his coat was so dirty that he could've passed for a black bear.

You two escape through the tunnel. He signaled with his furry muzzle. *Get somewhere safe and do what you know to do. I'll keep the acalicas busy.*

"Thank you," I said, and reached up to put my hand against the side of his face. His fur was unnaturally soft—almost airy somehow. I couldn't believe I was *actually* touching him. I couldn't believe I was standing face-to-face with this legend among legends!

He nuzzled me affectionately, his blue eyes glowing even brighter. Then he signaled once again with his head. *¡Dale! Go! You don't have much time.*

CHAPTER THIRTY-FOUR

The tunnel El Cadejo had dug was dark and a little narrow, but we both managed to crawl our way through pretty easily. We came out along the edge of my neighbor's yard, then quickly hurried back around to the front of my house, where we jumped on our bikes and hauled butt back to Mrs. Wilson's.

There we spent the next twenty minutes trying to figure out a way to destroy La Uña. We tried stabbing it, smashing it with a hammer, dropping it onto the driveway from my bedroom window—even tried melting it in a pot of boiling water. Nothing worked. In fact, the more things we did to it, the stronger the crystal (or whatever that thing was made of) seemed to get. When we finally got around to trying one of Mrs. Wilson's extra-sharp butcher knives on it, La Uña's *edge* reduced the knife's *blade* to metal shavings after just *two slices*. The thing was incredible.

"It's indestructible," I said, tossing the ruined knife onto the countertop. "It's literally *impossible* to destroy. . . ."

Violet paced the kitchen. "There has to be a way. . . . We're just missing something." Suddenly, she whirled to face me. "I know what we need!"

"A nuclear warhead?"

"No, *cookies!*"

"*Cookies?*"

"Yeah, you know, chocolate chip? Almond?"

"I know what cookies are, Violet. But what's your plan? To give it sugar diabetes?"

"Funny, but no. What I mean is, *I* need a cookie. . . . I think better on a sugar high." She peeked into the pantry. "Plus, nothing beats a soft and chewy double chocolate chip."

"I don't think we have any, though. Mrs. Wilson is more of a waffles-and-tea kind of gal."

"That's okay. I like them better from scratch, anyway."

"You bake?" Was there anything this girl didn't know how to do?

She was grinning when she glanced back at me. "Oh, do I ever."

Ten minutes later Violet bent to look through the oven window, then stood up, frowning. "The cookies aren't rising properly," she said. "Something's wrong."

"Maybe we found the one thing you don't know how to do," I teased.

She studied the bag of all-purpose flour she'd found in the pantry. "Doesn't seem like it's expired. . . ."

"It's not. Mrs. Wilson just used it. I saw her put some in her lobster bisque, like, two days ago."

"Really? Must be a weird recipe. I don't think you put flour in lobster bisque." Violet sprinkled a little on her fingertip and touched it to her tongue. "Funny, it has the same consistency as flour, but it tastes like lemons. . . ." She frowned. "Does Mrs. Wilson mix something into this? Because the smell is a bit o—"

Her gaze wavered. Her lips twitched. She staggered back from the counter, making a low, choking sound in her throat, and then suddenly collapsed.

"Violet!" I scrambled to her side, knocking over one of the kitchen stools. "Violet, can you hear me?" I pulled her into a sitting position, and then I almost passed out when I saw that her lips had begun to turn blue. *She must be having some kind of allergic reaction!* I thought as a flood of terror rushed through me. "Violet, talk to me!"

"She can't," a voice said.

I looked up and saw Mrs. Wilson standing in the doorway to the kitchen.

"Mrs. Wilson, thank God! She—I don't know what

happened to her . . . but she doesn't seem to be breathing!"

"That's because she's not. The flour she ingested was infused with a rare herb not found in this world. The cells of her body are currently gliding *gently* toward a state of suspended animation. But she'll be fine."

Um, *what?* "Just call 9-1-1!"

"I'm afraid there's nothing they can do for her. . . . There are few ways of extracting a cursed compound from a human body, and you won't find the necessary tools in this world. Guess she shouldn't have gone nosing around in my pantry."

"But Mrs. Wilson—"

"Oh, stop calling me by that *wretched* name," she hissed. "Human names are so dull. So *boring*." Her lips curved into a wicked grin. "Call me *La Cuca*."

CHAPTER THIRTY-FIVE

Before I could say anything, her form began to change. Her legs grew out several inches. Her hunched-over back straightened. The flabby skin of her face and neck smoothed like a skin cream commercial on time lapse, the wrinkles vanishing from around her eyes, from under her chin. Her once-frail-looking shoulders doubled in size. Newfound strength seemed to surge into her arms and legs, and the muscles there turned all hard and veiny. Her hair color also changed, becoming a rich dark blond as it grew out of her head, almost down to her waist, and she let out a peal of evil laughter that reverberated through the kitchen as if being blared from a giant amplifier.

"Oh, to be free of that pitiful form!" she shouted, lifting her hands triumphantly. Green light blazed from her eyes like twin beacons. "¡Por fin!"

I was almost too stunned to speak. Feeling like I was in a dream, I said, "You're her. . . ." The lady Sihuanaba had wanted to get revenge on. The one El Sombrerón was trying to find La Uña for. "You're that crazy old hag from the legends. . . ."

Only that wasn't entirely accurate. Sure, in a couple myths she was to have transformed herself into a harmless-looking elderly lady to trick her victims, but in reality she was the most widely known and widely *feared* witch in all of Hispanic mythology! Legends of her snatching misbehaving children right out of their beds, of luring them away from their homes with treats and rhymes—many times even *eating* the kids!—were known from Portugal to São Paulo.

In some of the stories she was a huge-headed ghoul with fiery eyes. In others she was an alligator-faced woman who specialized in brewing mystical potions. In one medieval myth she'd even been described as a fire-breathing dragon!

And as I stood there, almost close enough to reach out and touch her, I realized something else, something that made all the little hairs on the back of my neck prickle with fear: She'd never been just some old made-up character from a myth—some make-believe bogeywoman that parents used to scare little children into behaving. No, she was real. As real as I was. As real as my abuela had made her seem in the stories. And worse, I was staring right into the burning eyes of the very source of all those terrifying tales. Into the eyes of the most terrible witch in history.

For a moment I was so frightened I hardly even knew what to say. Then, shaking my head, I finally managed, "What do you want? I mean, what are you doing here . . . ?"

"Me?" La Cuca said innocently. "Ay, nada. I'm just here to cut out your heart and steal your powers."

Cut out my heart and steal my powers? "Uh, sorry to disappoint you, lady. But I don't have any powers for you to steal. I'm un equivocado. I'm sure you're familiar with the term."

La Cuca sighed. "Ay, and you're as dull as my *royal* pain-in-the-*nalgas* sister, aren't you, pequeño?"

Wait. Sister?

And suddenly I saw it. The same long, slender physique, the same glowing green eyes—even the same haughty, I'm-just-a-wee-bit-better-than-you tone of voice.

"Oh my gosh, you're Queen Joanna's sister!" I shouted. "The black sheep she mentioned."

La Cuca's lips split into an evil grin. "And *you*, mi niño, are the fifth born from the beginning of time, the last of your kind—a Morphling."

"Oh, that's awesome!" I said. Hey, anything was better than being un equivocado.

"You *do* also realize it's the reason I've embedded myself

into your little life and am now going to kill you, ¿sí?"

"Not so awesome, then. . . . But wait! The oracle *specifically* told me that I wasn't the Morphling. He seemed pretty positive, too."

"Of course that's what you were told, because that's *precisely* how I made it appear!"

"What are you talking about?" I said.

Her grin widened, turning maniacal. "You see, my sister and her band of *idiotas* believe only in the strictest interpretation of prophecy; they're closed-minded burros, if you haven't realized it by now. All I had to do was concoct a potion to make you manifest something other than what was prophesied in the picto-prophecy regarding the Morphling, and they would have no clue what to make of you. Which is exactly what I did—no small feat, mind you. . . ." When I didnt' say anything, she rolled her blazing eyes and shot me an annoyed look that bordered on a snarl. "Oh, don't look so empty-headed! Don't you get it? The poison your little friend accidentally ingested is the potion I crafted for *you*. I slipped a few teaspoons into that lobster bisque you loved so much and allowed your body's natural defense mechanisms to take care of the rest, to develop a perfectly genuine-seeming manifestation. Ingenious, no?"

Aw, dang. That was pretty slick. "Damn that delicious bisque!" I gritted my teeth in frustration. How was this possible? How could I have spent all this time living with her and never once have had the slightest inkling that something was up? That something just wasn't right about good ol' Mrs. Wilson? All the signs had been right there. Her freaky doll collection. Her obsession with keeping an eye on me. The pair of witchy cauldrons I'd found under the sink. Even the boxes and boxes of little kids' toys she was always trying to get rid of at the local flea market—the toys of kids she'd probably only recently *kidnapped*!

How could I have been so blind . . . ?

La Cuca tipped her head back in throaty laughter. "Oh, you *are* funny. . . . I have to admit that. And because you've never failed to entertain me, I'll be sure to tell your parents that you died bravely—that is, before I kill them and everyone else you love."

My parents. She knew where they were. I felt my hand tighten into a fist at my side. "What have you done with them?" I growled.

"*What have I done with them?*" she echoed mockingly. "Whatever do you mean? They've been right here with you the entire time . . . under the same roof, even!" She gestured at the pair of dolls sitting on the half shelf over the sink, and the sudden realization made my stomach twist: She'd turned my mom and dad into dolls! It seemed ridiculous, I know, but there was no denying it. The resemblance to my parents was *unmistakable* . . . even down to the tiny freckles on my dad's nose and the way my mom twisted her hair into a knot over her shoulder.

"I kept them alive for leverage's sake . . . in case you needed a little *extra* motivation. But their usefulness seems to have run its course."

"Undo whatever you did to them!" I shouted. "¡Ahora mismo! Undo it *right now!*"

"Ugh, so demanding . . . so *American.*" She opened her mouth wide, and a column of purple fire erupted from between her teeth, sizzling through the air. It struck me in the center of my chest, lifting me off my feet and slamming me into the wall. My head cracked against the doorframe, and I crumpled to the floor with a muffled moan as picture frames rained down on me.

"Hope that wasn't *too* hot," La Cuca said. She stalked forward, her strides long and easy, wisps of black smoke curling up from the corners of her smiling lips. "I held back as much as I could, but perhaps my eagerness got the best of me. . . . I've been looking forward to this for quite a while now—decades, even."

I groaned and rubbed my aching chest, which burned like I'd gotten tagged by a flaming boulder. The front of my shirt was in tatters, singed all the way through. The skin underneath, however, wasn't too bad—definitely a little redder than usual, but not much worse than a sunburn. "*What are you talking about?*" I choked out.

She gave me a funny look. "You honestly never wondered why your abuela taught you all those tales? Why she insisted that you memorize all those old and forgotten myths?"

My abuela. How did La Cuca know about her?

"You thought it was all just to entertain you? Merely to teach you a life lesson or two?" La Cuca's gaze sharpened on my face. "Allow me to tell you a little story about your beloved abuela. See, your grandmother, much like you, was a bit of a nuisance in her younger years. One day, during one of her many trips to South America, she happened upon a village that was under attack by a *legendary* bruja. Your grandmother, ever the meddler, decided to team up with a local chullachaqui in order to kill that wise and oh-so-beautiful witch." She paused. "Can you believe it? Your sweet little abuelita, a cold-blooded killer? In any event, your beloved granny happened to fall in love with that foul creature, and she soon bore a child . . . your mother.

"Now, unbeknownst to your abuela, the witch she had killed was *particularly* difficult to keep dead for reasons we won't get into right now, but suffice to say that when she returned from La Tierra de los Muertos and learned of all that had transpired since her most tragic death, she was beyond furious. However, once her anger subsided, she realized that your grandmother had actually done her a *wonderful* favor! Because now instead of having to travel the world killing chullachaquis to prevent the birth of the fifth Morphling, she could simply stalk a single family, wait for the Morphling to be born, *and then* kill it. So that's what she did, eliminating your abuela only once she was able to confirm that the Morphling had indeed been born into her familia."

"You're lying," I said. She had to be. "My abuela wasn't killed by . . . by some *witch*. She died because she was old."

"Ay, not so, pequeño. But hold on. . . . My story isn't finished yet. See, there are only three things you must understand to follow my little tale. One, romantic relationships between humans and chullachaquis are extremely rare; that is to say, I could count how many there have been throughout human history on my fingers and toes. Two, the number of these unions that have resulted in offspring are even *more rare*; those I can count on just one hand. And three, of those unions that produced offspring, a Morphling has always—and yes, you heard me right, *always*—been born into that family. Not always the first generation, not always the second, but at some point—and always within five generations—a Morphling has indeed been born of those bloodlines.

"To make a long story short, Charlie, that was why your abuela taught you all those legends. She knew all this; she understood that one day a Morphling would be born into her family tree. Furthermore, she realized that once La Mano Peluda became aware of the child's existence, they would undoubtedly send all manner of damned creatures to kill it. She told you the stories—like she told them to your mother before you—in order to prepare you. So that you'd be able to defend yourself. And if you happened not to be the Morphling, like in your mother's case, she expected you to pass those same stories down to your children and so on."

I was shaking my head. She could yap all day if she wanted to; it wasn't going to make me believe her. I mean, why should I trust some evil witch? "Like I said, you're lying. Plus, I don't care what you say. . . . My abuela died of old age."

"Because that's what *I* wanted it to look like, idiota! I didn't want to spook your parents and have to track you down all over again. But believe me when I tell you how your grandmother died, because *I* am that witch from my tale, and *mine* was the last face your precious abuelita ever saw before I *snatched* the life out of her!" A grin spread slowly across la bruja's face—one as genuine as it was wicked—and the ground seemed to tilt beneath me.

I could feel the cold fingers of dread and disbelief tightening around my insides, and when I finally found my voice, it was barely more than a whisper. "You killed my abuela . . . ?"

"Sí, I did. You see, pequeño, our lives have been entwined long before you were even born. And fortunately for me—but not so fortunately for you—I now possess the very object I've been searching for, the object that will put an end to our decades-long game of cat and mouse." Grinning, she strolled casually over to the counter and picked up the cursed hunk of crystal. Immediately, it grew into a crescent-shaped dagger in her hand. The curved reddish blade glowed darkly, as if the forging flames had been somehow trapped in the crystal, and the smoky tendrils I'd seen churning inside now swirled around its hilt like a swarm of angry wasps. The thing looked deadly. *Wicked* deadly.

La Cuca's grin finally blossomed into a full-blown smile. "Beautiful, isn't it . . . ?"

"Put that down," I warned her.

"Ah, but I cannot comply. For it is this blade that makes it possible for me to cut the heart out of a Morphling in such a way that I can still absorb its powers. Your parents and abuela knew this, which is why they stole it from me and hid it all these years. But thanks to you and your little girlfriend, La Uña has finally found its way back to its

rightful owner and will now fulfill its *delightful* purpose!"
Her smile had turned vicious again. It made me think of a
venomous snake preparing to strike. "Oh, and don't worry,
Charlie. I'll dispose of your parents and your little amiguita
as humanely as possible once I'm through with you. However, in your case, I'm afraid it won't be nearly as painless. I
hear having one's corazón cut out of one's chest can be *quite*
the excruciating experience."

"You're not going to hurt them," I growled as I hauled
myself painfully to my feet. "You're not going to hurt any of
us, you stupid witch!"

"Ay, Charlie, don't take it so personally. It's not like you
will be the first Morphling I've ever killed . . . though you
will certainly be the *last*."

So she's the witch from the legends of the Morphling, too, I
thought. And hadn't she already said as much?

"'The age of La Mano Peluda is upon us," La Cuca
purred, satisfaction filling her voice. "And your death shall
usher it in." She knelt beside Violet, trailing a razor-sharp
fingernail along the bottom of her neck. "Oh, and I lied,
Charlie. . . . Your little friend isn't fine. In fact, she's dying.
The compound she ingested is actually highly corrosive
and *highly* poisonous. She's so close to the other side now,
you have no idea. . . . Shall I not thrust her over?"

"Get away from her!" I yelled. "¡ALÉJATE!" Suddenly

a rage like I'd never known before ripped through me, angry and hot, like acid boiling in my veins. I cried out as feathers burst through the skin on my arms and shoulders, as a familiar tingle pulsed at my temples: the horns growing out of the sides of my head. And then, wings—huge white wings!—exploded through the back of my shirt.

"¡INCREÍBLE!" La Cuca marveled. "So much power contained in such a *puny* little vessel!"

I cried out again, and a blast wave of energy rushed out of me, blowing out the windows of the house and tearing huge chunks out of the walls. The freshly washed spoons in the sink jingled and jangled. Every single light bulb in the kitchen suddenly exploded in a glittery puff of glass.

"¡Sí!" La Cuca cried, her eyes growing wider, crazier. "Sí, keep going! Unleash the monster within!"

I squeezed my eyes shut. My whole body was pulsing with energy. Vibrating with it. I could feel a flood of something like electricity surging through me, racing through my bloodstream, sizzling along the surface of my skin. Strength buzzed in every muscle of my body. My fingertips tingled. My bones burned like coals beneath my skin. I'd never felt so alive. It was as if I'd been plugged into a vast and limitless ocean of raw power, and now that power was flowing through me, the cells of my body conducting it like trillions of tiny copper wires.

When I opened my eyes again, I saw that the witch was still smiling, still watching me with that awful glowing gaze. Meeting it full on, I lowered myself into a semi-squat and said, "La Cuca, do me a favor. . . . Think of a smooth comeback and imagine me saying it in a cool superhero voice."

Her forehead wrinkled in question. "Why in the worlds would you want me to do that?"

"Because that's usually what happens right before the good guy hands the baddie his or her butt on a platter." And I flung myself at her, ready to claw-punch her through the wall, ready to claw-punch her *to the moon* if that's what it took.

Only I didn't even make it five feet before the witch raised her free hand and some invisible force seized me, freezing me in midair.

"Going somewhere?" she asked mockingly.

With a yell of fury, I struggled wildly against the invisible hold, but it was useless. I couldn't move—couldn't even *blink*. I could only watch as that crazy witch stalked toward me, smirking evilly.

"You've been a bad boy, Charlie Hernández." She held her free hand out lazily between us, and the tips of her fingers began to glow as if they'd been dipped in purple fire. Tiny licks of flame danced along her nails as she took aim at the pair of dolls on the shelf, at my parents, and my blood went cold. "Shall I make them pay for your behavior? Shall I make you *watch* them pay . . . ?"

"Stop it!" I screamed. "Please just stop . . . *STOP!*" But there was nothing else I could do to save them. Nothing I could do to save Violet.

Nothing I could do to stop this psycho witch from killing *everyone* I loved.

La Cuca's eyes, lit with triumph, found mine. She whispered, "Say adiós to them, Charlie. . . ."

But no sooner had the words left her mouth than there was a knock at the side door. I turned to see a couple of delivery people standing in the doorway—a rail-thin guy in an El Tri T-shirt, Marlins cap, and ratty jeans and a woman wearing black visor-style sunglasses; they were pushing a dolly loaded with a huge wooden coffin.

"Who are you people?" La Cuca hissed, looking between them. "¿Qué quieren?"

"We got a delivery for 437 Giralda Avenue," the lady announced. They rolled the coffin inside and stood it up by the fridge. Neither one seemed to notice the blown-out windows, the ragged holes in the walls, or the fact that there was a kid hovering almost two feet off the ground in the middle of the kitchen. Guess they were too busy.

"Custom-made casket," the guy said proudly. "Twelve

foot by three with silver trim, silk lining, and our patented extra-triple-plush package."

La Cuca turned to me, disbelief etched in her face. "You ordered *a coffin* to our final, epic showdown? Is this your pathetic idea of a joke?"

"Me? What? *No.*" I mean, it would've been sort of funny. But I hadn't.

"Well, someone did," the delivery guy said, "and we sure as heck aren't taking it back. Thing's crawling with tarantulas...."

I felt my eyebrows screw up in a big question mark. Did he just say *tarantulas?*

The delivery dude grinned at me, a familiar ghoulish grin, then flipped open the lid of the coffin, and a swarm of huge black spiders poured out like a mini tidal wave of darkness, flowing across the cracked tile floor and slinging their silky webs at La Cuca. Clearly caught off guard, the witch fumbled back on her heels, slicing at the spiders with the cursed dagger. Then she shrieked and tripped, dropping out of view behind the island.

"Charlie!" the delivery guy called, yanking off his cap, and I instantly recognized him—it was the calaca from La Rosa!

Stunned—*beyond* stunned, really—I shouted, "What are you doing here?" as he and the lady scrambled over.

"She glimpsed your future earlier today," the calaca

said. "She saw you'd be in trouble. We got here as quickly as we could."

I shook my head. "She? Who *is* she?" Then the lady took off her glasses, and I instantly recognized her, too—the teary eyes, the puffy red nose, the straight, jet-black hair. "¡La Llorona!" I yelped. I turned to run, but the calaca grabbed my arm and spun me back around.

"Charlie, she's with me! It was her idea to come help you!"

Now *that* stunned me. "¿De verdad?"

"Yes, for real!" La Llorona cried, sniffing back tears. "You're mi hijo! I couldn't let some crazy bruja cut out your heart and *feast* on it!"

"But you do realize I'm not *actually* your son . . . ," I couldn't help pointing out.

"Biologically, no. But you do feel that special mother-son bond between us, don't you?"

I didn't want to hurt her feelings, so I went with: "Eh."

"Good enough for me!" she said with a beaming smile. She had a nice smile, actually. A little toothy and watery, but still nice.

"Your little visita to the Crying Shack got us talking again," the calaca admitted happily. "We'd been broken up for a few weeks, you see. Maria can be a bit gushy from time to time, if you know what I mean. . . ."

"I'm not gushy!" La Llorona shot back. "You're just emotionally *dead* half the time!"

The calaca sighed. "I'm not emotionally *dead*. Though I should point out that *all* calacas, myself included, are *physically* dead; our emotions, however, are perfectly *alive*."

"Then how come I've never seen you cry, huh? Not even once!"

"Because I don't have tear ducts, woman!" He took a breath, trying to compose himself. "Look, now is not the time for this. My eight-legged friends won't keep La Cuca busy for long. Charlie, you have to stop her. *You* have to end this."

"But I don't think I—"

The calaca raised one huge fist between my eyes, and I shut up. On his pinky finger glinted an old brass ring. A familiar design had been carved into the metal: the horns and feathers. "I've always believed, Charlie. . . . Fear may have blinded me—even twisted my actions—but in my corazón, in my *heart*, I have always believed."

"And so have I," La Llorona said.

The calaca cupped my face, framing it between his bony hands. "Charlie, so many of us have been waiting for this day. Waiting for longer than we can remember. Now is the time of the Morphling. Now is *your* time. *End* this. Termínalo. Do you hear me? Stop La Mano Peluda! Put an end to their reign!"

"You're the only one who can do it," they both started to say, but suddenly their mouths stopped moving as their hands and faces began to glow. Dimly, at first, then building in intensity until their clothes caught fire and their eyes began to melt in their sockets. In a last desperate act, they threw their arms around each other an instant before disintegrating into fiery ash.

Half-frozen with fear and shock, I looked around. Saw La Cuca standing on the opposite side of the kitchen, grinning, one burning finger aimed in our direction.

She killed them. The thought went through me like ice water. *That crazy witch killed them both!*

"You murderer!" I raged, feeling another rush of fury blaze inside me. "You're nothing but an evil, heartless—"

And that was as far as I got before the witch once again seized me in her invisible grip. My arms were pinned tightly to my sides. My elbow joints began to bend painfully in the wrong direction. I could feel her hold tightening around my body like a lead belt. I tried to scream but realized I couldn't even suck in a breath!

Less than a foot away, La Cuca stooped to pick up the mystical dagger, her eyes glittering with bad intentions. "I'll try not to make this *too* painful, Charlie. . . ." Straightening, she raised the dagger between us, and the sight of its curved, wicked point sent my panic into overdrive. I kicked and bucked and squirmed, straining with every fiber of my aching being. But it was no use. It felt like I'd been wrapped in an invisible straitjacket made of steel!

The witch studied my face for a moment with an eager look in her hungry green eyes. "Cálmate . . . relax." Her voice dropped, becoming a low, ultra-creepy hiss as she touched the tip of the dagger to the exposed skin of my chest. I don't know how it was possible, but the crystal felt simultaneously flamethrower-hot and freezing, numbing my skin almost on contact. I hissed in pain and surprise, making La Cuca laugh softly under her breath. "Duérmete, niño, duérmete ya . . . Que viene La Cuca y te comerá."

My throat tightened. I knew that lullaby. It was pretty well known, actually. My abuela had even sung it to me once or twice, putting me to bed with it when I was little. It basically went like: *Sleep, child, sleep already . . . for here comes La Cuca and she'll eat you up.* Something told me this lunatic recited it to all her victims. And just thinking that sent a spear of fear through my heart.

So, this is it, I thought miserably. *This is how it ends. How I die . . .*

And it certainly looked that way. But an instant before my life could begin to flash before my eyes—before I could even *close* my eyes—I heard the front door of the house creak open and a voice shout, "Charlie? Charlie, are you here, dude?"

CHAPTER THIRTY-SIX

lvin!. I felt a powerful rush of relief and then an equally powerful surge of gut-wrenching terror, realizing La Cuca would just as happily kill him, too.

"¡Madre!" La Cuca cursed. "What *NOW?*" Her furious gaze flew to the doorway just as Alvin stepped into view. He was holding an ice-cream cone in his left hand and licking sugary drippings off his thumb. It looked like vanilla and fudge. Al's favorite.

"Charlie—" Alvin's expression jumped from confused to freaked to curious before finally landing on googly-eyed fascination. His jaw dropped and his hand opened, releasing the ice-cream cone, which hit the ground with a sticky splat. "Dude, you're doing cosplay? Why didn't you *freakin'* call me?!"

In the instant La Cuca was distracted by Alvin, I felt her invisible hold falter and made my move. I lunged forward, swatting her across the face with one of my wings. It connected solidly, bone on bone, and La Cuca slammed sideways into the kitchen counter, sending plates and cups crashing to the ground.

"Alvin, run!" I shouted. "Get out of here!"

"But, dude, I came over to apologize for earlier," he said. "And how the heck did you just do that? Where's the fly system? I don't see the wires. . . ."

"There are no wires! And apology accepted. But you need to leave. Now!"

"But I want to play too!"

"Alvin, go! I'll explain later!"

"But—"

"*Run!*"

"*Fine*," he grumbled, pouting like a little kid as he bent to pick up his mashed-up cone. "But I'll be right outside if you need me."

"Yep!"

As La Cuca regained her balance, she snatched one of the short-handled paring knives from the butcher's block and sent it screaming at my face. The blade blurred past me, grazing my ear, and buried itself in the wall behind me. Had I been standing another inch to my left, it would've taken my ear off. Two inches, and it would've all been over.

"I don't usually miss," she said.

"And I don't usually die." Huh. Not a bad comeback.

With another savage shriek, her mouth opened wide— and I mean *impossibly* wide, like she had alligator jaws or something—and a cone of purple flames shot straight at me. I dove to my left, just barely managing to avoid insta-death. The wall behind me caught fire. The little breakfast table was instantly incinerated. The stink of burning paint and wood filled my nostrils, scrambling my brain a little as I came up on one knee, preparing to dive out of the way of another blast if necessary.

It wasn't. Because La Cuca was bent over in laughter.

"¡Idiota!" she sneered. "You think you can avoid my blasts forever?" Her gaze narrowed on me, seeming to burn even brighter. An instant later, the entire house began to tremble, the walls turning transparent . . . and then we were standing in the middle of a huge cornfield, the endless rows of grain swaying back and forth around us in a gust of wind. I blinked, and then we were on the summit of a frozen mountain somewhere. I blinked again, and then we were in . . . *Barcelona?* I thought I recognized La Pedrera— that famous cultural center in Catalonia.

"YOU CAN'T EVEN FATHOM MY POWER, BOY! I AM THE MOST POWERFUL BRUJA IN ALL THE WORLD!"

The very air seemed to hum and vibrate with her power;

I could feel it flowing out of her like something alive and angry. It crackled around me like invisible currents of electricity. The next thing I knew, we were back in the kitchen of the house on Giralda—for the moment, anyway.

"*I AM THE MOST POWERFUL BRUJA IN ALL THE LANDS!*" she cried, and suddenly her body began to change again. The skin on her arms and face hardened and cracked. Its color ran out, turning first a sickly white, then a darker, muddier green. Bony scales appeared along the sides of her neck. They mashed up against one another, forming peaks and valleys that ran down her back in thick, scaly ridges. Then her head began to swell. Like a balloon. It expanded outward until it was about the size of a giant pumpkin, her eyes glowing so fiercely and brightly that the resemblance was impossible to miss—a jack-o'-lantern. That was what she looked like. A terrifying, maniacal, half-crazed jack-o'-lantern with alligator skin!

"THERE'S NOTHING—*NOTHING*—YOU CAN DO TO DEFEAT ME!" she bellowed. And she was absolutely right. I couldn't defeat her. She was too strong. Too skilled. Like the other Morphlings before me—the ones who had actually managed to beat her—I had to find a way to *trick* this witch into defeating *herself.*

And just like that, a plan began to form in the back of my head.

"Hey, I was wondering something," I said suddenly. "Can you fly?"

It stopped her. Like a pie to the face. "That's—out of the blue. . . ."

"No, I know. I was just wondering."

She looked confused. "Sí . . . of course I can fly."

"Well, I was just asking because you don't have any wings or anything, so it just doesn't seem like you'd be very good at it—or very fast."

Her mouth twisted into a humorless scowl. "Think again, runt. I am *very* good at it. And I am blazing *fast!*"

"Prove it, then. Race me."

"Race *you?*" She burst into laughter. "Actually, I think I'll just cut your heart out and call it a day."

I shrugged. "Might as well. I'd probably smoke you."

"YOU WOULDN'T STAND A CHANCE AGAINST ME!" she roared. "MY POWER IS BEYOND YOUR COMPREHENSION!"

"Then you shouldn't even break a sweat, right? In fact, I'll make you a deal. You beat me in a race—a *fair* race—I'll *let* you cut my heart out. Won't even try to stop you."

"And if you win?"

"How could I?"

A wicked grin split her lips. Arrogance and pride oozed out of her like a busted pimple. "Excellent point."

"Let's keep it simple. We fly straight up and see who can fly higher and faster. Cool?"

"*Congelado*," she sneered. Then she raised a hand, and the door leading to the yard tore off its hinges and went tumbling away down the middle of the street. "After you."

Once we were out in the yard, she said, "On your mark—"

"Too slow!" I didn't wait for her to count us down—just exploded into flight. I knew that would probably make her raging mad, and raging mad was just how I wanted her. La Cuca was on my heels in a blink, her face twisted into a furious snarl. *Perfecto*, I thought, and couldn't fight back a smile. We shot straight into the dark gray sky, twirling around each other like battling hawks as we climbed higher and higher.

My heart was pounding wildly. My entire body thrummed with each powerful beat of my wings. Obviously, I'd never flown before—not with my *own* wings, anyway—but it really did feel kinda like second nature. Like walking. Or breathing.

"Don't tell me this is all you've got, runt!" La Cuca hissed, and she put on a burst of incredible speed, pulling way out ahead of me. The witch was fast. Brutally fast. Even with my wings I knew there was no way I could beat her.

Fortunately, that had never been the plan.

"I'm just getting loose, witchy!" I gritted my teeth, put everything I had into flapping as the wind battered my face and La Cuca's shrill cackling echoed in my ears.

I have to push her! I reminded myself. *Push her to her limit!*

Up ahead, the clouds pulsed with arcs of blue lightning. Icy rain peppered my face and chest. I beat my wings harder, flying higher, faster.

"I hope you're not gassing out on me!" I called after her. "¡Te ves cansada!"

"I look tired to you? We'll see about that!"

We charged into the heart of the storm. Thunder rumbled around us like war drums, and gusts of updrafts tore at my wings, my clothes, my chest. Far down below us, through the swirling cloud cover, I could just make out the city of Miami spread out like a world of LEGOs. We must've been close to two miles up.

Just a little more to go, I told myself.

"Vamos. Let's make this a challenge!" La Cuca cried, hurtling through the air with such speed that a bubble of white vapor had formed around her feet.

I sort of remembered something from science class about how vapor cones were created by fighter jets when traveling at high speeds through moist air. This looked a lot like that, except I'd never seen a jet fly anywhere near as fast as she was. We soared higher, slicing through ribbons of wet black clouds. Then my wings caught an air current, shooting me forward like a slingshot.

"¡Hasta luego, muchacha!" I shouted as I blew past her. Higher and higher we climbed, rising so high that the air became freezing cold and impossibly thin. It was like trying to breathe through a straw! Almost immediately the muscles along my back caught fire, making every flap feel like it was my last. But I wasn't about to stop. Even if it took everything in me, even if it cost me my freakin' *life*, I was going to make sure that this witch never got a chance to hurt anyone I loved ever again.

"C'mon, Cuca!" I called tauntingly. "You have to be faster than this!"

With a hellish shriek, the witch tore past me so fast I wobbled in her current. I had to spread my wings out as far as they would go just to keep from being knocked out of the sky.

We were impossibly high now, high enough that my ears wouldn't stop popping and my chest felt like an elephant was using it as a seat cushion. My lungs were burning, begging for air. Worse, blackness had begun to nip at the edges of my vision.

Don't even think about passing out! I told myself. Not happening. Not now, not ever!

"C'mon, Cuca, show me the limitlessness of your

power!" I shouted, flapping my wings with every ounce of strength I had left. Which, by the way, wasn't much. Wasn't *anything*, in fact. Every cell of my body was in agony. My muscles burned like they'd been doused in gasoline and blowtorched. Still, I sucked in half a breath, sucked in what little air there was up here, and yelled, "Stop holding back, you cowardly old witch!"

"*OLD?*" La Cuca let out a hissing howl of fury. "I'LL SHOW YOU OLD YOU HAPLESS HALFLING! I'LL SHOW YOU SPEED LIKE YOUR PUNY MIND CAN'T EVEN POSSIBLY IMAGINE!"

There was a mega sonic boom as she shattered the sound barrier and then another one as she shattered some other barrier of physics.

And that's when it happened: The witch had picked up so much speed that all within a few seconds, she pierced the troposphere, passed through the stratosphere, and entered the mesosphere, where she suddenly began to glow like a miniature sun.

It was right then, right at that very moment, that she realized I had tricked her. That I'd been playing her this entire time.

"Cunning boy," she said through a vicious grin, and that was all she had time for before she was engulfed in a flash of fiery light.

CHAPTER THIRTY-SEVEN

U p until that very moment, I'd never truly appreciated how important school was. I mean, had La Cuca bothered taking a sixth-grade science class, she would've known that flying into the mesosphere is a big no-no because of the gas particles that exist up there. But she hadn't, and like a falling comet, the witch had been instantly incinerated.

Unfortunately, though, I didn't even get a few seconds to celebrate my victory, because just then my entire body gave out, and I started to fall. I had a moment to think about Violet, about my parents—even about my abuela and how thanks to her and all of the myths she'd taught me, I'd been able to make it this far—and I smiled. It was a tired smile. An *I did everything I could and I hope you guys appreciate it* sort of smile.

And then everything went black.

✦ ✦ ✦

I woke to the low buzz of conversation. Many voices, lots of people. Something long and wet and rough was being dragged gently across my forehead and cheeks. It felt like someone was doodling on my face with a scratchy paintbrush. Light stabbed through my eyelids, bright and hot. Somehow I sensed El Cadejo was near. I don't know how I sensed it. I just did.

Then I opened my eyes—and there he was! Licking my face with his beefy pinkish tongue, his blue eyes shining like stars. But as my vision stabilized, his form began to melt away. And by the time I had blinked all the fog out of my eyes, he was gone.

Dazed, I looked around me. I was lying in a crater the size of a swimming pool. The floor beneath me was all cracked tile and hunks of white limestone. There was half of a table to my left. The other half dangled precariously from the lip of the crater by one of its charred-black legs. I recognized it: It was Mrs. Wilson's—I mean, La Cuca's—dining table. Which meant that I was back inside the house on Giralda.

For a long moment I just lay there, staring up into the blue, cloudless sky, wondering how so much crazy stuff could have happened on such a beautiful day. Then I sat up—and immediately regretted it. Dizziness washed over me in waves. My temples throbbed. It felt like . . . well, like I'd dropped out of the sky and crash-landed in the middle of a kitchen. I checked my body for cuts or broken bones, but I didn't find any. No feathers or horns, either. Racking my brain, I couldn't come up with any possible explanation for how I'd survived the fall, but I knew El Cadejo had something—maybe *everything*—to do with it. I had to remember to ask him about it . . . that is, if I ever saw him again.

Still fighting dizziness, I pushed to my feet and waddled over to the edge of the crater. The crater itself was about fifteen feet wide and a little more than five feet deep, which meant I could just see over the rim of it. And what I saw were *kids*—dozens of them . . . *hundreds* of them. Kids of all shapes and sizes. Girls and boys. Prekindergarteners to high schoolers. They were wandering aimlessly through the house, most forming lines at the front door and filing slowly outside. All of them looked sleepy and confused and *completely* out of it. I didn't recognize any of them.

Where did they even come from . . . ?

Finally, I saw someone I *did* recognize.

"Alvin! Over here!"

Alvin spun around. When he saw me, he raced over with all the fleet-footedness of a one-legged turtle. His eyes were the size of melons, and he was panting like he had after our first one-mile run in third grade. Big, gasping breaths that made it sound like he was choking on a Snickers bar. (Which, by the way, had also happened to him in third grade—and only a couple of minutes after that one-mile run.)

"Dude!" he practically shouted in my face. "You were flying—I mean, you were FLYING!"

"Yeah, there are a few things I should probably catch you up on . . . ," I admitted.

"Oh! You think?" He searched my face, his brown eyes wild. "Dude, so you're like . . . like some kind of super freak then, huh?"

"Basically," I said, and realized I wasn't even the least bit embarrassed to admit it. Funny part was, just a couple of hours ago, I'd been too ashamed to tell him about my manifestations, too ashamed to let him see what I was becoming. But I wasn't anymore. See, at first (and like most people, probably), I'd assumed my manifestations were turning me into some kind of a weirdo. A freak. But what I *didn't* know at the time, what I couldn't *possibly* have known, was that it would be that same "weirdo-ness" (if that's even a real word) that would soon save my life—not to mention the lives of everyone I cared about. It had definitely taken me a little while, but I'd learned something fom all this: Somewhere between almost having my heart cut out of my chest by the evilest witch in history and waking up in the middle of this limestone crater, I'd realized that the things about yourself that make you feel awkward or different or drive you completely crazy are the same things that make you *you*. And you can't run away from who you are. You can't cry it away; you can't even wish it away. But once you accept yourself—*everything* about yourself (especially the weird parts)—you'll finally be free to be you. And that's a powerful thing. A *very* powerful thing.

And I guess you could say that I'd finally accepted *me*.

Still, I was surprised when Alvin said, "Man, oh man, oh man! This is AWESOME!"

I blinked at him. "So you don't think it's . . . *weird*?"

If possible, Alvin's eyes grew even wider. "*Weird*? Are you friggin' *nuts*? This is the best thing that's ever happened to me!"

"Uh, happened to *you*?"

He made a silly face. "You know what I mean. . . ."

"I do." I smiled.

"How long have you been like this, man . . . ?"

"Couple months now."

"Really? And why *the heck* didn't you say anything?" he burst out.

"I dunno. . . . I guess I thought you'd think I was a monster or something. I thought you wouldn't wanna hang out with me anymore."

He gaped at me like I'd just spoken the stupidest words ever uttered on planet Earth. "Bro, we're *best friends.* Hermanos. I wouldn't stop hanging out with you even if you grew a coat of fur, changed your name to Fido, and started chasing your own tail. Plus, do you have any idea how many *records* this can help us sell? We'll be the only band with a flying guitarist, like, *ever!* I can finally drop out of middle school!"

Yep. Typical Alvin. Always looking for an angle. Rubbing a spot of pain on my forehead, I glanced around at all the kids milling around. "Dude, who are all these people?"

Alvin shrugged. "How the heck should I know?"

"Charlie!"

I turned toward the voice. "Violet!" I was so happy to see her, so *unbelievably* relieved that she was up and moving and not lying dead and poisoned on the floor somewhere, that my heart almost exploded inside my chest. I scrambled out of the crater, and we ran straight at each other like one of those corny romance movies, except that instead of one of those spinning slo-mo hugs, we crashed together so hard we nearly went flying in opposite directions.

"You're okay!" I shouted.

"Yeah!" Her eyes were bright blue and shining. Man, it was great to see her breathing again! "And you? Are you okay?"

"Yeah, I'm good." I took a breath. Tried to slow my racing heart. "I got her, V. . . . I got the witch."

As soon as I spoke the words, I felt this enormous invisible weight lift off me. I could hardly believe it, but it was true. I'd defeated La Cuca. I'd defeated her and saved everyone I cared about. Dang, that felt good to know!

"Yeah, you saved us, Charlie!" Violet said, giving me one of her million-watt smiles. It was a smile that I didn't want to go a day without seeing. Not a single freakin' day!

I had just opened my mouth, planning to say one thing, then frowned, remembering something else.

"What's wrong?" she asked.

"I . . . I just wanted to say I'm sorry. For earlier. For all that stupid stuff I said."

"Charlie, forget it. You had a lot going on. I get it. It's okay."

"But it's not okay! I acted like a total idiota. You didn't deserve that. The truth is you're, like, one of the best and most loyal people I've ever met; I couldn't have asked for a better friend. . . ." And I meant it; she was awesome, and it felt great to get that off my chest.

Violet was still smiling, but I could tell she was fighting back tears now. "Think you might be giving me a little *too much* credit. . . ."

I took one of her hands. "Nah, it's true. You were

always there for me, Violet. And you never judged me. No matter how weird I got. You made me feel *normal.*" Which in itself was pretty incredible. And if I had to bet, I'd say it was how quickly and easily she had accepted me that had helped me—*eventually*—start to accept myself. I owed her a lot.

Violet squeezed my hand. "Well, that's what friends are for . . . or should I say, *pedal partners.*" Our eyes held for a long moment, and when I didn't say anything, her cheeks turned the color of the inside of a guava fruit, and she gave a little shrug. "What? You don't want to be my pedal partner anymore?"

That made me laugh. "Of course, I do," I said. Then I held out my pinky in the classic pinky-swear pose, and Violet hooked hers around mine.

"Pedal partners for life," she said, smiling bigger now, brighter.

And I was smiling too, as I squeezed her finger. "Pedal partners for life."

"Oh, and in case you're wondering who got the poison out of me . . ." She nodded back over her shoulder. "See anyone familiar?"

Squinting against the thick shafts of sunlight pouring in throught a ripped-open section of roof, I scanned the crowd and saw a tall, slim lady in a neat business suit making a beeline straight for us. "Queen Joanna!" I shouted. "What are you doing here?"

"Ah, ah, ah," she said, wagging a finger at me. "It's *Presidenta* Joanna. . . . We wouldn't want to confuse anyone."

And just like that I recognized her—*again!* She was the current president of Spain! The first female ever elected to that office. I *knew* I'd seen her before!

"And I'm not here in an official capacity," she informed us, "so let's try to keep it on the down low, as you kids might say."

Flanking her were two Secret Service–looking dudes in dark sunglasses, dark baseball caps, and even darker suits that had these sort of cool hoods. One of the guys was so huge it was almost ridiculous. Probably a retired NBA player, I thought. Except I didn't think even basketball players grew that tall. Then I caught a glimpse of a brown, leathery face peering out at me from beneath the bill of the cap and realized it wasn't just any old bodyguard type—it was Juan the basajaun!

Dang, I thought, *the guy really is super talented at going incognito!* Especially for someone of his overall size . . . and hairiness.

Behind him, kids were still streaming drowsily down the stairs and into the living room. The place was so packed, it reminded me of the Youth Fair on opening night.

"Certainly more of them than I'd expected," the queen said, glancing back over her shoulder.

"Joanna, who *are* all these people . . . ?" I had to ask.

"They're my sister's victims," she explained. "The ones she turned into dolls, anyway." Which explained the boxes and boxes of toys.

"Your sister, huh?"

Off my not-so-pleased look, she smiled and said, "We all have family members we're less than fond of. . . ."

Which I guess was true for most people. Except that most people didn't have proud, twice-cursed brujas with the nasty habit of kidnapping little kids in their family trees. "Espérate," I said, holding up my hands like a traffic cop. "So that giant doll collection of hers was actually all *real people* . . . ?"

"Sí, sí. In fact, it's quite a common practice in our culture for misbehaving children and naughty pets. Sort of a minor punishment. Like a time-out."

More like cruel and unusual. And now I felt *really* creeped out thinking back to one bored afternoon when the power had gone out and I'd spent, like, an hour or two fooling around with them, picking some up and making them dance and play-fight like I used to do with my action figures. I hoped whoever they were didn't remember. Or hold a grudge.

"But wait," I said as it hit me. "So then where are my pa—"

"Charlie!"

I looked to my left—and my entire world stopped.

"Mami! Papi!"

Instantly, my parents broke away from the crowds and ran to me.

"¡Mi hijo!" my mom shouted as she scooped me up in her arms. Her hug was crushing, squeezing every last ounce of air out of my lungs, but I didn't care. I squeezed her back, looking up at my dad as he wrapped his arms around both of us and began rocking back and forth.

Suddenly a flood of tears that had been building up for almost two months started pouring down my cheeks. I couldn't help it. . . . I didn't *want* to help it.

My mom sucked in a shaky breath as she ran her hand through my hair. My dad started crying. "We missed you so much," he whispered, pressing his forehead against mine. His entire body was trembling. His hands were as big and calloused as I remembered. "We missed you so, *so* much. . . ."

"I missed you guys too," I said. My voice wobbled like a busted tire, and now my mom was crying too. So was Violet. Even Alvin had teared up a bit.

So many different emotions were racing through me, I could hardly take it. Love. Joy. Relief. Happiness. My body felt impossibly weak and incredibly strong all at the same time. And even as I stood there, I knew that no matter how crazy the last few months had been—and they'd been *insane*—starting today, starting *right now*, everything was going to be okay. How did I know? Because we were a family again.

"Did you see the locket?" my mother asked, leaning back to wipe tears from one of my cheeks. "Did you find the map?"

I nodded, wiping my other cheek. "Yeah, what was that about?"

"It was your abuelita's," my dad explained. "The map was given to her by your grandfather. It was supposed to be a last resort. Somewhere she could escape to if . . . if *something* ever came after her. She passed it down to your mother once we had you."

"When we realized the witch had found us," my mom said, "we left it on your bed and then tried to lead her away from you. Our plan was to meet you back in the pasillo. For all of us to hide down there together. But we never got the chance."

My dad kissed me on top of my head, ruffled my hair a little. "Doesn't matter now," he whispered, his voice still thick with emotion. "You did good, Charlie. . . . Hiciste muy bien, mi hijo."

I smiled up at him through watery eyes and couldn't

look away. It was so painful to think that just a few minutes ago, that evil bruja had almost taken them away from me. Taken them away forever. Just the thought of it was enough to break my heart all over again, because I honestly don't know what I would do without my parents.

"I hate to interrupt this moment, Mami y Papi," I heard Queen Joanna say, "but I need to have a quick word with Charlie. Es muy importante, I'm afraid."

My mom looked up at her and nodded silently.

I nodded too. "Okay."

Joanna and I left the kitchen through one of the larger holes in the walls and walked out into the backyard, away from all the confused kids roaming around. At the far edge of the lawn stood a large tree I'd never actually noticed before. It must've stood close to eight feet tall and had a mass of beautiful purple flowers growing in perfect, crisscrossing patterns up its thick trunk. I couldn't remember ever seeing another tree like it. *Anywhere.*

As we got closer, the upper half of the trunk suddenly twisted around, and a green moss-covered face grinned down at me. A familiar face. Still, I almost had a heart attack.

"¡Madremonte!" I shouted. "What are you doing here?"

"She just wanted to apologize for how she treated you back at the Provencia," Joanna said.

"Sí, I was muy rude," she said. "I had no idea what a brave and special boy you truly were. And I had a terrible case of leaf blisters, so I might've been *un poquito* moody. . . ."

Un poquito means a little bit in Spanish, and that was probably *a little bit* of an understatement in itself—more like, *mucho, mucho* moody, but I was still grateful for the apology. "But I don't get it. . . . So you guys were just in the neighborhood or something?"

Joanna smiled. "No, Charlie. See, El Justo Juez and El Cadejo both thought it would be prudent to keep an eye on you even after we received the misleading report from the oracle. And yes, Ponce has been known to do that on occasion. He doesn't *exactly* trust me. . . . He's lost some faith in La Liga over the years. Anyway, El Cadejo volunteered to shadow you, while Juez attempted to apprehend El Sombrerón. We suspected that he might have some insight into La Mano Peluda's plans. Like most treasure hunters, he tends to deal in secrets as much as artifacts. In any event, Juez finally managed to capture him, and it was the enormous-hatted one himself who told us about La Cuca, how she'd embedded herself in your life, her plans. Apparently, one of his acalicas had overheard some rumors."

"Sí, once Juez told us what he'd learned, we got here as quickly as we could," said Madremonte. She looked at Joanna. "This was what? Twenty minutes ago?"

"Wait, so you traveled all the way from Colombia to Miami in *twenty minutes?*"

"I know. Slow. But there's been a lot of rain across South America, so the root system is pretty backed up."

I had no idea what she was talking about, but I wasn't about to ask. I wasn't sure my brain could handle the answer at the moment.

In the distance, a motorcycle engine revved and roared. I turned. Across the street, a big bulky dude dressed in head-to-toe black leather was straddling a sleek black bike. He raised a hand to his helmet in a salute before blasting off down the block, making me wonder who the heck he was . . . that is, until I saw a column of wispy gray smoke drifting out through the mirrored lens of his helmet.

Juez!

"But you got it done on your own, Charlie," Queen Joanna said, sounding like a teacher whose favorite student just solved their first algebraic equation. "We're all very thankful. And more than a little impressed."

"And you do know what you are by now, ¿sí?" asked Madremonte.

"Yeah, La Cuca told me," I said.

Queen Joanna smiled at me. A proud sort of smile. "That's why you've always liked animals. . . ."

"Wait. How did you know that?"

"Because all Morphlings do. Their collective DNA exists inside you. It's part of your calling. You're one with creation. A balancing force on the earth."

Aw man, that was awesome! And kinda mind-blowing, too . . . I was like a walking Noah's Ark or something. "I love that!"

"I'm so glad to hear that," Joanna said, still smiling. But then she and Madremonte exchanged looks, and the queen's expression changed, turning serious. "I hate to bring this up so quickly, Charlie—especially with everything that you've been through recently. But as it turns out, La Liga is once again in need of your help."

"Let me guess," I said. "Something to do with the Hairy Hand?"

"More like *everything*. There are sinister forces at work, Charlie. Forces even darker and more dangerous than La Cuca."

"Evil is gathering to the south," said Madremonte, "and beyond the sea."

"So, what's going on?" I asked.

The witch queen's eyes locked onto mine. "Have you ever heard of El Chupacabra?"

ACKNOWLEDGMENTS

A wise person once said that it takes a village to bring a book to life. And although that is certainly true, in the case of this particular book, it took a league. Not, as it were, a League of Shadows, but a league of wonderful and talented individuals whose selfless dedication to their craft has left me in awe.

What follows is my feeble attempt at a thank you.

To my editor and fairy godmother, Fiona Simpson, whose wit and boundless enthusiasm have made this entire process one I will forever cherish. You've not only made me feel welcome at Simon & Schuster, but you've also made me feel like family. How can I ever thank you enough for falling in love with Charlie and Violet and taking a chance on me? (HINT: I can't!) To my agent and fellow 305er, Rena Rossner—I have no idea how you find the time to do all the amazing things you do, but I am so grateful to have you in my corner. To my wonderful publisher, Mara Anastas, and to the incredible Aladdin team, Caitlin Sweeny, Sara Berko, Anna Jarzab, Alissa Nigro, Amy Hendricks, and Christian Vega—I can't thank all of you enough for your belief and support! To my copy editor, Penina Lopez, whose razor-sharp eyes could no doubt split a muki's hair, and to my production editor, the incomparable Elizabeth Mims, who has improved this book in two different languages—many thanks y muchas, muchas gracias! To Manuel Sumberac, my insanely talented cover artist, and to the creative powerhouse duo of Karin Paprocki, art director, and Hilary Zarycky, interior designer, who came together to create the most visually stunning book these two eyes have ever beheld—you three have truly surpassed my wildest imaginations! To my tireless publicist, Vanessa DeJesus—thank you so much for having my back. Hopefully one day we'll get to hang out at La Calaca and have some of those BBQ cauliflower nuggets you came up with!

Of course, these acknowledgments wouldn't be complete without a huge, misty-eyed thank you to all my family and friends. ¡Los amo a todos! Special shout-out to my cousin and all around e-ninja Alex (aka Dro, aka ShiningOutlaw), who has gifted me more electronics than I can count, including the Mac on which I'm currently typing this. Love you, cuz! Also, to my cousin Big Al, aka Don Alberto Corleone, aka Barbarossa, who's one of the coolest cats on the planet. ¡Mucho amor, primo! And I certainly can't leave out the two best primas ever, not to mention two of the fiercest hide-and-seek players I've ever had the privilege of running around my neighborhood with, Lauren and Alexandra! Or my favorite tía (you know who you are)!

ACKNOWLEDGMENTS

I'd also like to give a great big Lone Star State–size thank-you to the Texas Book Festival and the Tweens Read Festival, two can't-miss events for any book lover! Seriously, don't miss these!

I'd be completely remiss if I didn't also offer a very, very special thanks to all the teachers and librarians out there. You all are the backbone of civilization. The world can never thank you enough. (Or pay you enough, but that's a different topic.)

And lastly, but by no means least, a great big thank-you to you, wonderful reader—where would any of us be if it weren't for you?

GLOSSARY

acalica: a species of weather fairies native to Bolivia.

basajaun: huge hairy hominids that inhabit the dense forests of northern Spain (i.e., the Basque region). Often referred to as the "Lords of the Forest," basajauns are talented farmers, millers, and blacksmiths.

bruja: a witch or sorceress.

El Cadejo: a supernatural creature created by God to protect mankind. It manifests itself in the form of an enormous white dog. Tales of its heroics and benevolence have been told all over Central and South America for many years.

calacas: undead skeletons sometimes depicted as ferriers of the dead in Mexican and Latino culture.

El Cambiador: an extraordinarily gifted crossbreed who can partially manifest any animal trait found in nature. Spanish for "the Morphling" or "the Changer."

Cherufe: evil magma monsters that live deep inside active volcanoes in Chile. They are said to be responsible for earthquakes and volcanic eruptions.

chullachaquis: jungle dwarfs with the ability to take the form of both animals and humans. They are considered by many to be protectors of the Amazon. The only way to identify one is to keep an eye out for its backward foot.

comelenguas: literally translates to "tongue-eaters." These giant birds feed primarily on the tongues of cattle. Most sightings have been reported in Honduras.

La Cuca: a legendary witch and bogeywoman known by many names (Coco, Cuco, Coca, Cucuy). Her stories were first told centuries ago in Portugal and Galicia, where she was described as a fire-breathing dragon.

duendes: a race of gnome-like beings found throughout Central and South America and the Iberian Peninsula.

La Fuente de la Juventud (the Fountain of Youth): a magical water source capable of granting immortality.

jentil (plural: jentilak): race of giants believed to dwell in the mountainous regions of northern Spain.

El Justo Juez: a legendary Salvadoran figure who prowls the night on horseback in search of evildoers. His name translates as "Righteous Judge," and it is said that the night belongs to him and him alone.

La Llorona or "Weeping Woman": the spirit of a once young and beautiful woman who, in a fit of jealous rage, drowned her two children to spite her cheating husband.

La Luz Mala: unnatural glowing orbs said to lead unsuspecting travelers into danger. Most often encountered in the swamplands and marshes of Uruguay and Argentina. The name literally means "Evil Light."

Madremonte: the protector of the jungles and mountains

of Colombia. "Mother Mountain" is considered by some to be the personification of nature itself and sometimes curses those who steal their neighbors' land or harm animals.

muki: cave-dwelling goblinlike creatures found throughout South America. They possess the ability to transform rock into precious metals and are said to make pacts with miners—many times to the miners' harm.

nahual: a shape-shifting witch or sorcerer capable of transforming itself into animals, most commonly large dogs, jaguars, or birds. Legends of the nahual first appear in Mesoamerican culture.

Oókempán: a species of ogres with turtlelike shells on their backs. In Argentina and Chile, it is believed that any child playing unsupervised is at risk of being kidnapped by these monsters.

La Sihuanaba: a shape-shifting horse-faced demon. She preys primarily on disobedient children and unfaithful men. She is known by many names (Cigua in Honduras, Segua in Costa Rica, and Siguanaba in El Salvador), and her legend is told almost everywhere Spanish is spoken.

El Sombrerón: a fearsome bogeyman known throughout Guatemala and Mexico for braiding hair (both human and animal), wearing a ridiculously oversize hat, and serenading young maidens with his fabled silver guitar.

tartalos: a race of cave-dwelling one-eyed giants native to the Basque region of Spain. They are known for eating a sheep a day.

El Tucano-yúa: known in Brazil as the bird of the evil eye. Its beak is said to be so deadly that it can kill both humans and animals simply by being pointed at them.

zips: shy, spear-wielding, fairylike creatures most often spotted protecting herds of deer in Central America.

The adventure continues as brujas, zombies, and vampires stalk Central America.

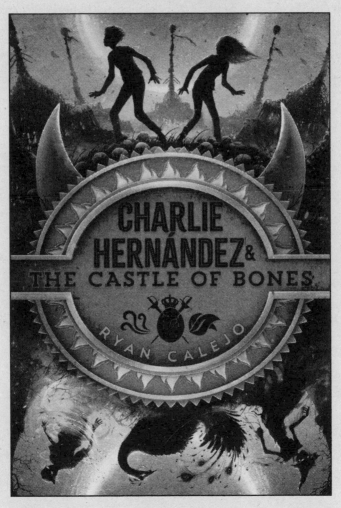

t was raining frogs. That's the first thing I noticed when we stepped through la bruja's mirror. Fat ones, green ones, black ones. They tumbled from the sky, bounced off the road, clunked off mailboxes. They croaked and chirped and peeped. They hopped through the tall grass like punch-drunk boxers.

One plopped down on the toe of my sneaker, glared up at me with its bulging, beady eyes, and said, "Rrriiiibbbbbiiitt!"

I stared at it for a moment, frowning, then squinted up at the dark churning clouds from where the slimy amphibians were falling in bunches. In *knots*.

My name is Charlie Hernández, and over the last few months, my life had been all kinds of freaky; I'd grown horns, sprouted feathers, teleported from South Florida to northwest Spain, made a quick stop in the Land of the Dead, and even faced off against one of the most famous and feared brujas in all of human history—but *raining frogs . . . ?* Yeah, that was new for me.

"Estamos aquí," said the witch queen, her green eyes blazing in the gloom.

I looked around. We were standing on the side of a narrow dirt track, smack-dab in the middle of . . . well, *nowhere*. A huge, grassy field spread out before us, flanked by walls of thick forest. Pines, maybe. The air was cold. The sky was dark, choked with storm clouds. Thunder rumbled in the distance.

"Where exactly *is* here . . . ?" I asked, but la bruja didn't answer.

Violet said, "And what's up with the *frogs?*" but she didn't answer that, either.

Maybe thirty yards ahead of us a strip of yellow crime-scene tape had been stretched across the field, from end to end, looped around the trunks of the nearest trees. A crowd of curious people was pressing up against the tape, shouting questions as a dozen or so police officers tried to keep them from busting through. There were even more people wandering aimlessly around; these were dodging the falling croakers while snapping pictures of the sky or recording the whole thing on their smartphones.

A couple of little kids in denim overalls were trying to catch the frogs as they fell. I watched one of them catch a plummeting toad in her front pocket, then start cheering and jumping all over the place like she'd just won the Super Bowl. Honestly, if I'd been about seven years younger and wearing overalls, I would've totally jumped in for a round or two. Looked pretty fun, actually.

Past the main crowd, more police officers were hauling heavy wooden barricades out of the backs of police vans, their flashing lights turning the woods red then blue, red then blue.

"Do not leave my side," Queen Joanna warned us. "And speak to no one. We cannot be seen, ¿me entienden?"

As we started across the field, the wind kicked up, shrieking through the trees and slinging the amphibians sideways now. I dodged one the size of a Frisbee, then wrapped my arms around myself, wondering where the heck we were and what the heck we were doing here; thanks to the police cruisers (which had the word "polícia" and not "police" emblazoned across the driver-side doors), I knew we weren't in Miami anymore, but that was about it. And that wasn't exactly a whole lot to go on.

"Are they gonna let us through?" Violet asked as we approached the barricade, but again Joanna didn't answer; she simply touched one pale, ringed finger to the golden brooch pinned to the front of her dress (it looked like some sort of butterfly, maybe—or a giant moth) and whispered,

"Vuela," which means "fly," and the pin's wings suddenly beat to life.

It rose silently into the air, a golden blur in the night, and then flew out ahead of us, floating lazily over to where the large crowd was pressing against the police tape. Leaving dusty, glittery trails, the pin began to fly circles above everyone's heads, and next thing I knew, all fifty or so people—cops included—were staring up at it, some pointing and smiling, others giggling with childlike wonder in their eyes.

They were all so mesmerized by it, in fact, that not one of them even glanced our way as we ducked under the ribbon of yellow tape and marched right past them, following the rhythmic swish of the witch queen's cape.

Yep, Joanna was awesome like that....

We'd made it maybe fifteen yards when a fat, bumpy, squishy toad plopped down on the top of my head and just sort of sat there like a warty green hat.

Glancing up at la bruja, I said, "So, about the frogs . . . ?"

"The dark magia in the atmosphere has begun to warp nature," she replied quickly. And pretty casually, too—like she'd just said, *Hey, your shoes are untied.* Or, *Hey, you dropped your pencil.*

Personally, it was my opinion that whenever the words "dark" and "magic" came together in a sentence, the entire situation should be taken a bit more seriously. But, hey, that was just me.

"So not a good sign then, huh?"

The queen stayed quiet, but the frog on my head said, "Riibbbbbiiittt," then hopped off, and I had to resist the urge to try to catch it in my pocket.

Up ahead, where the field curved out of sight, a man and woman in white lab coats strode into view, walking this way. They were carrying walkie-talkies and yelling into them in a language that was almost familiar. Portuguese, maybe?

"¡Escóndanse!" Joanna whispered, and we did exactly that, ducking out of sight and vanishing into the dark woods. Leaves crunched and branches made shifting patterns against the sky as we zigzagged through the trees, leaping logs and rocks. "Do not slow!" she ordered, and Violet and I weren't about to argue. Joanna, also known as the Witch Queen of Toledo, was one of the most powerful brujas on the face of the planet. Not only that, but she was the leader of the League of Shadows, which was sort of like a superhero team-up of the most legendary mythological beings—or sombras—in all of Hispanic mythology. The first time we'd met, she'd fed me worms, then tried to drown me (and basically *succeeded*!) But, surprisingly, it had all been for my own good, so I wasn't holding a grudge. She had dark auburn hair, long dark nails, and even darker lashes framing her glowing emerald eyes. When you topped that off with the golden crown she liked to wear and her elaborate, tiered gown the color of a midnight sky, she might as well have had a big neon sign over her head that read: SUPERNATURAL ROYALTY COMING THROUGH.

As we hurried through the woods, Violet shot me an uneasy look, and finally I couldn't take it anymore—I opened my mouth to ask Joanna where she was taking us and what in the Land of the Living we were doing here, but as we emerged from the trees, the words died on my lips.

My jaw dropped open. My toes seemed to hook themselves into the ground.

Before us, rising up almost as tall as the great trees that flanked the field, stood the most terrible thing I had ever seen—a thing so mind-bogglingly *awful*, my suddenly panicking brain could hardly make sense of it.

When I was nine years old, my parents took me on a trip to Spain. It was in early October, during the Concurs de Castells celebration, which is basically this huge festival where people get together to create these awesome body towers. Think cheerleader pyramids, but with a *whole* lot more people climbing all over each other, trying to see which team can build the tallest, most complex tower, or "castell." In Catalonia it was a centuries-old tradition, something everyone looked forward to all year. And *this* looked a lot like *that* . . . except a *nightmare* version.

This tower stood at least thirty feet high and was made up of the lifeless, shriveled-up carcasses of at least fifty milk cows. Most had been stacked flat on their bellies, one on top of another, but some were lying upside down, their bony, hoofed legs sticking straight up to support the ones above. There was also a whole mess of bones, big ones, picked clean of any flesh—spines and femurs and hip bones—which seemed to act like a kind of glue, holding the whole thing together. The air was heavy with rotting smells and hummed with the buzzing of flies. Everywhere I looked it was all slack jaws, bulging purple eyes, and the saggy black-and-white folds of dried-up cowhide.

It's a castle of bones, I thought dazedly. And even with my head spinning and my pulse thudding wildly in my ears, I was *positive* about one thing: This wasn't just a random stack of dead cows—no, this was something else, something dark and sinister and otherworldly.

And even more terrifying, it was *alive. . . .*

I could feel its presence like a physical force—like greedy, invisible fingers reaching out from deep within the bony pile, fingers that would grab me if they could—that would hurt me. Would hurt all of us.

"Oh my God," Violet breathed, staring up at it, shaking her head. "What is that *thing* . . . ?"

"The abomination you see before you, niños," said the witch, "has been called many different things by many different peoples. But it is most widely known as a castell."

I blinked, not sure I'd heard her right. "Hold up. You mean, like, *castell* castell? Like, the festival of *people pyramids?*"

"That festival began as a celebration of the day the earth was liberated from these ancient altars of dark magic. It is, in fact, its genesis." Sweat had broken out all over the queen's face. She wiped it with the back of one hand and stared down at me with eyes that seemed to swim in their sockets. Her cheeks were all red and blotchy. She looked tired—no, she looked *exhausted*. "We haven't seen one in many, many years . . . and . . . this one here in Portugal has many worried, for . . . for they are without question an omen of a rising evil."

As she spoke, the wind gusted, tugging at our clothes, and I was pelted by a hailstorm of frogs the size of quarters. One somehow managed to drop down the front of my shirt, and I had to shake it free.

Beside me, the witch queen made an odd, hacking, wheezing sound, as though she was having trouble getting air into her lungs, then began to back away from the terrible pile of bones. "Excuse me a moment . . . I . . . Perdónenme."

"Are you okay?" Violet asked her.

"I'm fine . . . no te preocupes por mi."

"Can we, um, *look around* . . . ?"

"Sí, sí, cómo no. That is why I brought you both."

As Joanna headed farther up the field, away from the castell, Violet began walking slow circles around the castle of cow corpses, looking it up and down with squinted eyes like some crime-scene detective on a TV show. Had this been anyone else, I probably would've laughed and told them to get real. But this wasn't just anyone; this was Violet Rey—or Ultra Violet, as I liked to call her.

Violet wasn't a Morphling like me, but she didn't need any special powers. Mostly because she wasn't your typical middle school student. Take a peek into her backpack and you'll find a pair of military-grade wire cutters, an extra-large can of pepper spray, and a professional forensics kit all tucked neatly beside her Hello Kitty pencil case and pom-poms.

Besides being the captain of both the debate team and the cheerleading squad, Violet was editor in chief of our school's newspaper (the *Leon Gazette*) and there wasn't much she wouldn't do to get a story. Including blackmail. Trust me, I would know. Violet was as tenacious as she was pretty, pretty as she was smart, and so smart she was practically a genius. Cool part was V wasn't one of those people who are all into themselves, either. She was caring, sensitive, *unbelievably* brave, and sometimes even motivational in an army drill sergeant sort of way.

In second grade she'd convinced me that I possessed the inner strength to do the monkey bars backward and using only three fingers. So I'd given it a shot, banged my head on the edge of the slide, spent the rest of that day in the nurse's office, and have been madly in love with Violet ever since.

She might not have been old enough to operate a motor vehicle, but the girl already had detective skills on par with Sherlock Holmes and it was mostly thanks to those skills that I was still alive. So I was happy to stand back and let her do her thing. Currently, Violet was wearing her cheerleading uniform—sneakers, white skirt, crisp white top with gray and blue stripes down both arms. Not exactly the ideal attire for going all CSI on a pile of dead cows, but somehow she made it work.

"Charlie, what kind of sombras could have done something like this?" she asked me, squatting down beside the castell.

I racked my brain. "Um, Dips, I guess. Those are vampire dogs. Obviously, a chupacabra, too. . . They're probably big and hungry enough."

"Check these out." Violet lifted a fold of skin at the base of a dead cow's neck, revealing a pair of marks—no, *holes*.

"How'd you see that?" I asked, stunned. It was like the girl had X-ray vision or something.

"I see everything, Charlie. It's my gift." She sank even lower into a squat, her face now less than three inches from the cow's.

"Ew, c'mon, V. . . stop touching it. It's *dead*."

"It's just a cow, Charlie."

"I know, but it's gross. . . ." And if I'd thought *that* was nasty, she then took her other hand and stuck two fingers into the holes in the cow's neck! There was this sick, sticky, squishy sound, and I nearly barfed on the spot.

"Definitely puncture wounds," she said. "About six inches deep." She jammed her fingers in deeper. A nasty yellowish pus gushed up out of the holes. "Make that *eight*."

"Please"—I burped, tasting this morning's breakfast (pork rinds and a chicken-and-egg empanada) in the back of my throat—"stop." Last thing I wanted was to barf all over the coolest girl in the world, but she sure wasn't making it easy on me.

Finally, Violet pulled her fingers out of the cow. She wiped them on the front of her uniform, staining it blood red and pus yellow.

Yuck and double yuck. "I think I'm gonna puke," I admitted.

V ignored me. "You think a chupacabra could've sucked this many animals dry? I mean, these things got slurped like—*like milkshakes!*"

I sighed.

"What's wrong?"

"I think you just ruined milkshakes for me. Like, *forever*."

She rolled her eyes. "Charlie, I'm being serious. . . . Could a chupacabra have done this?"

"Yeah, I mean, I don't know . . . maybe a pack of them?"

"And are they known to pile up their prey like this?"

"Nah, I've never heard of anything like this. . . ." And I was pretty sure I wasn't the only one either.

"Huh." Violet was down on one knee now, searching around the stinky, blood-spattered, fly-infested base of the castell as frogs hopped and croaked around us; this girl must've been an ER doctor in a past life, because she certainly didn't have any problem with blood or guts. Now, for the record, I wasn't squeamish or anything. Heck, just last summer I'd eaten an *entire* dung beetle on a dare. Okay, so maybe I hadn't *actually* eaten a dung beetle, but I *had* almost touched its nasty, armored insect legs to the tip of my tongue. And that had to count for something, right? Anyway, I had to draw the line on nastiness somewhere, and shriveled-up cow carcasses seemed like a mighty fine place to draw it.

"Oh, c'mon, V, get up. . . . That's *sooooo* nasty." I couldn't even watch anymore. Seriously.

"Interesting." She held up a hunk of wood—no, something else.

I squinted. "Is that—*a chancleta?*"

"Actually, they're called *clogs*. That's what the Dutch call them, anyway." She paused for a second, thinking. "Looks like Cinderella lost her slipper at the ball. . . . We should show this to Joanna. C'mon."

The Witch Queen of Toledo had been standing in the middle of the field, maybe thirty yards from the castell, staring up at the dark sky, which was still pouring frogs. Now she turned, and I saw surprise flicker in her eyes. "You two are still here?" she asked, sounding baffled.

"We, uh, never left . . . ," I couldn't help pointing out. *Geez, what's up with her?*

Violet held out the clog. "We found this near the castell," she said, and Joanna smiled weakly.

"That's very nice, mi vida."

"No, I mean—don't you think it's *odd?* Look at it. This thing's gotta be at least a hundred years old. And cows aren't exactly known for their footwear."

La bruja nodded like she got Violet's point, but her glowing green gaze had already drifted past her. "Odd, sí . . . but we have bigger problems."

I turned, trying to see what she was looking at. "Like what?"

"We're being watched."

"By who?" Violet asked.

The witch queen's voice dropped to a low whisper that told me I wasn't going to like the answer. "*Minairons.*"